DARING DUVAL

Center Point
Large Print

Also by Max Brand® and available from
Center Point Large Print:

Melody and Cordoba
The Winged Horse
The Cure of Silver Cañon
The Red Well
The Western Double
Son of an Outlaw
Lightning of Gold

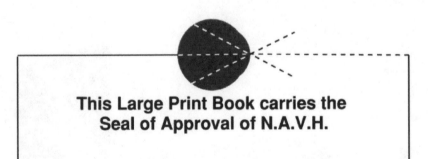

DARING DUVAL

Max Brand®

CENTER POINT LARGE PRINT
THORNDIKE, MAINE

This Circle Ⓥ Western is published by
Center Point Large Print in the year 2017 in
co-operation with Golden West Literary Agency.

First Edition
November, 2017

"Daring Duval" by George Owen Baxter first appeared
as a six-part serial in Street & Smith's *Western Story
Magazine* (7/19/30–8/23/30). Copyright © 1930 by Street
& Smith Publications, Inc. Copyright © renewed 1958 by
Dorothy Faust. Acknowledgment is made to Condé Nast
Publications, Inc., for their co-operation. Copyright © 2017
by Golden West Literary Agency for restored material.

Printed in the United States of America on permanent paper.
Set in 16-point Times New Roman type.

ISBN: 978-1-68324-589-6

Library of Congress Cataloging-in-Publication Data

Names: Brand, Max, 1892–1944, author.
Title: Daring Duval : a Circle V Western / Max Brand.
Description: First edition. | Thorndike, Maine :
  Center Point Large Print, 2017.
Identifiers: LCCN 2017029318 | ISBN 9781683245896
  (hardcover : alk. paper)
Subjects: LCSH: Large type books. | GSAFD: Western stories.
Classification: LCC PS3511.A87 D37 2017 | DDC 813/.54—dc23
LC record available at https://lccn.loc.gov/2017029318

Chapter One

In the spring of the year Duval came to Moose Creek. Between the tall, dark pines the underwoods were beginning to bloom with yellow green, as bright, well-nigh, as sunshine, and far away the dim avenues were streaked with color as though the sunlight had fallen through. Wings were beginning to whir from the southward. Every dawn was filled with musical chattering. In the marshes, too, the frogs were singing. On the hills, in the valleys, the cattle sleeked over the harsh winter that had hollowed their sides. Cows bawled down the wind for their calves. The young bulls challenged the old masters with great bellowings. In Moose Creek itself the screen doors were banging all day long as the children ran in and out from play. This was the season when Duval came down from the mountains.

It was old Simon Wilbur who saw him first.

Simon had gone hunting and his way had taken him up the weather-dimmed trail past his old place. He sat on the chopping block before the woodshed and took off his hat to the small breeze that managed to find its way through the forest. Deeper in, the wind was always still, but this was close enough to the open to allow even the mildest stir of air to enter, carrying the moist richness of the spring with it. The raw scent of young grass was in it as well as the delicate fragrances of the wild flowers. Simon Wilbur closed his eyes to breathe deep and see the image more clearly, and when he opened them again, he saw Duval come up through the trees from the creek trail.

He was amazed. No one used that path these days, and had not for years. But presently he forgot the strangeness of the coming because of the way this man filled his eye.

Later on, others were to feel the same thing, but though they were more talented in speech than Dad Wilbur, as they called him, they had his trouble in putting a finger on salient differences that distinguished Duval from other men. Certainly, from the limp brim of his hat to his spoon-handled spurs, he was dressed like any other cowpuncher of good taste. As for his appearance, he was a sinewy man who had come to the full of his strength—but Simon Wilbur would not have bet on his age within five years. In fact, there was nothing unusual about him, yet as Wilbur afterward expressed it, he felt at once that the stranger had "been around the corner and seen the other side."

When he saw Wilbur, Duval halted his horse, a good bay gelding that was perhaps a little too long in the rein to make an ideal cow pony.

"Hello," said Duval. "Now, this place I call something like . . ."

"Like what?" said Simon Wilbur, who really committed himself in the most casual conversation.

Duval looked at the stout little cabin, the wood and horse sheds behind it, the two great trees that guarded the path to the water's edge, and the meadows that descended the hillside, still dotted with a few big stumps. The second-growth saplings were coming up in clusters now, but still the fields were fairly clear.

"Like home," said Duval.

"Home," said Simon Wilbur, "is what you're used to. I seen some that needed three stories and an iron deer on the front lawn, and I seen some that only wanted the smell of fryin' bacon over a campfire."

Duval listened to him with a courteous smile of attention, but his head was raised as though he were hearing another voice—that of Moose Creek, perhaps, which was singing treble nearby and deep bass in the distance.

"That ground would raise crops, I lay my money," he said.

"It has," said Dad Wilbur.

"What sort of crops?" asked Duval. "Grain?"

"Rocks mostly," replied Simon.

Duval laughed pleasantly, a rich laughter much deeper than his speaking voice.

"A fellow could work here, and be alone, too," he said. "How's the house?"

"You don't need a key to get in," said Wilbur.

Duval dismounted with a clinking of spurs and, after throwing his reins, went at once through the cabin. He looked out once from the attic window.

"This would be tolerable warm in winter, partner!" he called.

"Oh, it's warm enough," said Wilbur. "In summer, too."

A little later, Duval came out again. This time he walked down to the creek and leaned there for a long moment against one of the great trees. The old path was quite grassed over now, except in the center, where many feet had worn through the surface soil to the gravel. Wilbur regarded the place with a half-happy and half-melancholy interest. It was as though he looked upon a picture of his young manhood out of the shadow of his age.

Then Duval turned on his heel. "Who owns this outfit?" he asked.

"Why, stranger?"

"I'm fixed to buy, if it ain't the price of a summer resort or a dude ranch. What would Mister Real-Estate Dealer say if I went and whispered in his ear?"

Simon Wilbur grew cautious. "There's a house here," he said.

"Kind of moldy, though," suggested Duval.

"There's some bang-up sheds, too, that cost a lot of makin'."

"They was made crooked, though," said Duval.

"And there's a hundred acres of land down there. . . ."

"Fit to raise rocks mostly," suggested the stranger.

Wilbur grinned in sympathy. "I own this layout," he said. "Twenty dollars an acre ain't too much, and I'd throw in everything else for another thousand, and never bear you no hard feelin's whatsoever because of your bargain."

"That's three thousand," observed Duval.

"You been to a right good school," said Wilbur.

"Sure, I been to a good school," said Duval. "And after addition they taught us subtraction."

"What you gonna subtract?"

"Rocks," said Duval, "among other things. I'll pay you fifteen dollars an acre and take the buildings throwed in. That adds up to fifteen hundred. Do you like it?"

Wilbur raised his hands and his eyes to heaven, and sat as still as a picture.

"My name's Duval," said the other. "Do we shake on it?"

"Fifteen hundred!" said Wilbur. "Young feller, I like you. I like your cut, and I even like your sassy way, but I'd hate to pay that much for a laugh. If I went home and faced Ma after makin' a deal like this . . ."

"She'd say she never knew you were a great businessman before. Look here. This land ain't been on the market because you didn't know there was a market. If I wasn't a dog-goned good man on a trail, I never would've tracked it down and got a chance to offer on it. Fifteen hundred dollars, and I leave it to you to fix the deed and the rest, or whatever you do when you buy land. Here," he continued, "is the coin in your hand."

Duval took out a wallet from which he shuffled a number of notes and displayed them to Wilbur.

"Two fives and four of a kind," said Duval, "is one better than a full house, and would get you shot in parts of the country that I been in. Make your choice, mister. Will you play this hand? There ain't a second deal."

"I'll play this hand," said Wilbur, and took the proffered money. He thumbed each note; he tested each slip of paper by making it crumple and snap out under the jerk of his hands.

"If you live near here and got a buckboard that I could borrow," said Duval, "I'd like to get down to town and buy some fixin's to go along with this roost."

Wilbur was glad to go. In the first place, he was convinced that the stranger would change his mind before he could get the money safely hidden away. In the second place, he was burning with desire to bring the tidings to his wife. Therefore, he streaked down through the woods as fast as his long, old legs would carry him. Only when he came to his new home did he check his speed a little, and, arriving at the back door, he spent a long time scraping his boots on the iron that was fixed there for that purpose.

"Is that you, Simon?" called his wife. "If you ain't brought back some meat fit for lunch, you can get yourself downtown and fetch up some chops."

"I ain't got no meat," said Wilbur, "but I don't reckon that I'll be goin' downtown."

He heard a stifled exclamation. Martha Wilbur rushed from the kitchen and stood at the top of the steps like a hawk about to pounce. She was years younger than her husband, but the washboard and many years of labor had humped her back and set her mouth.

"You won't go?" she said, controlling her voice.

"I reckon I don't feel like goin'," said Wilbur.

"You don't feel like goin'!" Martha Wilbur said, and tried to catch her breath to express herself in better words.

"No," said Simon. "I'm gonna drive the buckboard up to the old place."

"Are you gone crazy?" she said.

"No," he answered, "I just give the place away, and now I'm gonna loan the young gent the buckboard."

The wife came rapidly down the steps and,

taking him by the shoulders, looked earnestly into his face.

"You wo'thless old skinflint!" she exclaimed. "What've you been up to?"

"Givin' away the old place," he insisted, "and I got this in exchange for it." Slowly, one by one, he took the notes from his pocket and spread them before her eyes.

"Bless my soul," whispered Martha Wilbur. "Has somethin' worthwhile growed out of that place? You give him a promise to sell, wrote out, or something?"

"He didn't ask for nothin'," he said. "Maybe . . ." He waited, evil hope in his face, but unwilling to say the thing that was in his mind.

However, Martha shook her head with instant decision. "Them that don't ask for bills of sale are them that don't need 'em," she decided. "Him that paid you that money once won't never pay it twice, Simon. And if you lied to him about the ground, you better be movin' to a new county over the hills."

"I didn't lie," said Simon.

"Simon," she exclaimed, "I've lived with you nigh onto forty years!"

He seemed to accept the implication of this without resistance, but he added thoughtfully: "I didn't lie, because I couldn't. You'll know what I mean when you see him. Chickens don't lie to hawks, ma'am. No more could I lie to him."

Chapter Two

Later in that same morning, Duval appeared in the town of Moose Creek itself, driving Wilbur's roan mare and sorrel gelding hitched to the Wilbur buckboard, through the poplar grove at the head of the village, past the broken-down mill where old Lawrence was murdered for the sake of his pocket knife, past the Gilling blacksmith shop with its brand-new sign, past the Collum house, whose back porch overhung nothingness after the floods of the summer before when the river had torn away its bank. So he came down the single street, winding as Moose Creek wound, until he reached Lane's grocery store.

At the hitching rack, he tethered his team and went into the neatest mercantile interior that had ever graced Moose Creek. Linoleum was under his feet, its flowered pattern somewhat faded from vigorous scrubbing; all newly white-enameled, the walls, the ceiling, and the shelves were shining. Every jar of preserves stood in a strictly drilled line upon snowy oilcloth. The bins behind the counter for sugar, rice, beans, and flour carried not only their appropriate labels, but, like the walls, were freshly coated with the same glistening paint. All was white as snow, in fact, and, against that background, the labels of the canned fruits and vegetables and the translucent glasses of jellies made a little paradise of color.

A tall cowpuncher leaned at a counter toward the rear of the store, but he was the only human being Duval saw at first. For the girl who stood opposite was in white, also, and lost against her background. She was stiffly done up in a long apron tied about her waist with a gigantic bow. She had great white cuffs and a broad collar of starched linen. In short, she was so extremely speckless and stood so stiff that Duval could have been excused for thinking her no more than a model and imitation of a pretty girl, such as might be displayed with a face of pink and white in the window of a shop in a small town—*Fashions for the kitchen!*

Now, however, she raised her eyes to the tall cowboy. Duval, even from the distance, could note two things—that she was saying "no" and that her eyes were blue. No washed-out color, sometimes gray or green, depending how the light struck them, but blue of the sea, or of lapis lazuli, blue that could lighten or darken but never could change.

Those eyes had opened so wide that she seemed to be listening, rather than speaking. The man who heard her voice snapped his fingers impatiently. The sombrero he was wearing he pushed far back on his head, which was covered with closely curling black hair.

"I've run uphill for six months, Marian, and I ain't gonna run no more," he said. "There's some that like hunting for the sake of the walk and the fresh air, but I like the game that I kill. If you say no now, it's final and for good. You understand that? Wait a minute, I . . ."

"Charlie, there's another customer . . . ," she began.

"Dang the other customer," said Charlie.

She stood looking down, enduring, while Charlie leaned closer across the counter, making man's age-old mistake of logical argument where logic and argument never are wanted.

"Wait a minute and think. I've worked like fury for six months. I've piled up a roll. The old man'll back me. I've got a place laid out . . ."

His excited voice sank out of hearing, not from caution or embarrassment, but with a profound emotion.

He ended, and Duval, watching, waited to see compassion, pity, gentleness in the face of the girl, but he waited in vain. For again she looked up with the unmoved face of a doll, the big blue eyes opened. "No," she said. And something else that Duval could not translate from the movement of her lips—perhaps some trite expression of regret, an avowal of friendship, but no more.

The youngster who leaned on the counter did not wait for the end, neither did he say good bye. Yanking his hat deep over his eyes, he turned on his heel and strode rapidly down the aisle toward Duval and the door. His black eyes glittered as they came, shining at Duval with a promise of trouble if there appeared in the stranger the slightest glimmer of a smile, or even the faintest suggestion of interest, of curiosity, of scorn.

But Duval already was reading the labels on the shelf.

He did not look down from his occupation until he heard her voice before him, asking what he would have. It was a small voice, high and sweet, like the voice of a child. When he looked at her, he saw that her hands were like the hands of a child also—softly dimpled across the knuckles. Yet when he glanced at her again, he would have been surprised by so much as a smile, so doll-like was she. In this fashion, exactly, would a child of five have conceived the ideal woman.

Duval sat down on the high chair in front of the counter, and took out a list.

"Here you are," he said. "I'm opening up the old Wilbur place, and it's a bare cupboard up yonder. I want it lined, and if I've forgotten anything, you fill it in, will you?"

She considered this appeal and the list at the same time, tapping the eraser end of a pencil against her chin. It was a very complete list, she thought. She hoped that he would like the sort of bacons and hams that she carried. Did he care to see a sample of the flour? He did not.

"But you'll have to make a selection of jellies and preserves," she said. "Missus Morris makes this apple and quince . . . you see how clear it is, like amber, almost. But some people prefer Miss Lydia Stanley's apple jelly. Then there is . . ."

"Listen," said Duval. "I like jelly a little or a lot, according to the number of notches that my belt is out or in. You select me a couple of dozen, and throw in some preserves . . . you be the judge. A man has to eat. . . ."

From the corner of his eye he looked through the broad, front window of the store and saw young Charlie knock open the swinging door of Pete's Place, the saloon across the street. Like one sternly bent on an important march went Charlie, reaching for his wallet as he moved. And Duval, looking back at the girl, caught the movement of her eyes by which he knew that she also had seen. But not a shadow appeared in her face, not a tone of her voice altered. He determined to force the point.

"Listen," he said. "It looks to me like your partner, Charlie, is gonna collect some trouble, the way he sashayed through that door across the street. I hope he's insured against broken glass, ma'am."

She looked at him without the slightest emotion.

"A Nash is hard to break," she commented.

17

"Charlie is a Nash. I'll pick out the jellies and preserves, then. One glass of each kind until you've approved of them. Is there anything else? Or shall I start to fill the list?"

"A gent can't live on beef forever," Duval said, considering. "Lemme see. Between shifts some anchovies ain't so bad. Got any?"

"I can get anything you want . . . in a few days," she said, and looked up anxiously. Anxiously— for her business.

"All right," nodded Duval. "Vermont maple syrup will be the thing for hot cakes, and sardines with crackers would make any man a meal. A couple of hams, too, eh? Lemme think. . . ." Duval raised his lean, pale face and looked through the window at the sky. Happy thoughts could be traced in his eyes. "Tarragon vinegar. Is that in your stock, ma'am?"

"I'll order that, too." She was writing rapidly on a pad.

"And what about oil for salad. Real olive oil. Italian olive oil, please. . . ."

He was conscious that she had stopped writing and was looking up from her pad at him with ever so slight a puckering of her eyes.

"And English mustard?" she asked. "And a few cloves of garlic?"

He met her eyes fully, and at once they opened wide, guileless as the glance of a child. But Duval had heard enough to make him rise at once from the chair and curse the moment he had entered that store.

"Yes," he said. "If you'll fill out that order, I'll drop in for it later."

"Certainly," she said. "In twenty minutes, Mister . . . ?"

"Duval," he responded.

"Yes, Mister Duval. As you go out, do notice our new line of brooms and mops. Brown and Hardy's line, and the very best. Anything in which I can serve you. . . . In twenty minutes, Mister Duval. . . ."

She opened the door for him and smiled him out, a small, mechanical trade smile. And Duval found himself on the sidewalk. He turned up the street with long, slow steps, as one whose mind is profoundly occupied. He was heedless of the next two stores, but he turned in at the hardware shop, and then he sought the black-smith's, where in the rear yard he wandered among rusty second-hand plows, "better than new, because you can see what's the matter with 'em."

When he came onto the street again, the mind of Duval was more composed. The blacksmith followed him to the big sliding doors of the shop, for Duval's order had been comprehensive, from old pitchforks to be remounted on new handles, to plows and harrows, hammers, spikes. plowshares, and a score of odds and ends. The junk yard had been turned into a gold mine on a modest scale.

"You're here to stay?" suggested the blacksmith.

"Unless they drive me out," Duval said, with the faintest of smiles, and sauntered easily down the street.

He was himself again, but he had arrived at one ardent conclusion. After this day, he would never again enter the grocery store and submit to the examination of the big, childish eyes of the girl in white.

This determination completed his gathering peace of mind, and a lighted cigarette made him the old master of himself. He could look out now at the village and smile contentedly at the dark heads of the trees that rose behind it, along the bank of the creek, and at the first touches of green that were appearing in the front gardens.

So he went down to reclaim his groceries at the store, found them gathered near the door, paid the bill, bore them out to the waiting buckboard, and all without once meeting the blue eyes of the young girl.

He had heaped his purchases into the tail of the wagon when the explosion occurred in Pete's Place across the street.

It was like an explosion in more ways than one. It was a series of reports accompanied by wild howls, crashings of glass, splinterings of wood, and then through the battered door of the saloon poured half a dozen men, with the bartender last of all, his long, white apron blown up by the wind of his running and streaming across his shoulder.

And as the bartender ran, he was yelling: "Help! Help! Help! Get the sheriff! Help! Charlie Nash is loose ag'in!"

Chapter Three

It was apparently a well-known name in Moose Creek. An echo of it ran up the street and down: "Charlie Nash!"

Doors slammed, feet rattled down steps, a crowd was rapidly pooled in a broad semicircle around the front of the saloon. No one occupied the center of the street, but the fringes were well filled. Men, women, children came out to listen to the blind show. For inside the saloon, glass still occasionally crashed, a revolver exploded, and some yet-unbroken piece of furniture smashed.

"Poor Pete," said a man near Duval. "He'll be ruined."

"Where is he now?" asked Duval.

The answer came at once, for a bottle flew through the gaping, broken windowpanes in front of the saloon and was dashed to pieces in the road.

"He's busted into the cellar!" yelled the voice of Pete. "Ain't anybody gonna stop him? My gosh, I'm a ruined man! Ain't there any law? Ain't there any sheriff in this here county?"

"He ought to be stopped," Duval remarked to his neighbor.

"Sure, he ought to," said the other dryly. "Ideas

is cheap, but they's a premium on bulletproof men in this here town."

"He's most likely drunk," said Duval, "and couldn't shoot straight."

"That ain't the Nash way," said the other. "The more red-eye, the more they hit the bull's-eye."

"Do they?" Duval muttered, and straightaway turned and looked through the window of the grocery store.

He saw the girl within, not with hands clasped in terror and in horror, but mounted on a sliding ladder, stowing new jars in the dapper rows upon the shelves!

Duval smiled, but not with pleasure. He glanced around him at the gaping, uncertain faces of the crowd, then walked around its outskirts and straight up to the swinging door. Here he hesitated to pull his hat on more firmly.

"He's going in," gasped someone, and a murmur repeated the phrase. "Follow him up. Come on, Buck, you and me."

But no one stirred, and though Duval did not glance behind, he seemed to know that there was no help for him. He pushed the door open, and stepped inside.

Those who waited in the street heard what they had expected—a rapid tattoo of gunshots, and after that, a thudding and crashing—then silence.

"He's dead, the poor chap," said the blacksmith. "And I've lost the biggest bill that was ever ordered out of my shop. The poor sucker's been drilled in about twenty places."

"I told him," said another. "But he knew too much. Here's the sheriff. Hey, here comes the sheriff!"

The sheriff came on a running horse. He looked an impossible figure, with long sun-faded hair blown back over his shoulders, and the brim of his felt hat furled by the wind of the gallop. But the moment he dismounted, throwing his reins at the same instant, he was revealed as a little bandy-legged man. He went forward at a waddling run, firing questions as he proceeded.

The blacksmith became the spokesman.

"Charlie Nash gets on a rampage, shoots up Pete's Place, smashes things a good bit, I guess. Along comes a stranger by name of Duval and walks in on him. I reckon you'll find Duval a dead man inside and Charlie gone off the back way, or else dead drunk."

The sheriff ran straight on toward the door of the saloon, but as he came closer the impetus of his resolution or of his sheer motion wasted away, so that he was walking only slowly when he came to his goal. There, however, he did not stop, but, drawing a revolver from the holster on his thigh, he threw the swinging door wide, crouching to receive a shock.

What he saw made him straighten and run on into the place.

"I told you," said the blacksmith. "This Duval is laid out cold and the sheriff can start a long trail after poor Charlie Nash. Bad blood is sure to come to the top, in the long run, and Charlie's full of it."

The sheriff appeared suddenly at the door again, with an odd expression of bewilderment and disbelief.

"Who's this Duval?" he asked. "Who is Duval?"

At this invitation, the entire crowd swayed in closer.

"A gent you won't forget once you've seen him," said the blacksmith. "The right kind of a lookin' man, Sheriff. Ain't he on the floor, in there?"

The sheriff stepped back. "Come in and look," he said.

They poured in willingly. The entire street was emptied into Pete's Place, where they found plenty to look at in the shape of shattered mirrors, smashed chairs and tables, bullet furrows in the ceiling and along the floor, but not a sign of the dead body of Duval.

They spread eagerly. To the cellar they extended their search, shouting advice, opening every door, staring under beds, but still they found nothing, and gradually they flooded back into the main room of the saloon, where Pete now stood again, considering a little heap of seven $100 bills, together with a brief note, which said:

Sorry, Pete. If this ain't enough, let me know what else you want.

Charlie

The sheriff read this note and looked at the money, also. His bewilderment seemed to grow.

"I know Charlie and what Charlie can do," he said. "I've seen enough examples of that. Didn't he gut this place and the seven men inside of it? But Charlie's gone. What did you hear when Duval came in?"

"Heard guns, then a crashing. Then nothin' at all."

The sheriff closed his eyes and furrowed his brow with the most intense thought. "Duval comes in through the door . . . Charlie lets go at him. Duval dodges in close and takes the gun away from him . . ."

"Takes a gun away from Charlie Nash?" echoed Pete, aghast.

"Shut up," said the sheriff. "I know it ain't possible. But I'm sayin' what must've happened. Takes the gun away from Charlie, and lays Charlie out cold on the floor. Then jerks him up to his feet, half sober. Shows him what he's done. Gets the money out of him. Writes the note for him . . . you see the writin' ain't the same as the signature, don't you? Then shoves him out through the back door and gets him away." He paused and opened his eyes, looking around the saloon dizzily. "Where's Duval's horse?"

"He come in with Dad Wilbur's buckboard."

The sheriff went to the door, saying: "That'll be gone by this time, and nobody'll know where it went."

He was right, for when he cast the door open and stepped into the street, the buckboard had vanished. He went across to the grocery store and touched the brim of his hat to Marian Lane.

"You didn't see this stranger start, Marian?" he asked.

"I was busy in the store when he drove off," she said.

"When he drove off? Then you did see him?"

The long lashes that made a violet shadow on her cheek now rose slowly up and she looked at the sheriff gravely. "I've an idea," she said, "that it wouldn't pay one to know too much about Mister Duval."

"Humph!" he grunted. "Marian, if that gent's come to stay, I want to get some information, and I know that you can get what you want out of a man. You start him talkin' the next time he comes in and I'll give you something to remember me by."

"Of course," she said, "I'll try to remember if I hear him talk, but I'm pretty sure that I'll never have a chance to talk with him again."

"Hey?" he barked at her. "Now whatcha mean by that, Marian?"

"Well," she answered thoughtfully, "the fact is that I don't think he likes women very well."

"Is he as young as that?" grunted the sheriff, frowning.

"No, he's as old as that," she corrected. "What's happened to Charlie?"

"Been pulled out of the fire, thank goodness, by this Duval, from what I can make of it. But he ain't out of trouble yet. I'm gonna make this a lesson for him. It's jail for young Charlie for the disturbin' of the peace. Thirty days would do him a mighty lot of good."

He watched the look of the girl wander askance toward a corner of the ceiling.

"You . . . Marian Lane," he said sternly.

"Yes, Uncle Nat," she said.

"Will you wipe that baby look off your face," he demanded, "and tell me out and out what you had to do with this here affair?"

"I? What could I have to do with it?"

"You, you!" he insisted. "What did you have to do with it?"

"I only know that Charlie was in here just before."

"What was Charlie tryin' to buy? You?"

She nodded, and the sheriff grunted with indignation. "Takes his busted heart over to the saloon and smashes the furniture, eh? But I don't hardly blame him. If I was ten years younger, I suppose that you'd make me raise heck, too.

Maybe thirty days is too long. Maybe a week would do, or just a talk from the judge." He concluded solemnly: "Honey, what a terrible lot you got to answer for."

"Dear Uncle Nat," she said, "what have I to answer for?"

"Who sent Sam Barker downhill to drink?" he demanded. "Who made Josh Newman start for Australia? Why did little Carl Justin leave town? Both of the Wayne boys left the next month. And old Perry Booth got into such a way that he divorced his wife . . ."

"Do you blame all of that on me?" she asked.

"I do," said the sheriff. "I would rather have you out of town than Pete's saloon. And I mean what I say." Then he strode with his odd waddle to the door, but lingered there and finally turned back toward her again.

She stood with her hands clasped and her head hanging.

"You little wo'thless puss," said the sheriff. "You knew that I'd turn around, and you wanted me to see a picture, didn't you? Anyway, honey, you ain't quite as bad as what I make out, maybe. Come over pretty *pronto* and pick yourself out a puppy. The brown has a new litter."

He hurried out into the street, swung into the saddle, and was stopped by Pete, who ran hastily out to him.

"If you give Charlie a runnin' for this job," said

Pete, "he'll sure murder me. Leave him be, won't you?"

"I never lay no whip on a free puller," the sheriff said, grinning. "Don't you worry too much about what I'll do to Charlie, but think a mite about what he's likely to do to me. Howsomever, I can't lay down and let such things as this happen in the town, can I? Get up, Buck!"

He spoke to the horse, touched it with the spur, and instantly was at full speed out of the town and up the hill that led toward the old house of Simon Wilbur.

Chapter Four

Up through the spring rode Sheriff Nat Adare, following the dim old trail by the bank of the creek, and as he went, he took note of all that lay around him, but not with the eye of a lover of beauty, rather that of a hunter.

He came to the lower meadows of the old Simon Wilbur place, and, riding across these, he came to the front door of the cabin. A fragrance of cooking meat blew out to him, and the sheriff found himself a very hungry man. He dismounted, tethered the horse, and knocked at the door.

It was opened to him at once by the stranger. He never had seen the man before, never had heard the pale face described, and yet he knew with a perfect surety that this was Duval. Someone had said that, once seen, he never could be forgotten, or words to that effect, and the sheriff knew that it was true.

"You're Duval?" he said at once.

"And you're Sheriff Adare?"

"D'you know me, young feller?"

"As well, I reckon, as you know me, Sheriff. Will you come in?"

"I figgered on doin' that," nodded the sheriff.

"Bring your hat along with you," Duval said,

failing to move from the doorway, "but we got a rule here that visitors hang their guns outside." He pointed to half a dozen new, large nails that had been driven recently into the logs beside the door.

The sheriff considered them for a moment as though he were reading a page of print. "Most generally," he observed, "I aim to carry my guns with me. It's kind of a rule in my business."

"Why," said Duval, "likely it is . . . but it never does a gun no harm to get a lot of fresh air."

Nat Adare hesitated an instant longer, then obediently unbuckled his gun belt and hung it on the first nail.

"Come in," his host said genially. "You're in time to have chow with me, Sheriff."

"Thanks," said Adare. "I don't mind if I do. Am I smellin' venison or dreamin' by day?"

"This here?" Duval said innocently. "Why no. This here is something that I bought at the butcher's."

"Humph!" said the sheriff, and stepped through the door.

He saw that the place suddenly had become habitable. Two or three old, broken chairs had been revamped. The little table no longer staggered on three legs, and in the corner of the room the old stove that the Wilburs had abandoned as past all use had been made to support a roaring fire.

"Why, partner," said the sheriff, "you must have somebody already with you." He pointed at the two places that were set on the table.

"It's an old rule in my family," said Duval, "never to sit down without laying an extra plate. It's more sort of companionable, Sheriff."

"The same gent in your family fixed that rule, the one about guns and fresh air, I s'pose?"

"The same one. Dad was a great hand for rules, and mostly I find they come in handy. Gimme your hat. That's the best chair over yonder. I'll fix you a basin of hot water if you'll wash your hands. And can I put up your horse and give him a feed of oats?"

"Thanks," Adare said, sniffing again the fragrance of the cookery, and scanning the simmering coffee pot, the frying pan from which the rankness of cooking onions steamed forth, and other bubbling pots that made music, all in varying keys. "Thanks, Duval, but I don't take off my hat in no man's house until I've had a chance to speak my business. I don't eat salt and meat unless . . ." He paused and looked straight at his host. "Duval, what happened down there in the saloon?"

"Saloon?" Duval said in polite inquiry.

"What did you do to young Nash in Pete's Place?"

"Ah, yes," said Duval, recalling himself. "When I sashayed in there, I expected to have a handful of trouble, but the fact is there wasn't any at all."

"Humph!" said the sheriff. "Duval, was Nash there?"

"Perhaps he was," said Duval. "I dunno, exactly. I was sort of flustered and nervy just then."

"Guns went bangin' after you entered," observed Adare.

"Yes, they did," Duval said. "The fact is that I wanted Charlie Nash to know that I was coming along, and if he had any idea of getting out by the back door, that would be a good signal for him."

"Who wrote the note that Charlie left behind him?" demanded the sheriff.

"That's a thing that I dunno as I could say," replied the host. "Sit down, Sheriff. I dunno that any man gets very far by just standing around!"

The point of this remark made Adare grin broadly. "There ain't anybody else in this house, I s'pose?" he asked.

"It was a rule of my old man," said Duval, "never to lock no doors and windows. Locked doors keep the air out and the smoke in, he used to say. Maybe you've heard that saying, Sheriff?"

"I dunno that I have. Your old man must have been a rare one, eh?"

"The finest in the world," Duval responded. "Horses was his main hold, but he wasn't so bad with them, neither. He was full of ideas, but mostly he said that them that wanted to get along in the world had better keep their own floor swept and not mind about the neighbors'."

The sheriff winced a little, but then broke out into frank laughter. "Son," he said, "I like the way that you go about things. Who are you, Duval?"

"Me? Why, just an ordinary cowhand, Sheriff. Got a little stake and come along through the hills looking for a place to set up farming."

"Bein' off the main high road don't depress you none, I guess," said Adare.

"The old man always said," was the answer, "that a mite of solitude done a lot for a man's nerves."

"You don't look nervous, Duval."

"Don't I? I'm mighty glad of that. But I've been reckoned a tolerable nervous man, Adare. Off here by myself is the way that I like to live. The sound of the water, Adare, is a mighty soothing sound. Being off the road don't bother me none. The old man used to say that fast travel wasn't no good, except to them that had some place to go."

The sheriff smiled again. "Duval," he said, "where've you been?"

"Me? Up at the T Bar talking to the cows, walking in the mud, and going to get it at about four thirty in the mornings."

"What made you quit? Or was you fired?"

"I quit because God don't make a long enough

35

day to suit the boss of the T Bar, and he has to piece out with lantern light."

"I seen them kind of bosses," agreed the sheriff with enthusiasm. "Dog-gone their ornery hides. No other reason for quittin'?"

"Between you and me, speaking personal," said Duval seriously, "they got some pretty tough *hombres* up there on the T Bar, and a peaceful gent like me is always nervous around a place like that. The old man used to say that you don't need to light no fuse to set off a mean *hombre*."

The sheriff threw his hat in the corner and suddenly sat down.

"Call in Charlie Nash," he said. "Call in Charlie and be danged, you lyin', four-flushin', two-legged maverick."

The host accepted these strong names with a smile of perfect complacence. "It's all right, Charlie!" he called out.

And the rear door of the shack opening, Charlie Nash appeared with a wash basin in his hands. "Why, hello, Nat," he said. "When I get some hot water into this basin, it'll be about right for you to rub some of the harness blacking off your hands. How are you, old-timer?"

The sheriff looked without malice on the youth. A handsome lad was Charlie Nash and looked the part for which he was given credit around the town of Moose Creek, and over all the broad county thereabouts. For it was said that Charlie

Nash could drink more, fight harder, and lift a bigger weight than any man on the range. Supple, thick-chested, straight-eyed, he was one to have raced for a prize, or fought for it. He was marred in one place, however, for the keen eye of the sheriff found a slightly purple swelling just to the side of the square point of Charlie's jaw. It was, in fact, exactly on the place that prize fighters call the button, because even a tap there is apt to bring darkness.

Charlie Nash, unabashed, noted the direction of the sheriff's glance, and nodded as he put down the basin. "Sure," he said. "That's the place where he turned out the lights. Step up, Nat. There's the soap, and here's a towel."

The sheriff rose, and while he bent over the basin and liberally soaped his hands, his face until the bristling eyebrows were a fluff of snow, his neck until the suds filled the seams that checked it, he talked explosively between rubs.

"Now, boys," he said, "I'm in your hands. You've been and made a fool of yourself, Charlie. And maybe I'm makin' a fool of myself up here."

Here the host broke in quietly: "I reckon that you're wrong about that, Sheriff."

"Why, it's kind of likely that I am," replied Nat Adare. "The way that I figger it, you're sorry for that fracas, Charlie. Besides, I know what started it." He turned from the basin, dripping water on the floor and glaring at Charlie.

Charlie merely grinned. "You can talk right out," said Charlie. "He knows what started it, too."

"Dang," said the sheriff. "I've got soap in my eyes." And he raised double handfuls of water to his face and blew noisily into them. At last he turned, the water leaking from his face over his shirt front. "I reckon, Charlie," Adare said, "that you'll go back with me, and while I sit on my horse with my guns buckled on, lookin' plumb wild, you'll make a speech to the boys and tell 'em how sorry you are that you been a jackass, but the sheriff is gonna give you another chance after you've paid for the harm you done to Pete. And then you'll buy a drink all around."

"Make a talk like that . . . ," began Charlie Nash in great excitement, "I'd rather . . ."

"Sure you'd rather," the host said gently. "The old man used to say that the first speech was the first step up the ladder in politics, and it never made any difference what the speech was about."

Chapter Five

In this history of Duval, it would be of interest to maintain a daily chronicle, except that that would take too long. But, as all the people of Moose Creek maintain to this day, it was impossible to conceive of Duval without conceiving at the same time of his background. For, as they say, it was impossible to make a picture of the man by merely repeating his words and speaking of his deeds. Something was left over, some superior strength that, for a great while, seemed too big a thing ever to find labor that would seriously tax it. That labor was eventually found—but the story of that comes later.

Sooner or later all the chief men of Moose Creek went up to call on Duval. The more daring spirits among the boys used to venture there, also, and they found him plowing with a team made up of his saddle horse and an old brown mule he had bought from Wilbur, or else he was installing the second-hand furniture he bought out of the vacated Gresham house, or he was repairing the roof. Sometimes they found him gathering greens for a salad, or sowing flower seeds in small, femininely neat beds around the borders of his house. Of the evenings, it was known that he kept Monday for laundry work, and for the repairing of his clothes, but the other nights of the week he was glad to have visitors. They would come and find him beside a circular, burned lamp with a green shade, reading, and whoever arrived was certain of a welcome. Yes, day or night Duval was a cordial host. He never was at any labor so important that he would not pause from it and invite the guests to sit on his verandah, if the day were fine, and drink some of Pete's best beer—which was constantly kept cooling in the icy water of the creek—with sausage sliced delicately thin, or cheese of a quality unheard of before in Moose Creek. These repasts were talked of long afterward.

Sometimes late callers in the afternoon were asked to stay on for supper, which Duval prepared like a chef. He could make a man at home in one moment. His pale face was so full of courteous attention, and his gray eyes dwelled so carefully on every word, that each man felt he had been selected from many and placed high in the consideration of the new resident. There were two extra beds, also, which frequently were filled, and it might be said that no man in Moose Creek lived with less real privacy than Duval.

It became known that he was a thoroughly good fellow. He would go down to Pete's Place and drink his beer or his red-eye, up to a certain point, with any man. If the other fellow's pocket were emptied, Duval never permitted a scarcity of drink for all that. Cowpunchers who came in from the range and spent their month's savings in one grand party could be sure of a little present from Duval to pay for their lodging and buy their morning's drink that gave the world another color. Within ten days it would have been safe to say that he had become the most popular man in the district.

Yet, no one knew much about him. He talked freely of his garden, his farm, his work, his house, but he never chatted of his past, beyond his days on the T Bar Ranch, where the boss thought Providence had not furnished our earthly laborers with enough hours of daylight for their work. Beyond that, his life did not appear to be of sufficient interest to keep his attention. He preferred to listen, at any rate, and, of course, that is the greatest of all talents in the world. No matter how bent a visitor might be on extracting from Duval the story of his life, before long he found himself put off onto the tale of his own experiences, and who can resist the listener who seems to understand?

No one, however, could persist with the questioning of Duval past a certain point. It was not that his exploit in the saloon with Charlie Nash had given him a formidable reputation, for he was always the soul of good nature and gentleness, but behind the good nature, there appeared that quality of secret strength that

Moose Creek saw and appreciated, but could not define.

His peculiarities of behavior were few, but they were pointed. He kept close to his work, rarely going out, except to Pete's Place for an hour of an evening, now and then. He no longer came down to do shopping, because old Wilbur came by every day on his way to the stores. Whatever Duval needed was written down on a list, and this the old man carried from store to store, and brought back the needed articles in the evening. Neither did Duval ever go to the post office, for no mail ever arrived for him, a fact upon which the post-mistress commented at some length. Women, too, it was known that he despised. He could be lured out to visit a bachelor's house if only men were there. He would take a hand in poker and hold it until the cock crowed. He would play the piano for the boys, and sing the songs in a deep baritone that, like his laughter, was more profound than one would have expected from his speaking voice. But if there were women included, he was gone at once. No female footfall passed inside the gate of Duval's place, and no girl's voice sounded within the door of his house.

However, men do not object to a companion whose interest is not in the other sex. The peculiarities of Duval were to his honor. They increased his dignity and fortified his position in the community.

It was not from Duval that they learned the first bit about his unknown past. It was from chance.

In that chance, as in the first instance when he arrived in Moose Creek, there appeared Marian Lane, and Charlie Nash, and Pete's Place. There also appeared a stranger.

The latter had come into the Lane store. Most strangers who passed casually through the town generally did enter that store because of the freshness of the window, and the gleaming "city" brightness of the interior, the colorful rows of cans and glass jars, and, most of all, the flower-like face of Marian Lane in her fluffy dress of crisp petals, as it were. Men at a gallop of thirty miles an hour, as they passed that store for the first time, seemed able to look back into the remote shadows of the room and find the beauty of the storekeeper. They could not help reining up, then, and, turning back to enter, buy, stare, and buy some more. To attempt a little conversation, too, that generally froze as they faced the smile that strove to encourage them, but did not seem to understand.

Now, on this evening, the stranger came into the store and, like Duval on the first occasion, he found the girl talking with tall Charlie Nash. His fine fury, of course, had died long ago, and he had come humbly back with apologies and regained as much of a place with her as he ever had attained.

"Dear Charlie," she said to him this evening, "why do you waste so much time on me?"

"Because someday," said Charlie Nash, "you're gonna light up, and I want to be on hand to see the fire. Ain't that a good reason?"

This he said as the door opened, and the stranger came in. It was a very dark evening the sky being covered with low clouds that shut away the last light of the sun and made a lamp necessary in the store.

The lamp hung by three chains from the ceiling, and Marian Lane, squinting a little beneath it, watched the tall stranger come in, with his shadow stretching like a flat, awkward giant behind him.

"Gimme some canned tomatoes," he said, "and make it *pronto*. I'm rushed."

"Oh, yes," said Marian Lane. "For mulligan?"

She looked over her shoulder at him with that bright, childish smile that no man could understand, and that no man could resist. He watched with new interest as her small hands took down the can he required. He watched the faint pucker of her smile as she looked from the smallness of the can to the bigness of the purchaser.

"Yes," he said. "Mulligan. The danged hotel is filled up! There ain't any other place in the town where a white man can stay. But it ain't the first time that I've made home in a jungle."

44

Charlie Nash stood up from his counter chair and regarded the new man carefully. One does not use rough language in the presence of a girl in the West—certainly not of a stranger.

But this fellow was one who apparently made his own rules of conduct, wherever he went. His skin looked like brown leather, a little red-tinted over the bridge of the nose and across the cheek bones. He had a lipless mouth with a hook at one side of it, and eyes so filled with evil that they were unashamed of showing it.

He stared at Marian Lane, and she smiled dauntlessly back at him. It was for this cause that Charlie Nash often accused her of preferring the obviously bad ones to the best lads of the range.

"Well, I'll tell you," she said. "We have a very hospitable fellow who lives just out of town. He might take you in."

"I don't go battering doors for a bed," said the other ungratefully. "A horse blanket, and a swiped chicken, and a can of tomatoes will make me a supper anywhere, and a bed after it."

"Oh, but you wouldn't have to beg," she informed him. "Mister Duval. . . ."

The other reached a gloved hand across the counter with no hurry, but with inescapable speed. It settled on her arm and held her as though he feared that she would escape.

Charlie Nash doubled his fist and came cautiously nearer. He was famous for the strength of his punch, and he rarely had wanted more to use it than on this occasion. But down the right thigh of this traveler there was buckled a long holster out of the top of which blossomed the handle of a full-grown Colt .45. And Charlie was not carrying a gun. It was an act of penance to which Duval had persuaded him after the almost fatal incident in Pete's Place. So Charlie hesitated.

"Duval?" the fellow was saying. "You mean Duval?"

"Do you know him?" Marian asked.

"Know him? Him with the pale face and the gray eyes?"

"Ah, that's the man," she admitted. "You do know him?"

"Do I know him?" he said, releasing her arm, almost flinging it from him. "I know he's lower than a hound. I know he's a sneak and a yellow skunk. I know enough to tell you about him. Where's his house? Know him? Ain't I been lookin' and prayin' for months that I'd meet up with him again? Where's his house, I ask you?"

"Stranger," said Nash, "that there is a friend of mine. I don't allow no . . ."

He almost ran his nose into the end of a leveled gun. It appeared so suddenly that Charlie hardly had time to realize the seriousness of his position. Rolling his eyes in amazement, he saw Marian Lane exhibiting neither fear nor horror, but merely watching with a rather critical curiosity. That was for Charlie Nash almost as great a shock as the gun in his face.

"Fill your hand and then talk to me about your friends!" snarled the big man.

"I ain't heeled," declared Charlie, "or you wouldn't have caught me cold."

"You lie," the tall man said. "You're a sneak and a liar like your friend, Duval, that murders and then sneaks away out of the trouble that he's got comin' to him. I know you, boy!"

"Yonder," Charlie said with quiet fierceness, as though he could keep his words from reaching the ear of the girl on the other side of the counter, "is the only good saloon in Moose Creek. It's Pete's Place. You go in there and tell Pete that I sent you. He'll feed you the best in the place."

"And you?" asked the other, gradually lowering the gun, and finally dropping it into a holster.

"I'll pay the bill," said Charlie Nash, "after I've gone home for my gun and come back and laid you out. I'll pay for your drinks, and they'll be the last that you'll lap up around here, old son."

The other patted the butt of his Colt and nodded with an ugly smile that was almost approval. "I like to hear 'em talk up," he declared. "How long will you be gone?"

"Twenty minutes . . . a half hour . . . not more."

"I'll wait for you," said the tall man. "I'll have you first, and your friend afterward. Ma'am,

I've changed my mind about havin' tomatoes."

He left the can on the counter, unpaid for, and strode through the doorway to the street. They could see his profile as he crossed toward the saloon, and he was smiling broadly, like one who has newly heard an amusing story, but will keep the mirth of it entirely to himself.

"You'd better hurry, Charlie, if you want to get home and back in twenty minutes," Marian Lane said.

He started from his dream and glared at her. "What's in you, Marian?" he demanded of her. "What's wrong with Duval that you mention his name to every gent that comes this way? What's he done that you should have it in for him? Confound me, if you ain't the bottom of all the trouble that I have in this town!"

Chapter Six

When Charlie Nash had left, running through the door like a man pursued, the girl waited for another moment, then acted swiftly. She locked the front door of the shop, pulled down the lamp on its chains until she could extinguish it, and then ran back through the aisle of the store, swerving this way and that in the darkness to avoid every obstacle. She opened a rear door that led to her own room above, and, fleeing up the stairs, she was plucking off white apron and white dress as she went.

Now the door slammed behind her in her own room. She stood in the darkness, panting, fumbling for a match, and around her the rising evening breeze was whispering at the window curtains and stirring the pale sweetness of lavender.

The match broke in her excited fingers, but the next one spurted flames. The flame ran across the wick of the lamp, whose chimney she had tilted to the side. At first it squatted, then rose in an increasing wave of brightness as the wick was warmed.

By that light she dressed, stepping into a khaki skirt, thrusting her arms into a blouse, jamming a hat on her head. The slippers were kicked from her feet and short boots dragged on, while she exclaimed impatiently at this delay.

Then down the stairs she went, swinging herself through the doorway at the bottom by one hand, like a fugitive boy with a father's wrath behind him—so raced outdoors.

Behind her store was a small corral, where one rarely ridden pinto grew fat and sleepy, day by day. Now that his mistress came in dire need of him, he frisked at once to life, and scurried from corner to corner in the corral, throwing up his heels and grunting with content at this pleasant excitement.

She paused to consider darkly, then hurried to the shed and brought out a blacksnake. The first sound of its snapper was enough for the refractory pinto. He stood still, with head stiff and high, ears flattened. He was dragged in by the mane, saddled, bridled, and she was in the saddle.

She did not go up the main street of the town. It was her purpose to remain unseen, in all that followed, if she could manage it—unseen except by one pair of eyes. So she took the way she knew across the back lots, dodging here and there behind the back fences, stooping to keep from being knocked from her place by the low boughs.

In this way she came out upon the high road that climbed the hill, but even this she did not follow, preferring to plunge straight across it and take the dim trail by the bank of the creek. This was daring riding. Even by day it was a broken and difficult way, but she gave the mustang the whip and trusted to his brute intelligence, his more than humanly keen eye.

Rounding the second bend, he slipped heavily, staggering on the verge of the bank. So for a dizzy moment she saw the water beneath her, and felt that the roar of it was leaping up at her ear. Yet he recovered. As a jockey rides, crouched far forward, hands far out on the reins, so she rode, swayed to the side of the high horn of the saddle. Branches shot over her head. The broken ends of limbs torn off by wind or lightning reached at her with jagged points, but through the tangle of danger she rushed the pinto without flinching until she saw the meadows stretch at her side, and headed straight across them for the lighted door of the house.

When they reached plowed ground, it checked the pony so suddenly that she was nearly flung from the saddle, but she recovered in time to check him just beneath the house. There she dismounted and threw the reins. There for a moment she waited, breathing deep, replacing her hat in its proper position, relaxing from the strain of the gallop. Then she went to the door of Duval.

The evening was warm. A shower in the afternoon had purified the air without chilling it, and, therefore, the door was open, so that she could look in on Duval beside his green-shaded light. She had heard other men describe the details of his household appointments so carefully that she knew them now as though her eye already had rested on them. It was like a twice-told tale, one telling of which had come to her in a dream.

She saw the stove, the top of it carefully scrubbed clean of soot and grease stains—that famous stove on the naked, glowing iron of which Duval cooked his famous steaks. She saw the wood for the next fire stacked neatly at one side, the kindling in a tidy pile near it. The table on which those celebrated feasts were spread divided the room in two. That nearest the door was kitchen and dining room. Beyond, stretched the circular rag rug, rich with red and blue. A shelf of books filled a corner—why had no one told her of their titles? Three or four big comfortable chairs and a little round table with a lamp on it—the green-shaded lamp—and the pale face of Duval lost in shadow, the light falling only on his open book and the lean hands that held it.

She saw this in that instant she paused at the door, and knew that Duval had become aware of her before he lowered the book and looked up.

Now that the book was down, he came to her hurriedly. "You ain't come sashaying all the way up here through the night, have you?" asked Duval. "Not because of that tarragon vinegar? That could've waited, even if Dad Wilbur did ask for it again today."

"Why," she said, "it wasn't the tarragon." She drawled the words carefully. "It was a bit of news that I thought you ought to hear. News about a friend of yours."

"What friend?" asked Duval.

"Charlie Nash. A stranger came into the store this evening and happened to hear your name . . ."

"From you?" Duval asked mildly. But she felt the keen, gray eyes fixed on her steadily.

"I don't remember . . . Charlie, I think. It seemed to throw the man into a rage . . . a big, lean, ugly man, with a leathery face and a crooked, thin mouth. He wanted to know where you live, and he said such terrible things about you that Charlie . . ."

"Tackled him?"

"Ran straight into a gun."

"And Charlie's bare-handed," Duval muttered. "Bare-handed, on account of my advice. . . ."

"The stranger is waiting for him in Pete's Place," she added. "He'll be down there in five minutes, or so, I expect. Charlie will, I mean."

Duval reached a hat from a peg on the wall. "You rode up?" he asked in his gentle way.

"Yes," she said.

"I reckon you won't mind walking back, then," said Duval. "I'm kind of pressed for time." He was through the door as he spoke.

Marian, following a step or two, was in time to see him spring on the back of the pinto like a mountain lion at the kill, heard the grunt of the pony as strong knees crushed its sides, then the scuffing of hoofs that struggled for a footing in the loose earth, and horse and rider vanished in the gloom.

She started a step or so after him, but, reconsidering, she went hurriedly back into the house. She was frightened now, it seemed. She looked askance at the steep flight of stairs that led up to the attic rooms, as though they were letting down invisible dangers upon her. The door behind her and the door before, were open throats of terrible possibilities, so that she went on tiptoe, hands clenched at her sides, but still resolutely persisting until she stood before the books.

They were battered volumes. A worn set in blue buckram bindings were labeled with the title *Hakluyt's Voyages*. She saw a *Tom Jones* in two fat volumes. There was a narrow Marlowe beside it, then a book on woodland flowers, one on the game fishes of the Catalina Islands, Boccaccio wickedly set in a dark corner. . . .

She had seen enough titles, and, hurrying toward the door, she only paused to glance at the thick volume he had been reading as she entered.

It was the most self-revealing, the wisest of essayists, Montaigne.

"Cowpuncher?" she said in a whisper. Then, as though fear overcame her, she ran to the door, but paused there and looked back with a frown at all the room, as one striving to fit together the bits of a most difficult puzzle.

"Cowpuncher my foot," she said. "But what is Duval?"

She carried that question unanswered into the open night, then remembered the thing that might be happening even this moment in the village of Moose Creek.

That thought started her running, light as a boy, with a swiftly springing step, straight down through the perils of the dark creek trail. She knew what she would do, if only she could reach the place in time. As she ran, she listened for the half-stifled report of a revolver, heard none, and raced on still faster. Once, she stumbled over a projecting root and tumbled head over heels, but this did not deter her. On she went like a whirlwind, dodging the black trunks as they leaped up under her face, and so ran on behind the rear fences of the village on the creekside until she came opposite the back of Pete's Place. There she turned in.

Chapter Seven

She knew every feature of the place out of the exploits of her childhood, which had ended not so many years before. In those days, whatever a boy would dare to do, she would do, also. She even could lead the way into perilous adventures in the times when she wore overalls, a flipping pigtail—stuffed inside her jacket most of the time—and knees as often bruised and gashed as those of any headlong boy in Moose Creek. And, still, at times, she yearned for the years when she had worn her freckles with never a care in the world. Then came womanhood, and with a nun's cold finger touched her eyelids and her lips.

The old practice was gone, but still she knew how to climb up the brick wall that helped to keep the river at bay from the rear marshes of Pete's back yard. The top of it was not four inches wide, and there was a long fall to the water beneath, yet she stood upright, and walked easily along it, her arms stretched out on either side to give her balance.

She reached the rear wall of the house. On that roof, she once had hidden in an important crisis of a game of hide-and-seek, to the despair of every boy in the village. Now she worked her way deftly across it, lowered herself to the low top of the kitchen, and from this dropped again to the ground. She was inside the back yard of Pete's Place, without the use of a key for entering that sanctuary. And straight before her was an open window that allowed fresh air to blow in among the billows of smoke that filled the barroom.

The big stranger was nearest to her. She could have reached through the window and touched his shoulder. Beyond him stood half a dozen others with tall beer glasses before them, or little whiskeys, no taller than three of her slender fingers. These who stood farthest from her were dimly seen through the haze of smoke from swiftly burning cigarettes. But of one thing she made sure at once, if for no other reason than that the cynosure of all eyes was this newcomer— Duval was not there.

She rubbed her eyes like a child wakening from sleep, and looked again, searchingly, into every corner.

It was true. Duval had not come!

Hurriedly she strove to reconstruct or to adapt her conception of the man. But no matter what shadows she could admit into the picture, she could not think of him as one tainted by cowardice. Yet, when she looked again at the stranger, she was not so sure, for he seemed to Marian Lane the most formidable she had ever seen.

He stood now in an attitude of reflection at the

bar, which Pete polished solicitously before him.

"I seen you before, stranger, I reckon?" suggested Pete.

"No," said the other, "you never did, or you'd know me. I'm Larry Jude."

The girl, in the outer night, saw heads jerked back a little, as though the name had struck them with a physical impact. She herself thought she had heard it in the casual talk of men, or in the newspapers. She could not be sure, except that it was connected with brutal violence.

"There's one around here that's called a man," said Jude. "Duval."

Pete stood stiffly at attention.

"You know his house?" asked the stranger.

"Yes," said Pete.

"Man!" Jude repeated. "Boy-killer, I'd say!"

It was a fierce hour of trial for Pete. He grew pale, but he did not give back from his duty to a friend. "He's pretty highly considered around here," he said. "He . . . he's a friend of mine, in fact."

"A friend of yours?" said Jude. "A friend of yours?"

His great shoulders swayed a little forward over the bar, but Pete stood his ground, very white of face now. Jude, however, laughed suddenly.

"A boy-killer, is what I said. A *boy*-killer. D'you hear me? D'you all hear me when I talk?"

He threw up his head, and every man at the bar

started. Yet they kept their attention, in pretense, fixed upon their drinks, so that it was obvious that they did not wish to have the newcomer's eyes specially focused upon them.

The girl at the window, no matter what her excitement, scanned those faces critically and knew that she would remember them as men who had failed. For all of these men had accepted the hospitality of Duval either in his house or at this bar, or had listened to his singing and praised it, or won from him deeply at cards, or "borrowed" a stake to take them home.

She was hardly amazed when she saw them turn their heads from Jude toward the other end of the bar, for certainly they would have chosen to find another object of interest in that direction.

In fact, she did discern a new form just against the farther window. She could not see the face, but she made out the leisurely posture of the figure, one elbow on the bar and the hands loosely interlocked. Then, as by a single phrase one recognizes a piece of music, so she recognized Duval.

How he had come, she could not tell. There had been no noticeable swinging open of the door, but like a ghost he had melted into this room and materialized at the bar facing Jude.

She glanced back at that lofty man, and saw that from the moment of throwing up his head he had not stirred, except his right hand, which gripped the handle of his Colt. Powerfully it gripped it, the skin whitening over the knuckles. Except for that sign, he looked rather like a soldier, frozen in the attitude of attention.

So were they all, for that matter, from Pete to the least of the drinkers at his bar—one with a glass arrested halfway to his lips, one with a match flaming in his fingertips, but never approaching the cigarette for which it was intended. All of them men of stone, except that careless figure at the farther end of the bar.

He who held the match had his fingers singed, and started as he dropped the red ember. At that movement, the gun of Jude leaped almost from its holster—then slowly sank back again into the leather.

All the line at the bar slipped away softly, as though they would not attract attention, and flattened themselves against the wall. Their heads never had turned. At big Jude they cast not a single look, but kept their attention riveted upon Duval. Marian herself could hardly draw her eyes away until, as a rift opened in the smoke, she saw that he was smiling.

At this, with a gasp, she glanced back at Jude to see how he was taking it. First, she noted that the hand that grasped the Colt was trembling, and then she discovered that his coat across the shoulders was growing slack and tense in turns as he drew in great breaths. His head, indeed, moved a little with the greatness of his breathing. And all at once she forgot the brutality of this man, the savagery grained in his soul and sneering on his lips, as she would have forgotten the ferocity of a tiger, if she had seen it struggling against a torture. So, Jude was struggling. He was able and willing enough to risk his life in quick action, she could have wagered, but this slow torment, this mysterious strain of nerves and will against an intangible force was breaking him. He shuddered suddenly from head to foot. She could see his jaw sag and his tongue moisten his lips.

At that moment, Duval spoke. The sound of his voice made the gun leap again in the holster of Jude, but for the second time he failed to draw it clear. There was a different reason now, she could guess.

"And here's another Jude," Duval had said.

He walked slowly down the barroom, with his hands resting lightly on his hips—far, far from any weapon. Indeed, if he were armed, there was no sign of it. She noted now, as she wondered at the inhuman courage of this man, how he was dressed. Details of his appearance had not entered her eye when she saw him in his house, but now she was aware of common blue overalls cinched about the hips with a tanned belt of common hide, and of a flannel shirt that once had been blue, but was faded almost gray from the washtub. It was open at the throat, and the sleeves were rolled up to the elbows for comfort and coolness in part, no doubt, but in part, one would guess, because the sleeves had shrunk. He could have stood as the commonest plowboy on the range, had it not been for that indefinable thing that still she could not even name, but it was Duval.

As he came, the enchanted eyes of the watchers followed him. Big Jude shrank back perceptibly until his shoulders were pressed against the window and obscured her vision.

She could only hear the voice of Duval speaking terrible things in the most casual tone.

"If I'd had an idea there was more like the kid," said Duval, "I wouldn't have knocked him over to stop him. I would have killed him, partner. But I figured that he was the only one of his kind and that maybe the world wouldn't want to lose him. He'd go behind bars to be looked at, five cents a look. But now that I have a slant at you, I know it's a tribe, like the snake tribe, all poison and of no use, except they eat rats, and toads, and such."

The voice grew very near. With horror in her heart, and unspeakable shame, Marian saw the big shoulders of Jude strain still further back.

"But you've come hunting in the wrong place, Jude. Here in Moose Creek we don't keep rats and toads even to feed the Judes with. You'd starve here, partner. So leave your teeth behind you and . . . get out!"

Jude did not stir.

Marian, one hand pressed against her face, wondered how a brother of hers could have endured such a crisis, and if he would have acquitted himself better than this monster, Jude. But from her very heart rose a great revolt against the strength of the conqueror.

"D'you hear?" said Duval. "Drop your gun belt and move."

There was a heavy clatter on the floor.

Then she could see Jude stumbling toward the distant door, with the back of one hand raised across his eyes as though he wished to cover his shamed face from the sight of men.

He who stood at the very end of the line that was watching by the wall stepped out in the path of that retreat.

"A sneak!" he shouted. "A yellow sneak!" And he struck the big man across the face.

There was no answering blow from Jude, the tyrant. Instead, he shrank cowering to one side, and then ran—fairly ran! In his blindness, he struck the doorjamb, staggered, and then pitched forward into the street, with both his arms cast out before him as though the darkness were more precious than all the treasures of the world.

Chapter Eight

Not at once did Marian go, partly because she was too weak to move from her supporting hold on the window sill, and partly because an unhealthy fascination kept her there to look once more on Duval and wonder again who he could be, and what. She had seen murder done in the streets of Moose Creek. She had heard men scream and pray, and had watched them fight for breath— aye, and when she was only a child. But this was worse than murder that she had seen this night. Murder slays the body, but Duval had dared to put out his hands and lay them on a man's soul.

He did not allow the grisly suspense to end in any prolonged depression, but waved the spectators forward to the bar.

"We need to drink together, friends," he declared. "And you with us, Pete. I want to thank you." He reached his hand across the bar and gripped the most willing hand of the bartender.

"I should've said more," Pete said honestly. "I tried to say more for you, but I was plumb scared and couldn't choke out the words. D'you hear me, partner?"

"I waited out there beyond that window and watched and listened, mighty scared myself," answered Duval, "until I seen that all of you boys was behind me."

Marian, who eavesdropped, pressed her hands suddenly together, for she had wondered how he would do this thing and rescue their self-respect for the loungers in the room. But he had done it. There was not one of them that would not suspect the lie, but there was none who would not wish to believe, and so in time would end by making capital out of his real shame.

Yet, as she watched the actor, with lips compressed and blazing eyes, she admired him for the magnificence of that acting. He was stretching out both hands and gripping theirs.

"Good old Jerry! When I saw you, Mike, it gave me a lot of heart . . . and old Sam wouldn't let me down, I was right sure. Nor Josh, nor Cap Sloane, and Bud Granger never said no to a friend."

He stood by the bar and with a tender eye embraced their foolish, grinning faces. They began to excuse themselves for their great courage, their dauntless bearing—these sheep! They began to make small of their achievement. They began to tell this cunning man that what they had done was nothing compared to what they would have done if the need had arisen. They were only leading on that fellow Jude and were prepared to crush him when the master came in to act for himself.

So they lied to him, and half knew that he saw

clearly through their lies, except that his attention to each spoken word was so serious, and his eager eyes seemed to be reaping the harvest of their friendship.

Only Pete, who had dared to speak for his absent friend in the moment of need, now sat on a whiskey keg with his face in both hands, trembling.

"One of you come and pour the drinks," he said. "I'm tuckered out. I feel right bad. My stars, Duval, how glad I was when I seen you come in, but how scared, too. I didn't see how even you could handle him . . . and then to do it without nothin' in the way of a gun or a knife. Not with your hands, even! I'm kind of sick. Jerry, you take my bar, tonight, and if you don't charge for the drinks, I don't care. I'm gonna go to bed. I'm mighty tired." He left the room.

The girl heard him stamping slowly, sluggishly up the stairs to his room. With a warm rush of emotion, she said to herself that Pete was too good a man to be bartender in Moose Creek, or in any other town.

The street door was cast open again. This time young Charlie Nash came into the room, high-headed, bright of eye, like a thoroughbred groomed for a race, and expecting one.

"It ain't over yet, is it?" he cried. "That . . . that thing that I passed slumping down the street . . . that wasn't him, was it?"

They hailed him with a joyous shout as Jerry poured the second round and assured him that it was indeed *him,* and the him was none other than Larry Jude. But the master had met him, and faced him, and crushed him.

They reached their hands to Duval. They patted his shoulders, they waved in honor to him as though their hands supported standards. Ah, they were glad to look up to him as their captain now. How willingly they would die for the sake of this great man's friendship.

These thoughts Marian furnished to them, in her bitter scorn of the crowd as they flocked around Duval. They had not even noted that while he encouraged them, he had not tasted the liquor himself.

She saw Charlie Nash brush them aside and confront Duval.

"How did you do it, Duval?" he asked. "How did you do it, David?"

The girl, listening, was oddly startled to hear that name. For some absurd reason, it seemed out of place for Duval to have a first name like other men.

"All I know," Duval said in his quiet way, "is that he was here, and now he ain't. But how it happened, I dunno."

"He stood up there at the end of the bar . . . ," began Jerry.

Duval raised a hand that stopped this rehearsal.

"My old man," he said with a faint smile, "always used to say that the dirty laundry should be done up on Mondays, so's the rest of the week could be clean. Well, boys, this ain't Monday, you know. Drink hearty! Step up, Charlie, boy! Jerry, come here."

He drew Jerry aside, close to the window. Marian heard him say: "Don't take money for these drinks. But keep a reckoning, and let me know what it comes to, will you?"

"Chief," Jerry said, "what you say is all the law that I want for what's right and what's wrong. Hey, boys, drink up, and have another!"

"Let everybody that comes in have what he wants," said Duval. "Bottoms up, boys! Good luck all round. Who can start us a song? You, Mike. Start us a chorus, will you?"

The song began with a rouse. It rose to a roar.

When Marian Lane looked again, she saw that newcomers were surging through the street door to join the fun. But the whole aspect of the crowd had changed, unknown to itself. For Duval was gone.

While he was there, it had been a play upon a stage with a chief character present who was either a hero or a villain, she could not tell which.

But now it was simply a confused and stupid drunken party, and she hurried away with a sense of shame that she had remained so long. It was not so easy to go as it had been to enter. In the other days, when she wore overalls like the boys of the town, she had been able to swing herself lithely up from the ground to the projecting kitchen eaves, and from the kitchen roof to that above. But now it was a great strain.

Twice she failed in her effort, and then, resting, panting, she looked up to the broad, bright face of the heavens and told the stars that she was not half of what she once had been. This touch of scorn seemed to nerve her, and the third attempt was successful, and thereafter she rapidly gained the upper roof, stole along the gutter to the place above the wall, and lowered herself to it. She dared not walk boldly along it now, however, as she had done in coming. Something had gone from her in the meantime, and she had to crawl on hands and knees, gritting her teeth with self-contempt the while.

A moment more and she had dropped down outside the wall. She did not start off at once, but leaned against it for a moment, taking breath, adjusting herself to the miracle that she had seen. It was a bitter task, for she was one who professionally disbelieved in miracles.

However, she gathered herself together presently as one willing to leave some of the problems of today for the meditations of tomorrow, and started for home. It was not until she had made a step that she realized someone was standing before her, almost lost in the darkness of the trees—someone who must have been there all during the time she scrambled down the wall and then rested against it.

A scream leaped into the throat of the girl and died behind her set teeth. The impulse to run merely made her sway and was equally mastered. Yet she could not help drawing back from him, though Duval was no giant, and she knew it was he.

"Yes, sir," drawled the voice of Duval, "doggone me if it ain't hard to find a quiet place for a stroll around Moose Creek. A gent or a lady that kind of wants to promenade a bit, he has to look around for a place where there won't be somebody else."

"You saw me through the window," she declared. "But you couldn't have seen my face."

"There wasn't nothing to that," he declared. "But I thought that I saw something like a khaki sleeve and figured it might be you. So, I bring around the horse to give it back to you. And thanks a lot, Miss Lane."

He tugged at something—and there came the pinto, which had been standing all this time beneath the trees, at the end of the long reins.

"Them that start out on horseback hadn't ought to come back on foot," Duval said gently, "just because they loaned a horse to a friend. Good night, ma'am."

"Duval!" she called to him as he turned away. "Mister Duval."

He came back to her at once, though keeping his distance. It was hard to talk to him, but she felt that this was the time to make an effort.

And Duval, after one instant of pause, spoke to fill in the silence and put her at ease. She was grateful for that. "I haven't thanked you either for the pinto. He runs mighty straight and fast for me, though I near beaned myself on one of them branches."

"You waited for Charlie. Was that it?" she asked him.

"Why," said the drawling voice, "it was kind of partly that I didn't want Charlie busting into my party, and partly that I wanted to size up Jude through the window. It isn't an easy thing to be thrown into the ring with a gent whose style you don't know."

She knew it was not true, but that, as appeared to be the rule with him, he was hiding his real scorn of all other men beneath an apologetic manner. From the same source had sprung his desire to put the men of the barroom at their ease and recall their self-belief. For he who possesses the key to a treasure can afford to throw coppers to beggars.

Then all the other questions that had been brooding in her mind, not yet come to words, drew back, and became more nebulous than ever.

She knew that he had erected a wall between them, and she said simply: "Good night, Mister Duval."

Yet, as he went off through the night, there was fierce indignation rising in her. He had feared her because she had seen a little through him and his disguise that day in the store. If he despised her now in her new rôle as eavesdropper, she bitterly resolved to make him change his mind. So, jerking at the reins with cruel impatience, she started back for her house.

Chapter Nine

It is true that in the West, alone of all places in the world, a man is assumed to be innocent until he is proved to be guilty. And, in the West, it is even true that guilt of certain kinds does not make a whit of difference. It is also true that one good action will establish a Westerner for life. He is said to have been tested and to have stood the fire. But two such actions, in one small town, under the eyes of one audience, were more than enough to place Duval upon a pedestal. The uncritical audience of Moose Creek believed, and perhaps they were wise, that it is folly to criticize, and that it is infinitely better to live than to talk about living. With the exception of Marian Lane, who had no confidants, probably there was not a soul who felt that there was anything evil in the power of Duval. He had picked young Charlie Nash out of the slough and set him on the high road. He had met the juggernaut, Larry Jude, and crushed him in the palm of his hand.

Besides, he minded his own affairs but was willing to listen to those of others. He worked hard, improved his house and his fields, never wore a sour face about weather or people, continually smiled on the world, and, above all, treated his bad bargain with Simon Wilbur as a joke of which he, Duval, was the point.

The old man, pricked in conscience, had gone to offer a reduction in the price he had accepted, though in mortal dread of what his wife would say afterward. But Duval insisted that finished business is dead business, and must not be brought to life again.

Moose Creek learned of this and, adding it to the other established virtues of Duval, decided by an almost unanimous vote that the town had acquired an ideal citizen.

Nevertheless, no matter how greatly they appreciated Duval, they could not help being curious about him. He was, in Moose Creek, what reporters would have called "a headline every day." And when it was learned that Duval had been in New York before he came West, that he had there seen a beautiful horse at a horse show, that he had now bought that horse and was having it shipped to Moose Creek, was it any wonder that half of the town assembled on the morning the train was due?

When the train arrived, it was almost characteristic of Duval that he was not present and had sent down Simon Wilbur to bring the horse home. So, when the door was rolled back and the gangplank fixed, the representatives of Moose Creek saw a tall, lean, smooth-shaven man, who looked sixty but might be seventy, issue from the shadows of the car and lead down the plank a most disappointing chestnut mare.

It was true that she picked up her feet daintily going down the plank, but she had a long, ugly head, her withers were high, and her neck was painfully long. So were her legs. As Doc Murphy put it, if they had been cut off at the fetlocks, she would have looked "nearer to something like."

"Duval's been sold," was the opinion of everyone, except Pete, who walked around her with care, lifted her blanket, thumbed her shoulders, felt her bone.

The old man who accompanied her—a marvel to Moose Creek that any man should be so extravagant as to ship a horse from New York and a man to take care of it!—turned to Pete with a smile that appeared crookedly, and only upon one side of his mouth. He had a secretive way of winking and speaking from the side of his face opposite to that on which the smile appeared.

"You know a horse, I guess," he said. He immediately added that he would like to know the way to Duval's place, and Simon Wilbur at once took charge.

They went up the street, the two old men in the seat of the buckboard, and the mare led behind, going at a rather shuffling trot that knocked up the heaped and rutted dust into a cloud. She pulled back lazily at the rope, moreover, and with her lower lip flopping as she went by the grocery store, she looked to Marian Lane like a cartoon of a horse.

"What did he mean?" asked Doc Murphy of Pete. "What did he mean? As if we that been pretty nigh born on horseback didn't know a horse when we seen one?"

Pete grew remote and almost surly. "Aw, I dunno," he said. "Maybe she can move."

"Not more'n barely," Doc said. "You seen her go down the street?"

The answer of Pete was considered very odd indeed. "Picture horses never carried my money."

For Pete had been East, and had bet and lost his one big roll on the ponies. The name of the mare was considered odd, also. For her old groom had said she was called Discretion, or Cherry, for short.

But the general opinion was that Duval had been sold indeed. It was a complacently taken opinion, for though no one liked to see Duval injured, it was pleasant to know that he was human. It was like hearing that Rembrandt could not paint a house.

In the meantime, the buckboard jogged up the hill and Simon Wilbur tried his expert hand on the new arrival, the chestnut's guardian. The latter was perfectly willing to talk about himself, and how many years he had been a groom, and in what stables, but on the important point, which was Duval, he knew nothing. He never had heard the name before. He never had seen the man. He did not know whether Duval was young or old. All he knew was that he had been hired to take the mare all the way West.

"Is she worth it all?" Simon asked rather spitefully.

"Well," said the groom, considering, "she can jump enough to make the hind legs follow the forelegs."

Simon Wilbur fell into a disgusted silence, for he had expected to take home to his wife an entire story, and now he felt that he could bring only an installment.

At last they reached the old, sagging, wooden gate through which one entered the Duval place, and here Wilbur drew up.

"You'll be goin' back soon, I reckon?" he asked.

"I dunno," said the groom, who had said that his name was Henry. "Might be that he'd like to have me handle the mare for a few days and get her on her feet." Then he waved good bye to Wilbur and advanced through the gate, leading the mare. He took the trouble, however, to call out: "Hey, Duval! Here she is!"

His call was answered almost at once by a shrill whistle. And glancing back through a gap among the trees that grew thick at the margin of the property, Wilbur had an unexpected sight of the lifeless mare jerking away from Henry, the groom, and running across the meadows toward the house. She went with her head stretched out and with a long, bounding gallop so different from the gait of a cow pony that Wilbur laughed as he watched it. This singular stride faded her out of view almost at once, and Wilbur jogged on down the road, still chuckling to himself.

The way the mare had responded to the whistle had not surprised Henry, the groom, however. As she cantered away, he strolled still more slowly forward, giving his attention to the fields on either side of the driveway up which he was advancing, and even coming to a stop to watch the flight of a bird that rose nearby and shot up into the sky. One could not have said that there was peace in his face and that relaxation of the spirit that generally comes to those who are in the quiet of the countryside. Instead, he turned his head restlessly from side to side as though the grass in the fields, and the very trees, and the voice of the creek could tell him something as definite as words.

So, pausing, examining, he strolled on toward the cabin, which seemed to him a greater novelty than all else. This and the sheds behind it he stared at as if they were so many human faces, each worthy of separate consideration, each expecting something worth adding to his total. He rounded the corner of the house and came in clear view of Duval.

The latter was engaged in walking around and

around the chestnut mare, a task that she made difficult, for though she dropped her head to pick at the grass now and then, she insisted on following her owner closely, with ears that pricked with pleasure.

"Cherry hasn't changed a bit," Duval said, his back to the groom. "She gave you plenty of trouble on the way out, I reckon, stranger?"

"Oh," Henry said, "she's got a mind of her own, but I like folks that can think for themselves."

Now, at the sound of his voice, Duval stiffened a little, like one who hears something in the distance and fixes his attention upon it.

At last he said curtly: "Put her in the pasture corral over there by that shed."

"Certainly, sir," Henry said, and, taking up the lead rope, he took the mare toward the corral.

He coaxed her along with much patience, and this was needed, because she made stubborn efforts to leave him and go after Duval, who had gone into the cabin. However, Henry seemed unhurried. He humored her, and all the while with the same secret smile that he had worn before, as though he knew a jest that even a horse could appreciate if he told it.

In this manner, he brought her to the pasture, took off her blanket, looked into the little watering trough, and, finding that it was slightly lined with green scum at the sides, he emptied it and spent some time in scouring it clean. When he had pumped it full of sparkling water again, he left the corral and went with his usual lack of haste up the path to the house. When in front of it, he paused, surveying the big trees by the creekside with special interest.

"That pair by the path must be three or four hundred years old, sir," he suggested.

He received no answer. Again, the faint smile appeared on the face of Henry, and now he went in across the verandah, and through the doorway. Just inside of the shack he paused again, not to look at the owner, but to survey the furnishings, as though they told him more about Duval than the face of the man could do.

The latter, in the meantime, sat at ease in his most comfortable chair, with his hands inter-locked and his gray eyes quietly studying the groom.

"Henry?" he said at last.

Henry straightened himself. "Yes, sir," he said.

"A long trip, wasn't it?"

"A very long trip," agreed Henry.

"And after such a long trip," went on Duval in his gentle way, "Henry, what do you want to make it worth your while?"

At this, Henry no longer smiled his secret smile, but laughter rose up and shook him with a dry violence of mirth. "Why, sir," he said, "I ain't hardly had a chance to look around and see what's worth taking."

Chapter Ten

In spite of its oddity, Duval accepted the last speech with a nod.

"Sit down, Henry," he said kindly.

"Thank you, sir . . . I'll stand," said Henry.

"You have plans for returning at once, I suppose?"

"Me, sir? Not at all, sir. I was raised in the country . . . that's where I learned horses."

"Now I remember, of course. You've always said that horsemen have to grow up on the grass. But do you mean that you like it out here? Hardly that, Henry!"

"Why not, sir?"

"So far from the ponies? So far from the interesting big cities, too?"

"Old men go back to the soil, sir."

"But these big open spaces are only meant for people who have been born in them. Strangers never can quite adapt themselves to the range, Henry."

"No, sir?"

"No, as a matter of fact, they find the elevation a great trial. They're apt to grow short of breath. They're even apt to grow dizzy and fall from a cliff."

"Me," Henry said genially, "I've always been used to heights, sir."

"Ah, yes?" said Duval.

"Besides," Henry said, "I've got to be an old man, sir, and so I've left all my affairs in pretty good order."

"You're a wise man," said Duval.

"Left letters," said Henry, "to be opened a month after I left New York, unless the bank heard from me in the meanwhile. Letters about my will, and such things, sir. So it would be pretty hard to see how trouble would bother me, sir."

"Of course," Duval agreed. "You really should sit down, Henry. Out here one doesn't stand on formalities, you know."

"Just as you please, sir," said Henry, and sank into a chair.

"You think of staying on, then?"

"I don't mind if I do. As I was saying, I take to the open air, and it takes to me. You'd have room for me here, sir?"

"You can see for yourself that it's a small house."

"Well, I wouldn't want to crowd you, Mister . . ."

"Certainly not," Duval stated hastily. "I was only considering your own comfort, Henry."

"Ah, sir," said Henry. "That was always your kind way, sir."

"Besides, in this part of the country we don't 'sir' one another."

"Very good, sir. I'll remember that."

"If you insist on staying?"

"Insist? Of course, I don't want to press in on you, Mister . . ."

"No pressing in, Henry. Delighted to have you, of course. You have a bag with you?"

"Yes. Wilbur brought it up in his rig. I left it at the gate when I brought up Cherry."

"Henry, I'm a curious man and want to ask you a question. What brought you out with Cherry?"

The same secret smile that often before had twisted the face of Henry reappeared on his lips.

"That makes a story," he said.

"I'd like to hear it, if I'm not prying."

"Well, then, when the news came of your drowning . . . which was a shock to me . . ."

"No doubt it was," cut in Duval. "Go on."

"I remembered that you could swim only about twice as well as an otter. It was a half-mile pull to the shore from where that boat upset. . . ."

"No, nearly a mile."

"All right, sir, but I looked at the place and all at once I was sure that you could have made the land. Why didn't you, then? Because you didn't want to. Why didn't you want to? You were young, you felt your blood as much as any yearling just in off the grass. What would make you want to go off stage? Nothing, maybe, except a few debts. And it wasn't your style to scratch at the last minute."

"You're full of compliments," Duval commented. "But I'm still interested."

"Besides, the boat looked too small to beat you. I don't know how to put it any other way. When you hear that a selling plater has beat a stake horse at even weights, you know there's something wrong. I felt that way when I saw that boat. I told myself that it couldn't have beat you."

"Thank you," said Duval. "Go on, Henry."

"When your things went at auction, I was on hand, and I saw Slater and Grimm bid on the mare. Now, no matter what happened to the rest of the stable, and the house, and the furniture, and all that, I made up my mind that even if you were dead, you'd stir in your grave when Discretion was sold.

"I sat up there in the stand at the auction and watched them prance her up and down. They had a fool of a boy up that couldn't show her a whit . . . in fact, she never had right hands on her, except yours, sir."

A flash of pleasure appeared in the pale face of Duval. "She has to know that she's respected, but not feared," he explained.

"Right, sir," Henry agreed. "When the idiot of a boy showed her, he couldn't keep her straight, and she sky-hopped the jumps like a rabbit, it was a shame to see."

"The puppy!" Duval said angrily.

"Even that way, the bidding went to three thousand. But Slater and Grimm wouldn't let her go, of course, at that price. They entered her afterward in the Chester Point-to-Point and gave young Enderley the mount."

"He hasn't the strength or the brains for Cherry," Duval murmured.

"He tried to get both out of Scotch highballs," Henry said, grinning in his lop-sided way. "And he did fine up to the last half mile. Then the whiskey faded out of him. He rode her like a lump of lead and fell off at the last jump, when she was three lengths to the good. I wished he'd broken his neck. However, I knew that race would boost her price. I used to drop in at the stables of Slater and Grimm nearly every day and have a look at her and a talk with the boys. Then one day they told me that she was sold. A man from the West had seen her shown last winter, liked her, and now he bid up for her . . . bid high enough to make even Slater smile. They were shipping her out.

"Now, sir, I put two and two together and thought that it made a thousand. So I said I'd always wanted to take a trip West, and I'd go along with her, for the chance to travel, and no pay. Of course, they took me, and that's how I'm here. I knew, somehow, that if you were living, you were Duval. And so it turned out."

"So it turned out," agreed Duval without enthusiasm. He stood up suddenly. "Bring up your suitcase, Henry!"

"Thank you," said the groom, and went at once to fetch it.

Duval stood in the doorway of his house and looked out on the spring that had spread more thickly beneath the pines, the leaves of trees and shrubs turning a darker green. Through the woods, it was impossible to see so far through the transparent mist of coming foliage, but the farm was now embowered in impenetrable hedges. He was closed in, and that thought made him lift his pale face and look beyond the treetops to the mountains that walked off far-away into the sky.

Now Henry was coming up the path, leaning far over against the weight of his suitcase, his mouth compressed with effort. Duval hurried down to him and took the burden lightly in his hand.

"Whew!" Henry gasped, relieved. "I'm turning into an older man than I thought, sir."

"An old body with a young brain, Henry," said Duval, "is one of the highest-priced things in the world."

They chuckled together as they reached the house, and Duval laid the suitcase on the bunk in the corner of the room.

"Unlock it, Henry," he said.

Henry looked askance at him, hesitated, but then obeyed. He stood anxiously by.

"I'm going through it," Duval informed him.

"Sir?" said Henry. "Going through it?"

"Yes, stand away from me."

Henry, with a very dark face, stood back without a word, and Duval raised the top of the case.

All inside was packed very neatly, and with great care Duval lifted out article by article, until the case was half emptied.

Through the rest of it he passed his hands, feeling here and there until he touched something that seemed to tell him what he wanted to know, for he looked at Henry with the slightest of smiles.

"I thought so," Duval said, and drew from the suitcase a package wrapped in oiled silk, beneath which the texture of chamois showed through. As he fingered this, a faint gritting of metal on metal was heard. "I'll take this," he said.

Henry was biting his lip. "I don't know . . . ," he began.

"You don't understand, Henry," said Duval. "I lead a quiet life here, as you can see for yourself. A very quiet life. I'm rarely off the farm, in fact, but stay here most of the time, with no face to see, except those of the trees. When you realize that, Henry, I'm afraid that you won't find yourself as much at home here as you expected to be. Am I right?"

Henry sighed, but then shrugged his high, narrow shoulders. "Blood lines and performance is what I bet on," he said. "I'll stay here with you, sir."

"Very well, then. Your bunk is that one in the other corner. Take your stuff over there. You'll find some shelves behind that curtain. Get into old clothes. Everyone works in Moose Creek, Henry."

Saying this, he turned his back on Henry and descended through a trap in the floor, down a ladder into the cellar. There he dug a small hole in a corner next to the wall, placed the package in its wrapping of oiled silk in the aperture, and then covered it over and tramped down the moist earth. The remnant of loose soil he scattered here and there, before returning to the floor above.

There he found Henry apparently quite recovered from his blues. He already had changed into stable clothes and a pair of heavy boots. An old slouch hat was on the back of his head, and he gave Duval his twisting grin as he said: "It's time to work, sir. But I ain't seen a cow on the place. It's not a farm without a cow."

"I'll get one," said Duval. "I've always wondered what was missing, and, of course, milk is the thing."

Chapter Eleven

Woman, like the elephant, never forgets, and cannot forgive. So it was that Marian Lane, behind her emotionless property smile, was filled with bitterness when she remembered how Duval in their last encounter had checked and thwarted and scorned her by his superior wit.

He had given an acid strength to her old passion for discovering who Duval might be. She transferred a portion of her curiosity, naturally, to the very plain-looking chestnut mare that had arrived for him from the East, and promptly she decided that the secret virtues of that animal—since it was not to be expected that Duval would waste money and time on a thing no better than she looked to be—must be investigated. Not that she expected to learn much, but she was eager to learn a little.

She hit at once on a plan for making the investigation, and started to work on Charlie Nash the next time he entered the store.

"Poor Charlie," she said. "I suppose you're terribly embarrassed now?"

"About what?" he asked her.

"Why, the way everyone is laughing at your friend."

"You mean Duval, of course," said Charlie

Nash. "Nobody's laughing at Duval in this here town, honey. Unless it's you. And what's your call?"

"At Duval, and his mare," she insisted. "When I saw the poor, pitiful thing going up the street, I couldn't believe my eyes."

"Look here, Marian," the youth objected. "She's got points. She's got bone . . ."

"She's full of bones!" said the girl.

"And legs, too."

"Yards of 'em," she said.

"What makes you hate Duval so?"

"Hate Duval? What an idea! Why should I hate him?"

"I don't know. That's why I'm asking."

"Charlie," she said, "what a silly thing to say."

"It ain't silly. You're always taking a crack at Duval."

"If the mare's any good, Charlie, what is it good for?"

"You can't go on a man's looks," Charlie said stubbornly, "or on a horse's, either."

"But what is she good for?"

"How can I tell?"

"Does she look good for anything?"

"As I was saying . . ."

"Stuff!" said Marian. "He simply doesn't know horses, and you have to admit it."

On that range, this was far worse than saying that a man could neither read nor write.

"I'll bet she can run," Charlie said, desperate.

"How much will you bet?"

"Anything you want."

"I'll give you odds," she answered. "Two dollars to one."

"Who'd be the judge?"

"Why, there's the race at the end of the rodeo at Kendry tomorrow."

"You know Duval. He won't . . ."

"I don't know him at all."

"You know he won't leave the farm."

"He'll do anything for a friend, you always say."

"Well, and it's true. Everybody knows that."

"You're his friend, I suppose."

"I reckon I am."

"Then why don't you ask him?"

"Maybe I will. But he won't enter Cherry."

"Not for a friend?"

"Well, if I have a chance to see him."

"I saw him go into Pete's just this minute."

Charlie was cornered, and, sullenly swinging around, he crossed to Pete's Place and found Duval there, treating his new companion, Henry, to a tall glass of beer.

"Partner," said Charlie, "will you do something for me?"

"Anything I can," Duval answered offhand.

"Try that mare of yours in the race at Kendry tomorrow. I've bet that she could run." He saw the face of Duval darken, and added hastily: "I wouldn't bet she'd win. I know she couldn't beat Dave Shine's blood horse. But I've bet she can move a little."

Duval flushed a trifle. "I'd a pile rather not," he said. "Unless you keep me to that promise."

"I'm gonna keep you," said Nash. "Dog-gone it, man, I don't want to bother you, but you'd enjoy the rodeo, anyway. Will you come?"

"I've given you a promise," said Duval shortly. "I suppose I'll be there."

And he was.

Though, to be sure, rodeos did not seem at all to his taste, and he was nowhere to be seen with his mare until the very end of the bulldogging contest, in which Charlie Nash himself won glory and almost first place, except, as everyone said, that he had been thrown at the toughest maverick of the lot. But when the riders lined up for the race, while loud voices were shouting bets and offering odds, Duval appeared on Discretion in the starting row.

There were already eight known horses in the string and not a one but made Discretion look a sad thing indeed, especially when she grew excited and began to prance, throwing her long legs about. People chuckled as they looked at her—chuckled behind their hands, because those who had not come from Moose Creek, nevertheless had heard of Duval. His name had gone like magic over all the range.

Charlie Nash, grimly bent on supporting a friend who he had introduced to trouble, savagely bet a borrowed $100, and got odds of eight to one—high odds for such a race as this. Then he returned to the place where Marian Lane stood near the finish with a big black camera in her hands. She was setting up a tripod as he came near.

"It ain't gonna be such a close finish as all that," Charlie said gloomily. "They won't need a picture to show which one got first. When Dave Shine's blood horse gets warmed up, he's gonna swallow this whole field." He added grimly: "Then you'll feel a lot better."

"Why," Marian said sweetly, "it's no disgrace if poor Duval doesn't know horses. I'm sure he's shown that he knows a great many other things."

"You've got a mean way about you sometimes, Marian," the boy assured her. "What's Duval ever done to you, anyhow?"

"Hush," she said. "They're about to start . . . and . . . oh, he's left at the post. They ought to call them back and start over . . . what a shame! Will he pull up? Will he pull up, Charlie?"

She asked it eagerly as the starter's gun exploded while Discretion was turned broadside to the course. The rest swept away in a thundering line, while Discretion, floundering behind, slowly straightened and then began to labor after the field.

Her efforts brought great laughter from the spectators. It was like the running of a jack rabbit—a young jack rabbit that had not yet found its strength—so did the long, bounding gait of the mare impress the watchers, while the rest of the field scoured rapidly before her.

"And that's Mister Duval's fine horse," the girl said scornfully. "He ought to pull her up, even if he doesn't."

However, Duval was not pulling her up, though he made no effort to overtake the others, but simply had rode the chestnut mare. So the runners swung around the first half of the circle, to the point where the early leaders began to tire, and now a fine black stallion rushed out from the pack as though they were standing still.

A wild yell of triumph went up for that favorite.

"There goes Duster! There goes Shine's horse. The race is over, boys!"

The race seemed indeed over, as the last bend was rounded, when through the tiring pack cut a chestnut streak that seemed to make but one stride to two of the others. Duval, and Discretion, coming like the wind—so uncomfortably fast that all shouting ceased, and Charlie Nash, standing on the fence, raised both his hands, whispering: "Eight to one. Oh, you ugly beauty. Come on, Cherry."

Cherry came on, but not fast enough. Those who watched, wondered why Duval had not taken up his whip. Even hand ridden, she was making a race of it and gaining on Duster's frightened rider, but what if a whip were laid on her? Indeed, it looked as though her head were drawn in by the pull that Duval was giving her.

And Marian, crouched behind her camera, watched with parted lips and with hands gripped hard, as though she saw a thousand things more interesting than a mere horse race—as though, indeed, there were volumes of hidden meaning being revealed to her eyes alone.

The rest of the crowd gave tongue like a hungry pack—and as they yelled, the right rein of Cherry's bridle parted. They saw Duval sway back. They saw the mare dart ahead.

It was like the release of a stone from the hand of the thrower. With every leap, she gained momentum. Her long neck was stretched straight out, her ugly, lean head was snaky as she thrust forward, and the very wind of her going seemed to have flattened her ears along her neck. She looked no longer awkward. She was like a thing with wings, and every stroke carried her swiftly up toward the stallion.

He should have won, however, if the rider had done his duty. But just before the wire, looking back in fear at that sound of hoofs, the youngster let the stallion swerve.

That was fatal. Discretion shot under the wire, first by a head.

That, however, was not the important thing in the eyes of the winning rider, for as Duval looked to the side of the track in crossing the line, he saw the big black square of the camera aimed not at Discretion at all, but at the height of his own head. He jerked his face in the other direction, but, somehow, he knew that he was too late.

Already she knew too much, he guessed, and now she was well on the way to learning everything!

Back at the start, the girl was gripping the arm of Charlie Nash, who was almost the only voice to celebrate. He and Pete, the bartender, who, strangely enough, had chosen to bet on the mare of his own free will and not out of loyalty to the rider of Cherry.

"Listen to me, Charlie," Marian said. "Collect your bets tomorrow. I have to go home. I have to go fast. Do you hear me, Charlie?"

"Sure I hear you. Can she run, Marian? Can she run?"

"Like the wind . . . she's wonderful . . . only get me away quickly, quickly."

"Sure," Charlie said, sobered. "But what's the matter?"

"I forgot something at the store. Oh, make the horses fly on the way back!"

Chapter Twelve

It was night before the sweating horses of Charlie Nash brought the girl back to Moose Creek. He himself was serious enough before they arrived, and he would have got out of the buckboard in which he had brought her home.

"There's something wrong, Marian," he said. "You're sick, or something."

She laughed, and tried to make that laughter sound natural, but knew that she had failed.

"Maybe I'm about to be ill, but I'm not now," she told him. "You go along home, Charlie. There's nothing for you to worry about and nothing that you can help me in. Good night. I'm glad you made a big winning plus my dollar."

She was gone into the darkness of the store before he could answer, and then he heard the front door locked and double locked.

She herself, standing in a blue funk inside the big glass windows, felt, when she saw young Nash drive away, that she had stripped herself of her last chance of safety. Then she gathered her courage and went on about the thing she had planned.

She had no faith in the locked front door, though she did have some in the chain and bolt that she fastened across it. The windows she locked, also, and despaired of securing them in a better manner.

Then, lamp in hand, she walked back down the aisle, while the shadows rose and fell softly around her with every step she made. The rear windows she secured in the same manner. She would have gone into the cellar to fasten its two windows, also, but when she raised the trap to go down, something seemed to rush at her out of the darkness, the flame dwindled and turned blue in the throat of the chimney, and she dropped the door with a crash.

This also possessed a bolt, though it seemed to her now a most feeble one. She shot it home, and remained stunned with terror, feeling the noise of that fall still reverberate along her nerves. After that she had to pass through the door that led to the rear stairs, lock this behind her without the additional security of any bolt, and climb up to her own chamber.

The door stood wide open, and for a moment she dreaded to enter, leaning sick and helpless against the jamb, for it seemed that even if the rest of the building had been empty, here she would certainly find what she feared. But when she raised the lamp above her head, it showed her nothing but emptiness. She set her teeth, entered with a quick step, and closed and locked this last door of all.

There remained one last barrier that she could

erect against the world, and that was the open window, which she closed, and fastened the ridiculously weak catch that was supposed to keep it from being opened from the outside.

That done, she fell to work.

Adjoining her room was a small closet that she used as a dark cabinet. No one else in the town developed films and she derived a vitally necessary little income from this work. Rapidly she prepared the acid bath, immersed the film from her own camera, and then waited desperately until the proper time had elapsed.

A wind had risen. It was not strong, but it was sufficient to stir the shutters of adjoining houses. Once, in a neighbor's place, a window was drawn down in screeching protest, and the sound made Marian Lane sink against the wall, half fainting.

But the time ended. She forgot the small, pulsing sounds that continually seemed to steal up the stairs and stand listening outside her door. At last she could take the film from the bath and hold it to a light.

Her heart leaped in fierce triumph, for it was Duval's face she had snapped. Clearly, unblurred by all the speed of the horse, it stood before her, and she faced around at her door in victorious defiance, as though the thing she feared could look through the wood to see her.

There was still the printing to be managed. It was long before it was accomplished. Three copies she struck off, and, having made them, she sat down to write:

Dear Eleanor:

This is a hasty note, first to apologize for not writing for so long, and most of all to send you this snapshot. A strange fellow has come to Moose Creek and made a great place for himself here. You can see even from the picture, I think, that he's not a type, and in the flesh, he's a great deal more remarkable. He has a pale face and gray eyes. That's not much of a description, but if you've ever seen the man, it will mean a great deal to you. The reason I'm sending the picture, dear, is that I want to have him identified if I can. I don't want talk made, but if you could quietly show this picture to a few people you know, I'd be glad to hear if they know him. I have reasons for thinking that he's quite a horseman, and among your Long Island or Maryland friends who hunt and follow the races, there may very well be someone who will recognize him.

I know that you can manage this gracefully, without any embarrassment for yourself. You might say that this is a picture of the typical cowpuncher, who recently won a race in a rodeo at Kendry, in the Far West.

The real point is that I don't think that he's typical at all. However, start your little investigation for me. I'm eaten with curiosity to learn the result.

I intend to write to you again soon, and make it a real letter. What has stopped me so often with the pen in my hand is that the old, school days seem so sadly distant that it's like raising ghosts to talk with someone who knew them with me.

She hesitated for something else to say, then signed the letter, placed it with a print of the picture in the envelope, and sealed it and stamped it.

She had hardly ended, when the window was struck as if by a hand, and rattled so that the blood ran out of her brain to her heart, and she almost fainted. However, she heard the gale whistle in the distance and guessed that it must have been the wind that had made the disturbance.

Then she sat down to wait for the morning.

Of all the hours of her life there was none that compared with the strain of that long waiting. Listening with aching nerves, a dozen times she knew she heard the faint metallic rattle with which the front door of the store was opened, heard the unlocking of that at the foot of her stairs, and then again the pause of someone outside her very room. Once she could have sworn that she saw the knob slowly turned, and, gasping with horror, she picked up a small bulldog revolver and leveled it with both hands.

Nothing happened.

She assured herself that she was childish and a fool. No one was in the building and no one would come there. Yet she dared not even propose to herself to open the door and go down to the street to drop the letter through the slot in the post office wall. That would have to wait until the reassuring eye of day opened over Moose Creek.

But she wrapped herself in a bathrobe and lay down on the bed to rest, with a book—and with the gun. There was no rest. The print swam into a confusion of shadows, and every moment her haunted eyes were lifted toward the door, or toward the window.

It was like a blessing to her when she saw the gray of the dawn begin, but never had it lingered so slowly. Never had she so prayed for the honest sun.

At last it came. The rose died from the sky, the brilliant golden light was everywhere, and, springing up from the bed, she prepared to go down at once to the street.

With nervous hands she dressed her hair, put a hat over it, rubbed color into her cheeks, and then with much trouble looked at the shadows beneath her eyes.

Never had she wanted anything as she wanted coffee now.

First, she had to dispose of the two extra prints and the film itself. These she placed for the time being in the book that she had attempted to read that night, a much-battered old copy of *Lorna Doone* that she had taken because she felt it might give her ease from its very familiarity. She was ready now. First, she listened at the door. Then she boldly unbolted, unlocked it, and flung it wide.

Nothing happened. Only the breath of wind that its opening had set in motion entered the room, and now she nerved herself to go down.

She held herself very well until she was halfway up the aisle of the store, and then she went to pieces and fled to the big front door. She tore back the bolt and chain, but the key stuck in the lock, and terror gripped her by the back like a lion. Crouched then against the door, she looked back—but all was familiar emptiness. That moment the key moved in her trembling fingers, and she was free to stagger out into the freshness of the early morning.

So early was it that not a chimney in Moose Creek was smoking as she hurried up the street, and every step gave her additional confidence, additional courage, until in half a block the terrors of the night seemed more fatiguing than real.

She could almost have laughed at them by the time she reached the post office, but when she held the letter at the slot in the wall, she hesitated again. There was danger in it, no matter how broad the daylight, and as she remembered the pale face of Duval with its usual faint smile, she took a deep breath and told herself that the risk was not worth the profit, if profit there were in this business.

She turned away. She half crumpled the letter in her hand as she did so. Then the last impulse won, for she stepped back and, with a decisive flick, shot the envelope away—away into the hands of the law, which would cherish it, protect it, shed blood of brave men for its sake, if necessary. In that instant, she felt a warm assurance that she had gained a mighty ally and started wheels too huge for even Duval to stop.

Then lassitude overcame Marian Lane. She went dreamily back down the sidewalk, the loose boards creaking a bit beneath her step, and smiled vaguely at the open door of the store, remembering the horror with which she had flung it open only a few moments before.

She closed it again, yawned at the blank street, and returned upstairs for a cold plunge, then to breakfast quickly, and so to work before any early orders might come in, as they often did.

But life seemed a little blank and dreary to Marian Lane as she opened the door of her room and went in to prepare for the day, after such a night as this. She was unnerved, too, by an increasing pity for Duval, who had done no wrong, at least in Moose Creek. Here he was a hero, a champion of might, a tower of strength, a defender of the weak.

But she had hoped to take the hero in the palm of her hand and make him tremble.

Now that her mind was clearer, she wished suddenly to see how good a likeness she had taken, and so opened *Lorna Doone*, to find that the pictures and the film were gone!

Chapter Thirteen

It was so impossible that she laughed and stared suddenly out the window as though to ask the bright day how such a monstrous thing could happen when all the night had produced no harm. She told herself that she had really put them in some other place, and was opening the drawer of her writing table when she saw the letter that was placed on top of it.

It was written—or rather printed—in very dim ink that made hardly a mark on the surface. As a matter of fact, it seemed to have been done with a brush that possessed an extremely fine point, for some of the letters blurred one into another. She read:

Dear Marian:

As I watched you through the window last night and this morning, you sure made a mighty pretty picture. . . .

She ran to the window and jerked it open. The sill projected well to either side, and to the right it seemed to her that the dusty paint had been cleaned a little. On the rusted pipe that drained away the roof water, she told herself that there was a distinctly brighter place, where a hand might have grasped it for support. But how could anyone have climbed here from the outside?

She leaned out and stared down toward the ground. It still seemed impossible. There was a sheer drop of twenty feet. There was no possible way of mounting, except by the slight indentations between the boards and the drainage pipe itself. Hardly a sailor would have liked the task of making that climb.

But then to sit there in the cold wind through hours of the night and the morning! To remain there, certainly, until he had seen her putting the pictures in the book. That was broad day, and a dozen windows of neighboring houses gaped at him, yet he had remained there until she left the room. Then entered—then swiftly slipped down the pipe to the ground, leaving no trace behind him, except that the window was unlatched.

Thinking of this, she grew cold indeed to have made such a man her enemy.

She ran back to the letter, which seemed now even dimmer than before, and read it again.

As I watched you through the window last night and this morning, you sure made a mighty pretty picture. I was powerful tempted to knock on the window and tell you so.

He could have dropped his slang, she thought bitterly, if he had known that she had seen the titles of his books.

> That was a pretty clear picture that you made of me, and I didn't think that you'd mind if I borrowed the prints.
> But here I been looking into the book and wondering a pile if you ever read it before, because the girl in there is sure a winner. Which I mean, she's nothing but good nature and kindness and such. She don't seem to be full of nothing but trust, and I'd lay my money that she made men better . . .

It was certainly true that the writing was now so extraordinarily dim that she could hardly make it out. But with straining eyes she found her place again and struggled on.

> . . . and never made a poor cow-puncher burglarize snapshots out of a girl's room and then go and rob the federal mail which is what I have to hurry and go do before the folks get up. But in the wind-up, I got to say again that you made a mighty pretty picture lying on the bed and pointing that gun at the door

that maybe you didn't notice that the caps was all pulled?

Respectfully yours,
Duval

She could make out the last words only by using a bit of imagination.

But now she hurried to the little revolver and opened it. It was quite true. Every cap had been removed from the cartridges, and she might have pulled the trigger as often as she pleased without firing a shot! It changed her picture of Duval suddenly and completely.

He had returned from the rodeo faster even than the sweating horses of Charlie Nash. He had entered the store, he had been to her room, he had found the weapon and made it harmless. Then he had slipped out from the building.

Why had he done this, then, rather than encounter her suddenly in the dark and take the camera from her with all its evidence that he so much dreaded?

Perhaps he had feared that her outcry would raise the neighborhood. Yet a man who could do what he had done that night would hardly have hesitated for such a reason. There were such things as clothes thrown over the head of a victim, stifling all sounds before they issued from the lips. And Duval, she somehow knew, would be a master of every such craft.

Or if he simply had appeared before her in her room, that moment when she raised the lamp above her head—if she had not died of fright, certainly she would have been incapable of any utterance, or even of flight. Then he could have taken the camera from her nerveless hand.

It was not that he wished to keep his agency in this matter a secret, for had he not written a letter and signed it with his name? Perhaps, she thought, it was a strange weakness, an odd compassion in this singular man that had prevented him from appearing before her in the dimness of the store. He had spared her that shock, even though it made for him a night and a morning of so much danger, of so much serious crime. At this thought, a queer smile came to the lips of the girl, lingered, and slowly died there.

She thought, with a start, of hurrying to the post office to give warning of what might be attempted, but she saw at once that this was impossible. Totally impossible, and all that had happened on this night, together with Duval's confession, could never be mentioned to any other human being in the world.

He, with a cunning insight, had known it, and taken that advantage to leave the letter behind him.

She picked it up again, but to her amazement, she found that there was hardly a trace of anything upon the smooth paper, and that trace, real or imagined, now vanished under her very eyes.

How he had mixed that mysterious ink, she could not guess, but she told herself that there were a thousand accomplishments of Duval that must be behind locked doors from any investigation of hers. At least there was one secret that they shared, and she laughed a little grimly as she thought of it.

Here, however, her reflections were interrupted by a rattling of the street door, and she flew down the stairs to find old Jud Parker waiting there with an urgent order for ham. They had run out. The infernal dogs had got into the smokehouse and ruined a hundred dollars' worth of the best smoked meat in the county, and now the best he could do would be to give the men a late breakfast. The confounded dogs, he wished they'd never been born.

She brought him what he wanted, and then raised her most innocent eyes to his face. "Ah, but the poor things," she said. "They didn't know that they were doing wrong."

The hard face of the rancher softened as he looked down at her. "There you go, Marian," he said. "Always thinkin' kind thoughts . . . always doin' good deeds. It ain't in you to sow no mischief in this world of ours."

Chapter Fourteen

In the dusk of the day Duval came from the horse shed where the mule and the saddle horse had been duly stalled and fed. He had worked hard that day, but his step was light as he carried a bucket of water in from the pump, and his whistle was so shrill and gay that Discretion neighed from the pasture and came to hang her head over the fence at him.

He came in to find the steam of great cookery ascending from the stove, and old Henry perspiring before it.

"Too much food for tonight, Henry," he remarked. "There's work for me to do. And I can't overeat."

"Night work?" Henry asked, his eyes gleaming under their white brows. "I could tell you about some night work that's been haunting me all the afternoon."

"You can? You always were a prowling old cat that woke up at sunset. What is it now, Henry?"

Henry extended a long-handled granite cooking spoon. "Yonder, over the hills . . . ," he began. He choked with a sudden emotion.

"You look as if you were going to cry, Henry. Who do you want to do now?"

"Thousands and thousands," murmured Henry,

"and a safe that would fall down like a house of cards if you blew at it. If you touched it, it would open its door to shake hands. It's a fine safe, a good safe, an honest safe, it's a safe that makes friends."

"Business is as business does," said Duval. "You old scoundrel, where have you been?"

"I've been over the hills and far away," said Henry. "I might've known you wouldn't talk to me about it. Two weeks' pay and a lot of extras for about eleven hundred men . . . two weeks' pay and a lot of extras, I tell you. Do you hear me?"

"Oh, I hear you clearly enough. You want to take more scalps, Henry? I should think that you'd be willing to retire, by this time, and rest on your laurels."

"Business is as business does," Henry said, turning back the remark upon its originator. "The fact is that laurels ain't ham and eggs, sir."

"Ah," said Duval, "but you could stay here with me and grow to a ripe old age, vegetating in the green fields, milking the cow, making the excellent butter that you alone know the secret of, spreading an atmosphere of the home all through the house, Henry. You have just the touch for that."

"Stay here with you," Henry said slowly. "Aye, and maybe I would. Maybe I would chuck the other thing and stay here with you, but how long'll you be here?"

113

"I? Why, forever, of course. Isn't this my home, Henry?"

"Your home," said Henry gloomily, "is somewhere between the *Rue de la Paix* and Timbuktu, and right well you know it."

"Tush," said Duval. "I much prefer it here, Henry."

"You'll be off," remarked Henry. "Stay here, I think I could." He lifted his head and looked with narrowed eyes through the doorway at the rosy sky above the treetops. "This'd be a place to live and die in. Seein' things grow up out of the earth and die back into it, I mean, till the growin' and the dyin' of men don't matter so much. But . . . you won't stay long. You'll be flying as fast as steam'll take you . . . in a week . . . in a month . . . as soon as the wind stops blowin' and the dust settles down a little."

"What dust, Henry?" Duval asked softly.

The older man grinned. "I don't know nothin'," he protested. "And I don't want to know. I'm not that much of a fool. Only if you'd listen to me, I could tell you of a way to spend a night that would be worth somethin' to both of us."

"Could you?"

"I'm sayin' so."

"Henry, there's nothing in the world that really interests you except the elbows and the cops."

"Me?" Henry said, amazed.

114

"You! You can't get along without 'em."

"Without that mangy lot?"

"Of course you can't, and you'll know it if you think for a moment. What would you have for spice in life, Henry, if half a dozen detectives weren't nosing about the country for you all the time?"

"They'll never get me again," Henry said solemnly. "Never again."

"How old are you, Henry?"

"Risin' fifty," Henry said, without blushing.

"Rising it so far it's out of reach and sight," said his companion. "How many years have you spent in jail?"

"Oh, a few stretches. Maybe twenty."

"Twenty years in jail, and you'll be ten more if you live that long."

"No," Henry said as gravely as before. "I keep a gun now and not for the other guy but for myself. The next time they grab at me, they'll catch nothin' but air. I don't figure on dyin' in the stripes."

The way he spoke made Duval, it appeared, put off his casual and caustic speech.

"What's your scheme tonight, for some other night?" he asked.

"For this night, and no other," said Henry. "I've been over to the Broom and Carson Company the other day. I've seen their office. Why, any fool could walk into it, and, once inside, there's

115

the safe that fills the whole end of a room. Its own weight is breakin' it to bits. It sags in the middle as if it had colic. I tell you, it's mine and yours, if you'll come with me. If you won't, I'll go by myself."

"Will you?" asked Duval.

"I will. One taste of soap and soup would knock the whole face off it. There's a couple of hundred grand inside it, or I'm a fool and a liar."

"What would you do with it, old fellow?" asked Duval.

"What would I do with it? I'd find a way to use it. I might buy a farm beside yours, and settle down here."

Duval smiled. "They'd have you in two days, probably."

"The dicks? Nobody knows me in this neck of the woods, and that's one thing that put the idea into my head, I tell you. I'll have it as easy as walk. I'll bring it back. . . ."

"Not here, Henry."

"Not here?"

"No. If you go for it, then keep away from me," Duval insisted.

"I'd be missed and suspected, then."

"It's true," Duval muttered. "You infernal old troublemaker, keep quietly at home. If you want money, you have a gun at my head. How much will you take?"

"Money?" Henry said. "Money?" He laughed

softly. "It ain't the money. You know that. It's the feel of the game. It's the night, and the listenin'. It's the creak of a floor under your foot. It's the whisper that sneaks up behind your back and puts a chill down your spine. It's the long chance . . . and then maybe empty pockets and maybe full. But the game is the thing that I'm after. You know what I mean."

Duval sighed. "I'm going to make you change your mind," he declared.

"Change it? I can't change it. Dyin' wouldn't change me that way."

"Kinkaid would, though, from what I hear of him."

"Kinkaid? I never heard of him."

"Neither did I, except in the distance. He's a man-catcher, Henry, who works for the fun of the game, just as you work for fun at the other end of it. It's no more fun for you to crack the Broom and Carson safe than it is for him to catch you for the same job. He's gone three years on nothing but one trail, they tell me. I've been hearing about him for two weeks, off and on. Tonight, I'm going out to meet him."

"Goin' to meet him!" exclaimed Henry. "Are you crazy?"

"I'd be crazy not to. He's to be at the dance tonight. He's likely to hear something about me there. Well, I don't want that. I don't want him to get suspicions of his own and . . ."

117

"What if he knows you?"

"If he knows me?" Duval shrugged his shoulders. He had been undressing as he talked, and now was preparing to step into a galvanized iron tub, into which he had poured his bucket of water and a hot bottle from the stove. "If he knows me, that's guns, Henry. But he's all Western. He's lived here, worked here, grown famous here . . . and that's why we don't hear more of him in New York and other places. But I want to walk under his eyes, be introduced to him, shake hands with him. Then he's not likely to think I'm dangerous and worth a little study. I don't want to give him the trouble of coming to find me, Henry, if you can understand."

Henry nodded, with open admiration in his eyes. "If I had what you've got," he said, "I'd have the world. I'd have the crown jewels of England out of the tower, and take 'em away in a grip at noonday. I'd walk into the Bank of England and take away the heart of it with a ten-ton truck. Why, there ain't a thing you couldn't have, fixed the way you are."

"Then why don't I have it, Henry?"

"Because," said the other, "you're too good to be bad, and too bad to be good. That's the straight of it. Hurry up. I'll lay out your dark suit. Are you going to slick up?"

"About halfway. That's all."

"And you're goin' to the dance, too? You really mean it?"

"I mean it, and you are going to stay home."

He paused in soaping himself to level a forefinger like a gun at Henry, and the latter grinned with enjoyment.

"Sure," he said. "I'll be home. I'll be here when you come back." But his keen eye flickered away from that of Duval.

The latter, though he marked the sign well and understood it, said not a syllable more on the subject. He dressed rapidly. They sat together through dinner, chatting of the farm, of the horses, of the peculiar ways of the old mule, and most about Discretion.

They sat long.

"How did she come by that name?" Henry asked at last.

"She's the finest thing I ever owned," said Duval, "and therefore I hunted about for the best name I could find."

"Salvator . . . ," said the old man. "There's a name for a horse."

"A big, round Roman name for a horse," said Duval. "But Discretion, Henry, is a better name. Because discretion is a thing that you keep in your head wherever you go. It keeps you from the wrong chance. It tucks you into bed at night. It keeps guns out of your hands, or if one is put there, it makes the bullet go home. Discretion makes your voice and your footsteps soft. Discretion keeps you home at night."

He raised a finger as he said it, and old Henry, lowering his eyes, sat quietly, rubbing his chin.

Chapter Fifteen

It was a big dance, a dressed-up dance.

Spurred boots and bandanas and rough shirts remained in bunkhouses, and from the pegs on the walls wrinkled, unfitted suits of blue serge were taken down, brushed with a fond hope that the spots of yesteryear might not show their faces, and sorrowed over, because old sins would not be hidden. However, there was nothing for it but to don them. They washed in tubs of cold water, those men of the range, and scrubbed themselves with laundry soap, and rubbed themselves dry with harsh cotton towels. They dressed with care. They donned fancifully colored shirts. They buckled chokingly high turnover collars around their bulky necks, and then stood before dim, little, cracked mirrors, tiptoe, with agonized effort, while they tied neckties of white, with little streaks of colored flowers down the center.

They brushed their hair and cursed and watered the tangles that insisted on standing upright in spite of patient labor. Their faces were red with shaving and with work, when at last they squeezed their feet into old shoes, and blacked the dingy toes of them, letting the heels take care of themselves.

After that, miserable, pinched in many places,

they passed one another in review. They told each other that they looked "fine," that they "certainly looked fit," and that they would stop the show when they began to prance. Then they climbed into carts, into buckboards, and drove from five to thirty miles to attend the festivities.

The orchestra began to moan at eight. New arrivals were still coming in until after midnight, shrugging their shoulders, gripping their hands to get self-confidence, and working their necks uneasily up and down inside their collars.

They found an orchestra, tired but enduring, supported by certain quantities of whiskey and unlimited applause. They found a big barn floor polished with wax, ground in by a bale of hay drawn across it by volunteers earlier in the day. There were bunting streamers stretched across the rafters, Japanese lanterns burning dimly, low down, lamps bracketed against the walls, and a thin haze of cigarette smoke that seemed to grow thicker as it mounted toward the shadows of the loft. They found a gay crowd, moreover, that made up for the shaky music, the dimness of the lights. For those who had worked so hard to get here refused resolutely to have a bad time. They found, moreover, at this dance, a king of the ball, named Richard Kinkaid, and a queen, also, who was Marian Lane, as a matter of course.

They found one stirring bit of gossip, as well, that somehow seemed to reach every ear, male and female, the instant a newcomer entered the hall.

"Dick Kinkaid's taken a tumble at last."

"How come?"

"Watch him and Marian Lane. Look at his grin. He ain't smiled for seven years, they say. Looks like his face'll crack tonight."

They looked with awe and with delight, for the thing undoubtedly was true. The great Kinkaid at last showed one touching human strain.

He was an Ajax of the mountains, lofty, nobly made. He was no boy, but well over thirty, and with a dozen years of big achievements behind him. The weight of their accomplishment showed upon him, but that was not the shadow that lay on his face. For he was one of those who, it seems, are forever on the frontier of the world, loving trouble for its own poisonous sake and hunting danger as lovers hunt for their beloved.

There are ever two classes of these men—those who carelessly defy the law and make their own rules of living, and there are those more cautious spirits, though equally grim, who exercise their strength in defense of the law. But both classes have at heart the same overmastering desire—the desire for combat.

Richard Kinkaid was of the second class. But all men, whether good or evil-doers, found it equally hard to look into that dark, stern face, for his eye was always quick, and with or without his will, it was forever looking for only one thing—offense.

It was hardly a wonder that women had meant nothing to Richard Kinkaid. His life was lived among men, his battles were, of course, with them, and where his fights were, there was his heart, also.

Tonight, however, the unexpected blow had fallen, and he, looking down at Marian Lane, as many another man had looked, suddenly began to wonder if that delicate and doll-like face could be lighted by any real emotion, and if those wide, childish eyes could begin to have a woman's meaning.

So he found himself talking, and she listened. He spoke of the only thing he knew—his battles, his rides, his conquests. He was not vainglorious, but, in speaking to her, it seemed to Richard Kinkaid that he retasted the fierceness of the fighting, that all drab commonplace disappeared, that the rides on staggering horses through snow, through iron mountain passes in the wind and rain, through the blasting heat of the desert now were glorified.

The frown that made the crease between his eyes relaxed. And Kinkaid began to smile, for she, also, was smiling up at him, speaking very little, but listening, listening, and seeming to drink deep of all he said.

What could he do, then, but talk? And as he

talked it seemed to the manhunter that he had invested some of his pains and some of his glories in her. He danced a little stiffly, clumsily. Then, several times, he sat out with her and told her why he had come to this place—because even if his coming were known, certain men for whom he was looking, might perhaps appear here, drawn by the irresistible lure of pleasure, and hoping somehow that he would forget. He laughed a little as he said this, and the ring of iron was in his voice again, as when he spoke of his wars.

Now and then he left her, shamed into it by the furtive circle of youths who perpetually lingered near, unwilling to draw down his anger by an interruption, but delighted at the sight of Marian Lane. The instant he withdrew, partly with sadness and partly with contemptuous pleasure, he noted how they closed around her—dogs, after the wolf had stalked away.

Once, lofty in the distance of a corner, he overlooked her in the crowd of suitors for a dance, and he told himself that one of these would have her at last. But, oh, the pity of it, when she was meant to be the wife of a man. No wonder that her face was blank and her eyes brightly empty when she talked with such as these.

It was late in the evening. Rather it was early morning, when the next interruption came with the entry of a new excitement. It sent a buzz around the hall, and the murmur came even to the ears of big Richard Kinkaid, as he stood talking with Colonel Hope, old, gentle, chivalrous, famous from the Indian wars.

"What are they all talking about?" asked Kinkaid. "Who are they looking at?"

He himself had been occupying the forefront of attention up to this moment, but it never occurred to Kinkaid that he was jealous of such notoriety. He would have said that he was above such a thing. However, it is undoubtedly true that from the very first instant he felt a pinching of the heart as the colonel answered.

"By my stars, I didn't expect to see him here. This is a greater surprise than your coming, even. Because you've showed yourself at these places before, Kinkaid. But, unless I'm seeing dreams, that young fellow yonder . . . that one who has just come in . . . d'you see him?"

"No," Kinkaid said untruly.

"Look again. You can't mistake him. Rather tall . . . not huge like you. But tall, with a pale face. That's the man of Moose Creek."

"Are they raising men in Moose Creek these days?" Kinkaid asked with his usual half-suppressed sneer.

The colonel did not appear to understand the slur. He went on enthusiastically: "By George, that fellow has the real steel in him. He's the one who took young Charlie Nash . . . good lad but wild . . . and took his gun away from him . . . dodged bullets to do it, mind you . . . confoundedly heroic. Took his gun away, laid him out, took him home, and sobered him up . . . made his peace with the sheriff . . . made Charlie his fast friend for life. Confoundedly fine, I call that. A fellow in ten million. Why, Kinkaid, they love that lad in Moose Creek! I don't blame them. I wish we had him in our section of the country."

Kinkaid, in fact, had noted this newcomer the first instant he entered the room. He followed him now as he passed across the floor. A dance began, a tag dance. The man of Moose Creek was dancing, his lady remaining safely in his arms, untouched by any hand.

Yes, even as they would have avoided offending Kinkaid himself, so they avoided this other, this slighter, this younger man, this unknown.

"What's his name?"

"Duval."

"I never heard of him before," Kinkaid said bluntly.

"Then you've been out of touch with this section for a good many weeks," the colonel commented with equal frankness. "We've been talking about nothing else. Graceful couple, aren't they?"

Kinkaid looked at the girl, and his heart leaped amazingly, and then fell like a stone. For it was Marian Lane in the arms of Duval, and truly they made a graceful couple. His own heavy strength was suddenly a mantle of lead that he would have cast off, if he could, to be light, to be free, to be a part of the dance, as was this young man.

They came closer. As she had looked up into the face of big Kinkaid, so now he vowed she was looking up to Duval, except that now she talked, and the man listened, and laughed frankly with her, and seemed at ease beyond imagination.

Kinkaid would have been far more interested, if he could have heard their conversation, for Marian Lane was saying: "And the letter was delightful, except . . . you need not have written slang, I saw your books in your house."

"Then there's one more weight off my mind, and soon we can talk freely. As friends, even?"

"How long were you waiting there outside the window?"

"Not long. I merely went up for a glance."

"But suppose that I'd gone down in the dark and mailed the letter?"

"Poor Eleanor would never have had it. I was waiting in the lower store."

"How did you get in?"

"I can't confess. I may have to come again. But I knew you wouldn't go out."

"Did you?"

"Yes, certainly."

"Why?"

"You were afraid. I saw from the size of your

eyes that you were frightened of the man outside your door."

"As if there was one there."

"There was, for a time."

She shuddered in his arms.

"Yes," he explained. "I thought you deserved a little suffering. So, I came up the stairs at one time and stood for a while, breathing rather hard from the climb. That was early in the evening when I suspected that you might really go out as soon as you'd written the letter."

She drew a quick, deep breath. "You didn't want me to go then?"

"I should have had to meet you in the dark. I didn't want to frighten you as badly as that. Simply give you waking nightmares for a little while."

"Why couldn't you have robbed the post office, as you did later?"

"Because the postmistress was up playing cards with a crony. I'd made sure of that before."

"But when the day came . . ."

"Yes, then I climbed up again and looked in time to see you confide the secret to *Lorna Doone*. Poor Lorna! She never would have approved of such an evening, do you think?"

"Even Lorna would have wanted to know who is Duval."

"A poor farmer who works hard."

"But he's something else."

"Nothing that has harmed you."

"Who is Duval?"

"Have you made a fight out of it? Will you never give in?" he asked her.

"I don't think that I can. I want to know."

"Suppose I start prying into Marian Lane?"

"Oh, I'm open as the day. The whole range knows everything about me."

"About beautiful Marian Lane, hard-working Marian Lane, gentle Marian Lane, cold-eyed Marian Lane. But there is another side, I suspect."

"What other side?"

"They never have seen her with ghosts in her eyes, as I have. They never have watched her slip like a graceful little cat at night across the roof of Pete's Place. What would they say to that? What would all the honest boys say?"

"That I am a seeker after truth, if they only knew."

"Truth is fire," he said. "It burns many hands, even calloused ones. I've come here tonight to beg for a truce. You see that I don't stand on pride. I beg for forgiveness, and forgetfulness. I've come all this distance to see you and ask you to be a friend, instead of an enemy. Do you believe that?"

"In part," she answered. "And was it also in part to see Dick Kinkaid, the manhunter? I'm sorry the dance is over. That's where I want to sit . . . over in that corner. . . ."

It was Kinkaid's corner, and toward it he took her, realizing that the appeal had gone unanswered and that it was indeed war to the knife. But now he was before Kinkaid. He could hear the last words on the lips of excellent Colonel Hope—and they were something about that ghoul of a man, Larry Jude.

Then he stood before Kinkaid, and a great hand of iron closed over his with unnecessary force, until he raised his head.

So, for the first time, each looked into the eyes of the other steadily, remorselessly, never giving way, until a longer pause would have called attention upon them.

They separated, but each was absent-minded, thoughtful, one of Kinkaid, and one of Duval, though the colonel, in his gentle way, was striving to make cheerful conversation between them.

The next dance started. And away went Marian Lane in the arms of the great Kinkaid. She was talking to him now as eagerly as he to her.

"You know this Duval pretty well?" he asked her.

"I don't know him at all," she said. "But he's wonderful, isn't he?"

"Humph!" grunted Kinkaid.

"And how I should like to know who Duval really is," she said.

"Would you?" answered Kinkaid. "Then I'll tell you that you're going to, and going to hear the facts from me. He's got an eye in his head for one thing."

But the last words were nothing more than a mumble, intended for his own ears alone.

Chapter Sixteen

The cream of a country dance is always the last of it, when the older people who give it sanction and dignity have gone home, and the orchestra has played itself into some degree of abandon, and the crowd that is left is thinking of nothing but the joy of motion.

Pretty Marian Lane was still there, as though she had no store to open in the morning. Strange to say, big Kinkaid also lingered, and the late dancers almost forgot to look at him with awe. It was almost as remarkable a thing that Duval was also present.

He was everywhere.

He danced only that once with Marian Lane. After that, he was interested in every girl present, as it seemed, for he danced with each in turn, and between dances he appeared to discover great charm in round-backed old grandmothers who sat along the wall as chaperons. He talked everywhere, not overflowing with talk, but simply with that keen and attentive interest that made each companion certain that Duval came to her with eagerness, and left her with regret.

He was not with the women alone, but also in the anteroom—once reserved for saddles and such gear in the days of the barn's real

133

usefulness—where he found the men between dances hastily smoking cigarettes. He lounged and talked with these. He walked up and down with young Charlie Nash, arm in arm, and Charlie was obviously proud of this distinction that was given him. He submitted, also, to a good deal of bantering upon the obvious pleasure that he was getting from the dance.

"He wants somebody at his stove besides a man to cook," said a cheerful cowpuncher, "and so he's come out here to find somebody. He's a dog-goned practical man, ain't you, Duval? I was the same way, once. I was the same way, and I went out to collect myself a wife. I got myself all engaged up to a fine girl that wasn't either wind-broke or spavined. She was sound, and her best point was her teeth . . . I mean they was the most to see. I give her a ring that I was keeping for a friend of mine, and the next Sunday I go to call on her and she throws the ring at my eye and don't miss it. It appeared that I was a mine owner and a dog-goned rich one, that night I danced with her . . . and when she learned that I was a low-down ornery cowpuncher, it riled her a good deal, the time she'd wasted on me. She had a fist that would've looked good on the handle of a fryin' pan, or carryin' a five-gallon bucket of clabber to the pigs, or pitchin' winter feed to the weeds off the stack. But when she tried to put that fist on the end of my chin, I turned around and run for it, and she nigh caught me at the gate except that I jumped, and so I got away with everything except a part of my clothes. When you go to get yourself a woman, Duval, you take my advice and practice up a mite on jumpin'. But why ain't you ever come out before?"

Duval explained that he would have been pleased enough to do so. But he had to work. The farm was young. It needed infinite care. But he at last had a great idea. He was going to raise asparagus and make a fortune in this manner.

They listened to him with their eyes upon the floor. It was not the first extravagant scheme he had hatched. Once, he was going to buy lean young cattle from the southern drives as they came north toward the grasslands in the summer and put them in sheds to be fattened.

When he was asked what he would feed them, he assured everyone gravely that he had just learned that cattle loved cabbages, and that he had a scheme for raising cabbage on his farm, and such tons of it that he could afford to buy the cows and make them fat from the crop. He was hardly dissuaded from this foolish notion, when he decided to put in an apple orchard, pointing out that one tree might produce fifty bushels of Winesap apples, and at $2 a bushel, with very little cost of care except for spraying and plowing, he would be able to make, literally, thousands of dollars a year. From this, also, he was persuaded, largely by Charlie Nash, who pointed out that he would have to wait forty years for apple trees to grow to a fifty-bushel size, and finally by Simon Wilbur, who proved that apple trees would not grow at all in that soil.

Now, he had struck asparagus, and the cow-punchers bit their lips to keep from smiling, until Duval heard the orchestra begin and hurried off to find a partner.

"Look at him," said hard-handed Murphy of the Salmon Tail outfit. "There he goes, the straight-standin'est, square-shootin'est, most out-gamin'est man in the range, bar none . . . the smartest, keenest, brightest, wisest, patient-est, hard-workin'est man, too. Yet he's got so dog-goned little sense about business that one of these here days we're gonna see that place auctioned off for debt, and poor old Duval will be there as bright and cheerful as ever, smilin' at everybody, and never lettin' anyone see that he's eatin' his heart as he watches the stuff being auctioned off."

"Shut up!" said Charlie Nash. "Ain't I been thinking nothing but that same thing these here last weeks?"

"How does he keep goin', Charlie? He ain't made a cent out of that fool farm, and he's spendin' all the time at a terrible rate."

"I dunno," Charlie admitted. "But he told me once about a terrible fine evening that he had

136

at roulette up Montana way, before he quit the T Bar place. And I reckon that's why he's still flush. Spending his capital on you and me and all the other boys, and never complaining because he doesn't get anything back. Why, boys, may heaven send Duval a woman with a business head that'll take charge of him."

Murphy laughed, and others joined him.

"Who'll take charge of Duval?" they asked. And Charlie Nash agreed with them, half sadly and half with a fierce pride.

"I saw him stand up and look Kinkaid in the eye," he said. "There wasn't any backing up. Kinkaid seemed like he'd been hit with a lead pipe. He wasn't used to having gents eye him that way."

They chuckled. The whole range was proud of its new champion, rejoiced in his valor, thanked him for his kindness, admired him for his wisdom, and loved him more than ever for his folly.

But what they did not understand at all was the thing that Marian Lane suggested to Charlie Nash, as they were dancing together still later that morning. He had gone over the great good points of his friend as a disciple and a worshiper, in an outburst from the heart.

"Of course," said the girl, "but suppose he's thought out all these things before? Suppose the farm's only a blind, and the other things all done for a game? I don't think that anyone in the world could ever have been such an idiot as to plan to fatten cattle on cabbages . . . certainly not a smart whip like Duval. You can think what you please, but I know that he's laughing at us a lot more than we're laughing at him."

She compressed her lips a little and waited for Charlie's explosion of wrath. It followed at once.

"I never seen such a poison-mean nature like you got, Marian. Everything you don't understand, you're against. It's a wonder to me you don't hate the birds, because you can't fly like them!"

At this moment, a man ran into the room shouting in a loud voice: "Where's Marshal Kinkaid? Where's Dick Kinkaid?"

The orchestra slackened, almost died out, and fell into a softened discord, without any tune except that in the violin, while the messenger blundered across the floor, and, finding Kinkaid in his corner, bellowed: "Mister Kinkaid, trouble's poppin'! They've cracked the safe of Broom and Carson, and they've got clean away with a hundred and eighty thousand dollars that there was inside of it! They've got clean off, and nobody knows where they've gone or who they might be except that one of them had hurt himself in the hand and left some red marks . . . !"

Kinkaid took his informant under his arm and departed from the room with him. Duval disappeared at the same instant. He headed back across the hills toward his home as fast as a horse could trot between the shafts of the borrowed buggy of Simon Wilbur. Sagging to a jog on the upgrades, rattling down the farther slopes, Duval drove into the gray of the dawn, and the pink of the morning, and saw the bright golden rim of the sun stare out over the hills before he drew up at Wilbur's.

There he hastily stowed the buggy, and led his horse back to his own corral, and then went softly down the path to the cabin.

The front door was open, as it was their custom to leave it in all except the windiest weather. Duval walked freely in and found old Henry asleep, smiling at his dreams.

"Henry!" he called. "The sun's up, and the cow is waiting for you at the barn."

"Hello," Henry said. "How was the fourteen-carat marshal, and did you bring home his watch and chain, or wasn't there even that left of him, when you got through?"

"Did you think that I went there to fight him?" asked Duval. "I went there to let him see me and to try a game of bluff."

"That worked? I never, in all my life, saw a better pokerface than yours, in a pinch."

"Nothing works with Kinkaid," Duval said frankly. "He doesn't care a whit for anything but his gun, and you can't bluff a man who has nothing on the table but iron and gunpowder. He has to have a weak spot."

"Not lame nowhere?" Henry asked, sitting up with a yawn.

"The girl?" murmured Duval suddenly. "Is that a chance?" He snapped his fingers and laughed through teeth that almost met. "I wonder," he said softly. He added: "How was the night with you, Henry?"

"Lonely, a little. I took a walk."

"As far as what?"

"Oh, up the road and over a coupla hills. That's all. Then I come home and I'm asleep before I know it. I'm getting old, I tell you."

"Aye," Duval said sternly, "you're gettin' old."

"Now what's the matter?" asked Henry.

"When a man's hands begin to slip, it's time for him to call himself old. Let me see yours."

Henry stood up from the bed, his long shanks looking as spindling as those of a child as he stood before Duval, but his hands were behind his back.

"What's the lead?" Henry asked angrily. "Because I barked my hand openin' that fool of a latch on the gate when I come home. . . ."

"You rattle-headed bungler," Duval said. "You driveling, out-of-date cracker of penny banks for children! You've left your mark on the Broom and Carson safe, and Kinkaid is going to run down the trail to my house and snag us both!"

Chapter Seventeen

It was a long and jagged rip on the inside of the left forefinger. Duval bathed it in hot salt water until the face of Henry wrinkled with pain. Then he dressed it with care, making the bandage as secure as possible, but also as thin.

"There'll be no trouble," Henry said reassuringly. "I've torn my finger on that sharp notch under the latch. What's wrong with that?"

"Kinkaid," Duval said.

"Kinkaid may be keen, but what would ever bring him here?"

"Robbery or no robbery, he'd come here anyway to see me. And you live with me, Henry, I suppose?" He added: "What the deuce made you do it, after I'd warned you?"

"It was the face of that safe that kept lookin' in on me," confessed Henry. "I went to bed and put out the light. I was ready to go to sleep. I was asleep, when I seen the safe like the face of a friend, winkin' at me. I got up and lighted the lamp, seen your chair, and went back to bed again . . . but all the time I was feelin' the long green under my fingers, rustlin' and crunchin' in my hand. I felt like a starved cow when it sees green grass on the edge of the road. Pretty soon I was in the saddle on Cherry, and headin' it over the hills . . ."

"Cherry?" groaned Duval.

"Why not? What else? The mule?"

"Why not? Because there's nothing like Cherry on the whole range!"

"She didn't talk," Henry said, grinning, "goin' or comin'."

"She had to step on the ground, though!" Duval said.

Henry stared in consternation.

"What did you do with her when you got there?"

"Tied her in a clump of poplars about a furlong from the finish."

"That's better." Duval nodded. "Did you leave any fingerprints in that blood?"

"I wiped every mark. Didn't have time to get all of the blood away, but every mark was wiped over."

Duval nodded again, and Henry, his eyes smiling with contentment, went on: "The night watchman was strollin' around the place the whole time. Once he stood for about ten minutes lookin' through the front window. I had the door of the safe open, by that time. When the can opener said hello to it, it answered right back. It swung open so fast I thought it was goin' to talk French. But the watchman didn't see anything. He was lookin' at his own ideas of the world,

I suppose." He chuckled. "Here," he said, as Duval finished bandaging the finger. "Here's the stuff." He started to raise the thin straw pallet from his bunk, but Duval stopped him with a word.

"I don't want to see it."

"Hey, what?" Henry demanded, amazed. "It won't hurt your eyes. You get your percentage, anyway. . . ."

Duval raised one finger. "How long have you known me, Henry?"

"Twenty years, sir. Nineteen, to be on the dotted line."

"Did you ever see me mix drinks?"

"No, sir."

"What am I?"

"The champion . . ."

"Farmer?"

Henry grinned. "I'll eat the crops you raise," he said.

"But am I a farmer?"

"You have the look and the lingo when you want to put it on."

"Just now, Henry, I'm a farmer. I never do wrong. I love the law, and I read the Kendry *Evening News*. D'you understand?"

"You're buried, you mean?"

"I mean that I'm a farmer and nothing else. If that satchel of yours were filled with selected diamonds, I wouldn't have as much use for them as I would for ten pounds of oats. Once more, Henry, I don't mix my drinks."

Henry gasped.

"But you have," went on Duval, "and there may be the dickens to pay. If Kinkaid isn't here before the morning's over, I don't know men and their faces. Go get the shotgun and start hunting."

"Huntin' what, sir?"

"I don't care what. Go and shoot a few shells at the air, if you want to, but don't come back till noon. Scout this place as if it were filled with wild Indians before you show your face again. That hand of yours mustn't be seen. Is that all clear?"

"Clear as glass, sir. I'll tell you how it was. The thin steel plate on the outside of the . . ."

"I don't care a whit how you cut your finger. The point is, that the thing was done. Now get out of here, and take your boodle with you. Hide it wherever you like."

"Look here," Henry began with a sudden defiance. "You think it's a grocery store till that I've cleaned out, but it ain't. There's a hundred and eighty thou- . . ."

"Green bits for rabbits," said Duval. "Go try to find the rabbits with that gun of yours. Start moving, and move fast. You're trying to shoot some sort of meat for us. You understand? Go on, Henry. You can have breakfast and lunch together, when you come back. Take

144

some hardtack in your pocket. Now, get out!"

Henry departed swiftly enough. At the verge of the blossoming brush, he paused reluctantly, satchel in one hand and gun in the other, to look back toward the shack.

Duval watched him from the door and called guardedly: "Whatever you do, don't decide that you can run away from trouble and bolt. The telegraph is faster than your long legs, Henry."

Henry waved. The next instant, the green of the shrubbery and the foam of the blossoms had closed like water over him, and he was gone from view.

Duval, after this, started his breakfast, stripped, and ran for a plunge in the icy brook. He came back from this well wakened and keyed for the day. He dressed while he ate, and before the sun was lifted high enough to begin warming the earth, he was out with horse and mule, running a small, heavy harrow over the plowed ground in the lower meadow, while a dozen blackbirds followed critically, watching for worms and grubs.

The air was still cool, but warm enough to redouble the fragrance of the pines, when he heard the hoof beats of a horse pause at his gate, and then saw the lofty form of Marshal Richard Kinkaid coming up the path between the fields.

He appeared to even better advantage now than

he had done the night before. He wore a loose, unbuttoned coat of a dull plaid, a blue shirt with a bandanna knotted about the throat, the knot at the back of the neck and the red dappled silk flowing down over his breast. His gun belt sagged far down over the right thigh, where it supported a long holster whose black surfacing had been worn to a shining brown in most places. He wore chaps of strong, tanned leather, deeply scored everywhere from the knee down by the brush through which they had been plunged in many a hot ride. It seemed to Duval that he could see the shrubbery dashed apart before him, and washed together behind his flying horse.

But above all, the massive form the marshal was crowned and completed by the high sombrero that he wore, in the Mexican style. His only ornament was the band of priceless gold-work that encircled the crown of the hat. His left hand was sheathed in a glove as thin as a weevil's skin, to borrow the poet's simile, but the same hand carried the glove for the right. That hand must always remain bare. Duval knew. He could tell by the sun-blackened state of the skin that this was the case, as he halted the team at the end of the land and waited for the big man to draw nearer. By some vital inches he had been overtopped the night before, but now the lofty hat added to the difference.

146

The marshal did not shake hands. Instead, he waved the glove briefly.

"You don't take days off, Duval," he commented. "Dance all night . . . work all day."

Cheerful, friendly words, but spoken without the slightest softening of feature. The frown of stern and rather contemptuous thought remained stamped upon the face of big Kinkaid.

"Same to you," Duval said. "You mean Broom and Carson Company, I guess?"

The marshal responded obliquely: "Hired men ain't their own masters, you know."

"You had breakfast?"

"No."

"Come up and I'll give you a hand-out."

The lips of the marshal parted, and then closed. "No," he said. "I gotta lose some weight. I'm getting too fat for the horses that I can buy. But I'd like to have a talk with you, and set down a minute." Plainly, his first impulse had been acquiescence.

"Sure," said Duval.

He left the team. They would amuse themselves in their own way, the mule standing with one hip sagged down, and ears cocked awry, the saddle horse picking at random blades of grass that showed under the sods of the plowed furrows beside it. There they would stand all day in the sun, if need be. So Duval was free to take his formidable guest up to the house.

Before they went in, Kinkaid paused in front of the verandah step and turned his grim, handsome face toward the bubbling of the river, and then to the banks of foliage that hedged in the farm.

"Quiet, here," he remarked. "You could hear yourself think in this here place, Duval."

"Aye," said Duval, "there ain't many comes up the road, excepting Wilbur. Go on in."

The marshal entered, stooping his head lower than need was to pass beneath the cross-beam of the door. Inside, he removed his hat, almost reluctantly, and Duval could not help feeling that the reason for this seeming reluctance was that without hats they were more nearly equaled in height.

He pointed to his own big chair, and the marshal sat down in it. He filled it completely. In a way, he was more imposing as he reclined in the chair at ease than when he stood erect, hat and all, for in this relaxed posture the imagination of the spectator was excited as to the possibilities of the colossus in action.

Never before in all his days had Duval seen such a body, such a face, such gleaming, steady eyes, which laid a weight instantly upon him.

"Coffee, anyway?" Duval offered.

"Coffee?" repeated the other, his eye flashing hungrily toward the big blackened pot upon the stove. Then he shook his head. "I don't need anything," he declared.

But Duval, alert before, was tenfold keen thereafter, for he knew that the marshal had some point in refusing to taste, beneath his roof, either food or drink.

Chapter Eighteen

Whether in the Christian grace or the pagan libation, all peoples at one time or another have attached some religious significance to the partaking of food, and in the West there is still a trace of the same influence felt, though it appears there rather as a vague superstition. No man could say exactly what it means, or of what importance it may be, but he who enters the house of another and hangs his bridle on the wall, he who eats bread and tastes liquor, has in some mysterious manner established a bond between himself and his host. His host is placed under a certain duty, and so is the guest.

To Duval, closely watching, it appeared undoubted that the marshal had felt some obscure qualm of conscience, and if he had guessed at once that the visit was not altogether friendly, his last doubt was now removed.

The esteem that he felt for the physical and mental powers of the marshal was not without some return, he was soon aware, for though Kinkaid managed to cover much under a casual manner, still there was a question and a faint doubt in his eyes, such as appears when a man is not entirely sure of his surroundings. It was plain that the door behind him and the window in front were both in his mind, as he faced Duval. But, more than this, there was something in his host that he could not fathom and that he was hungry to get at.

"You been up at the Broom and Carson place, I suppose?" Duval said purposely, taking up the question that was most in his mind.

"Yeah. I been there."

"That's a clean-up," Duval said thoughtfully. "You take a clean-up like that, it's worthwhile."

"What good does it do the crook in a penitentiary?" asked Kinkaid.

"Why not? Maybe he gets fifteen years. Good behavior, and he's out in ten," Duval explained. "Well, when he's out, he goes back to the place where he's cached the coin, picks it out of the ground, and he's fixed for the rest of his life. Ten years down, and everything else on credit is pretty soft, I'd tell a man."

"Some of them figure it that way," the marshal said without interest. "This was an old hand, though, and nobody young enough to want to risk ten years in jail."

"Old fellow, eh?" Duval said, bright with interest.

"Yeah. Pretty old, I reckon."

"Well, dog-gone me if I see how you tell his age," Duval said, as one prepared to admire brilliance beyond his own scope.

"Well, he didn't have too much time on his

hands, but everything he done was neat. Laid the drawers and the trays out in rows, and didn't ruffle everything up. A young crook leaves a messy job. The old boys, they're likely to have a sort of pride in appearances, if you follow my drift."

"Sure," agreed Duval, "I could see how that might be. Still, you might be wrong."

"Maybe. Anyway, I'll have him before long."

"Good!" Duval said. "If they go around busting safes, it's better to keep money buried in the ground than investing it in banks."

"Sure," agreed the marshal. He paused, letting his eye rather covertly drift about the room. "You done a pile of dancing in your time," said Kinkaid, apropos of nothing.

"I've done some when I was a kid."

"You can step," the marshal said absently. And suddenly he was looking at Duval with an open, flaming envy in his eyes, so extremely patent that Duval had to look out the door to avoid appearing to recognize it. He felt an odd pang of superiority, amusement, and pity combined, for he saw with this touch of human nature that the great Dick Kinkaid, the stern marshal, the slayer of men, was in some respects as much an envious little boy as any other human in the world.

"Partly," the marshal began again, shrugging his heavy shoulders, "I come here on business.

I've heard that you got a mare that can outrun the jack rabbits."

"She's fast," admitted Duval without enthusiasm.

"In my line," said Kinkaid, "I need a fast one. I'd aim to buy that mare, Duval."

"Would you?" Duval said. "But she ain't for sale. Besides, she wouldn't carry your weight, I reckon."

"I'd like to see her. Maybe I could make you an offer."

Duval did not hesitate. There was not likely to be a man in the West who would refuse to offer his horse to the admiration of even the most casual passer-by, let alone such a celebrity as Kinkaid. He went out at once with the big man and took him to the pasture.

She was grazing on the far side, and at the whistle of the master she tossed her head and came to him with her long, bounding stride.

Kinkaid looked at her with a critical eye. "Rawhide and cat gut," he said. "She's twice what she looks. She could carry me, Duval."

"Maybe, Kinkaid, but don't you go tempting me. I like that mare a lot."

"I'll tell you," said the marshal. "Without no trial, without looking her over, I'll pay you down five hundred spot cash for her."

It was a large price, almost a staggering price on a range where a tough mustang, broken to the saddle, could be bought for $50, and in Mexico for less.

Duval, entrenched in his part, saw that he must appear to be tempted, so he said: "It's a lot of money, Kinkaid. But look here . . . I was flush last winter and had a bust clean to New York. I saw a horse show there and she done fine, the way she slid over the jumps. I couldn't get her out of my head. So, I sent for and got her when I was flush again. It cost me a lot of money, and a lot of thinking, too."

"Well," Kinkaid said impatiently, "lemme try her, will you?"

"Sure."

Kinkaid brought up his own saddle from the powerful animal he had been riding, and this was cinched on the back of the mare, then the marshal mounted. He simply jogged her down to the bottom of the path, then turned her and galloped her back to the pasture at full speed.

His eyes gleamed as he dismounted, but his deep voice was quiet as he said: "A thousand dollars, Duval."

Duval looked around him at the pitiful farm on which he appeared in the eye of the world to be pouring forth all his might of labor for what niggard results. Almost the price of that farm had been offered to him for the horse and now the marshal went on to expand upon the thought.

"You gotta have more acres. You can get 'em

with this money. Take a gent like you that'll be marrying before long, he's gotta have more land than this to keep a wife, and maybe kids."

"Yeah," Duval agreed grudgingly. "But look here, Kinkaid. There's some things that you can't get with money. Suppose you seen a man with a fine son. Would you put a price on the kid?"

"Suppose I wanted him, why not? Suppose that I could give the kid a fine home, and everything that he wanted, and a reputation. . . . Why, I'd make this here mare famous, Duval. If I could fork her, the crook I started after would think that the wind had blowed me over the hills." After a pause, he added: "I'll come up a little. I'll give you twelve hundred iron men for her."

Duval shook his head.

"Oh," said Kinkaid, "money don't mean much to you, eh? Maybe I was wrong. I thought that you was a small farmer, Duval. Maybe you're just a banker taking a vacation?"

At this slowly drawled suspicion, Duval felt himself weaken. Certainly his own attitude was going to be hard to understand if he held out much longer. But he knew it was not merely for the pursuit of criminals that the other wanted the horse. He had some purpose in the back of his mind that was not to the advantage of the present owner of the mare, though what that purpose could be, Duval was unable to decipher. Unwillingly, too, he admired the liberal methods by which Kinkaid had fairly cornered him. All that was left for him to do was to growl: "You could buy a whole cavvy with that there money, Kinkaid. Leave me be with my horse and buy a herd."

"I'll make you a last price," said the marshal. "I want her, and I figger that I ought to have her. What good is she to you? She ain't for plowing. You don't often go out, except down to the village, I reckon. She's nothing to you but something to look at . . . and I'll pay you fifteen hundred cash on the nail for her."

Cold perspiration burst out on Duval. He was silenced and sick at heart.

"That," went on Kinkaid, "is what you give for your house and your whole farm. You can have twice as much of a farm, now. If farming is what you're really interested in."

"No," Duval declared, "I can't let her go."

But he said it faintly, for he realized that this refusal would make his whole position seem absurd. No farmer in his apparent condition could afford to throw away such a tidy little fortune as this.

Kinkaid did not appear to have heard the refusal. He had taken out a long, fat, pigskin wallet, and, unfolding this, he drew out a stack of bills, oddly neat and crisp. From them he took two $500 notes, and after these, some of smaller denominations. He packed the stack together neatly, and offered it to Duval, who reached for it, hesitated, and then took it in his hand with another speech of refusal on his lips.

The marshal, however, seemed to take the conclusion of the affair for granted. He turned to the mare and looked her over almost spitefully now, scowling at her long legs and skinny, reaching neck.

"She's pretty lean," he objected. "I'd like to put fifty pounds on her, but I reckon that she's one of them skinny ones that never get fat. Here you, Cherry, stand still." He raised his voice loudly as he delivered the order. The ears of the mare flattened, but she was still.

"I'm late," said Kinkaid. "Here . . . sign this. It ain't very regular, but it'll do for a bill of sale, maybe." And he placed before Duval a slip of paper that read:

For value received I, the undersigned, have sold the chestnut mare called Discretion to Richard Kinkaid.

Duval, with the marshal's fountain pen in his hand and the paper resting on top of a post, hesitated long, with bitterness in his heart. He had been trapped, and sign he must, so the pen slowly traced his name—*D. Duval.*

He passed it back and thrust the sale money down into his coat pocket. Looking up, it seemed to him that he had surprised a faint smile upon the lips of the other.

But the thing was ended. The mare was gone. Kinkaid was riding her down toward the gate!

Chapter Nineteen

What is more stifling than for a strong and brave man to be forced to control his anger? So it was that Duval choked with his wrath as he looked down the path after the marshal. That half-suppressed smile suggested many things—that the marshal might have guessed that $1,500 was hardly a third part of the price of the runner, and, therefore, that there was almost as much of the fox as of the lion in the composition of Kinkaid.

At any rate, he had come, he had seen, and he had conquered, in the course of a scant half hour. It was as though a charge of enemies had swept over Duval, and left him crushed in the dust. He had all the feeling of the vanquished—humiliation, rage, and helpless despair.

Cherry was gone forever!

Such a procession of pictures then passed through his mind as had not been in it for many a day, for he was seeing all the days and the ways of Cherry, from her spring as a foal to her wild days as a two-year-old, when she had been tried for the track and found just short of the right foot, and then the dark days of her three-year-old form, when she was neither hunter nor racer, but simply a long-striding hack, pleasant to drift with across the countryside. In those days, their affection for one another had become fixed. He rode her not because he valued her, but because he loved her wise, ugly head, and her imperial ways, and she loved him as only a good horse can love her master. In her fourth year began her glory, and this was her fifth.

But now she was taken out of his hand by the coin and the cunning of Kinkaid, lost to him forever, and he actually had signed the document that divided them!

So thought Duval, as he looked after the marshal, and suddenly he roused himself, and forced his lips to smile. He made himself whistle cheerfully as he went back to the plow team, and in a few more minutes, he was singing as he followed through the dust of the rattling, dodging, jumping harrow. But for all of his change of face and front, there was less security for Kinkaid's future at that moment than there ever had been before.

Kinkaid himself had ridden down to the village, and there he stopped in front of the grocery store to buy some dried meat for his food supply. Not that he needed the meat, but that he wished to accomplish a double outside purpose. One was to allow the people of Moose Creek to see what he had done. The other was to personally inform Miss Marian Lane.

The crowd was gathering the instant the

marshal appeared on the chestnut, but for the moment he had enough to do in meeting the girl.

She finished serving a customer, but her eyes and her smile were both for Kinkaid as he strode toward the counter. And then she saw the mare tethered in the street just as he gave his order.

It was the sweetest pleasure to Kinkaid to see the consternation, almost the fear, in her face.

"You borrowed her?" she gasped in explanation.

"I bought her," said the marshal. "I needed a fast horse, so I bought her. I want two pounds of dried beef and a pound of hardtack."

She went to fill the order. "Poor Duval," she said as she brought the order to him and wrapped it up. "Poor Duval. Is he as broke as that?"

But he saw, with relief, that it was not real pity that was in her voice, but merely the semblance of it. Really, there was sheer excitement, and she looked at him as though he had accomplished some wonderful thing, far beyond the mere purchase of a horse. She, too, knew that Duval had been vanquished, and the thought made her eyes shine.

And the heart of the marshal was filled with surety and with peace. He had thought, the night before, that Duval had danced his way into the very heart of the girl. He assured himself now that there was no fear whatever of that danger.

"You paid, then?" she said.

"Fifteen hundred," the marshal answered carelessly.

He did not look at her as he gathered up his parcel, but he knew that he had made a point, and a great one. Such a sum of money as this was not spent, in that range, for the sake of a riding horse.

Then he went out hastily. He knew that he could not make effects by mere conversation. His rôle with her must be that of the man of action, who performs three deeds to every sentence that he speaks. But as he reached the street, he felt confident that he had done more than a little to establish himself in her eyes.

From the crowd, too, he received the same murmur of wonder.

Pete came out from his place of business, wiping his hands on his white apron, and gaped like a child at the mare and her new rider.

"Borrowed?"

"Bought," said the marshal.

"My gosh," said Pete. "Poor Duval! Is he gone bust, already?"

But Charlie Nash, dark with doubt, shook his head. "There's something behind it," he whispered to himself. "There's gonna be trouble. There's gonna be big trouble. There's gonna be trouble that Moose Creek never seen the like."

The marshal, content, went whirling out of town with the long-striding mare half extended, swaying him forward, even then, at an amazing speed. In this gait, he held her for mile after mile, and then he sprinted her up a sharp slope, and at the top of it reined her in and listened carefully to her breathing. She was well covered with sweat, but then the day was warm. Her breathing was slow and easy, and she went up well against the bit, plain token that she was fit for further effort. Kinkaid drew in a breath so deep that it crowded his shoulders back, and made him sit the saddle like a conqueror returning from the battlefield. He felt, in fact, that the battle already was won, that he had demonstrated his superiority over Duval in this entire transaction, that he had staggered the faith of Moose Creek in its hero, and that he had fixed the attention of Marian Lane entirely upon himself.

The latter was, for the moment, the most important thing that he could do. It seemed to Kinkaid, indeed, that this was the most important object toward which he could strive, at that time, and he smiled with a grim self-content. Other men devoted a vital portion of life to the pursuit of the woman they wished to marry. He, having found her, would, in a few days, brush from the stage all other contenders, and take her if he chose.

He was not, in fact, a self-important ass, but he had won so often in other fields that he could not conceive of defeat.

As for Duval, it seemed patent to the marshal

that the mare was not too expensive, even at $1,500. How much had Duval paid for her, then? Why did he let her go at no profit, or even at a loss? Obviously, simply to maintain his rôle as the simple farmer of no resources. That rôle, then, was a farce, and something lay behind Duval more than the eye perceived. That, then, was the reason that Marian Lane had begged him to find out more about the stranger at Moose Creek.

The marshal literally laughed aloud, for he began to see that this was not only a woman for his heart but also a companion for his brain. The thought enriched him already, in prospect. She was one who would know his problems, understand them enough to give keen feminine suggestions, here and there, and, above all, enough to admire the talent that he expended in his labors.

He wakened from his daydream with a start to find himself almost in the act of riding past the Broom & Carson place. He turned in hastily, biting his lip, and straightaway began his investigation.

To the amazement of the distressed Mr. Carson, who was frantically walking up and down inside, the celebrated marshal paid not the slightest heed to the interior of the shop, but he went out to a certain patch of poplar trees that he had located when he first cut for sign around the place.

There he had found the grass trampled, and

leading from the trees back into the woods there were more hoof marks in the grass. They had been made by a trotting horse, and the length of the stride was what had made him think at once of the mare of Duval, now celebrated on the range for her long action.

He trotted the mare in a parallel course, but when he dismounted for measurement, he discovered that the slipping of the hoofs in the grass and the fact that that which had been trampled down in the morning already was springing up straight again, made it impossible for him to make any accurate measurements for comparison.

He looked next down the back trail, striving to find a distinct print of a hoof, but that was almost equally difficult.

There were plenty of dim impressions upon dead pine needles; there were scratches on rocky surfaces; but there were no real prints. He had been working for at least an hour in this patient fashion, getting no results, when he was aware that he was being watched from behind his back. When he turned sharply about, he saw a tall man with a gloomy face, a big fellow whose thin lips were hooked in the curve of a perpetual sneer.

"Hello!" said Kinkaid. "What are you looking at, stranger?"

"I'm lookin' at a man waste his time, Kinkaid," said the other.

The marshal took no immediate offense.

"Can you do better at this job?" he asked.

"Tolerable," said the other.

"That's what you say."

For a reply, the other carelessly raked the pine needles that lay before his foot. "Look here," he said.

The marshal obediently went to look, and there he found the complete and delicate outline of a near forehoof, the very nail holes being clearly indicated.

"That's what you want, I reckon?" said the stranger.

The marshal, without an answer, brought up the mare at once, and caused her to step with the left forehoof exactly beside the former mark.

The instant the impression was made, there was no need for measurement. The two were identical to the spacing of the nail holes. There was the same rather large spread of hoof. The same distance between the open ends of the shoe. In all respects the two were identical, and it was established that moment beyond cavil that this mare, earlier in the morning, had been ridden to the poplars, held there long enough to trample the grass down, and then brought back through the trees.

"Duval was at the dance," said the marshal. "Who are his friends in Moose Creek? Because I got an idea that one of 'em is a fellow with a hurt hand, just now."

"There's an old man named Henry that lives with him," said the stranger.

"Tell me," said the marshal with interest, "who are you? If you got eyes as good as this, I could use you, friend, and pay you good for your time, too."

"I got no use for money on this job," replied the other sourly. "I'm in it for the sake of doin' what I can to Duval. My name is Larry Jude."

Chapter Twenty

The conclusions of the marshal were prompt, definite, and strong. Mr. Henry, as he learned, had accompanied the mare from the East. Since Duval in person could not have committed the robbery, and since the mare was most apparently ridden by the robber, therefore, Henry was the guilty man.

He did not go in the daytime. He went after dark to the house of Duval. It was not by the gate onto the road that he approached, but from the side, cautiously squirming his way through the hedge of shrubbery now advancing with the season into big leaf.

He had tethered his new mare fully half a mile away for fear she would whinny as she approached her former home.

Once inside the hedge, he took careful account of his bearings. Before him were several fences, surrounding the corral and the straw stack, that leaned in a lop-sided manner toward the south, under the pressure of occasional north winds. Beyond the bars of the fences, he could see the lamplight shining through the window of the cabin, and as he was looking at it, striking across the field with a pleasant golden shaft, the marshal found himself unusually thoughtful and depressed. For he was remembering with an uncanny vividness the pale face and the gray, unflinching eye of the stranger of Moose Creek.

This state of mind did not last long. He went deliberately to the first fence, and slipped between the bars, crossed it, and was going through the straw stack enclosure, when the whistle of a quail from the hedge disturbed him.

He flattened himself against the straw stack and whirled, gun in hand, as though enemies were already charging upon him. But then he heard the call repeated, and a distinct, though soft, rustling of the foliage far behind him.

He analyzed the notes of the whistle with care, but it was the perfect call. Four short notes in a quick ripple, and after the last a slight break in the rhythm and the final touch.

Yet the marshal waited, to make surety doubly sure. He knew that he was now invisible, pressed as he was against the side of the stack. He felt the chaff work loose, and stream down inside his shirt collar, working deep against his skin. However, despite this discomfort, he remained for a long time in this manner, motionless. Then he started again for the house, but not in a straight line. He first got out of the straw-stack enclosure, and stole down toward the side of the horse shed, inside of which he heard the horse and the mule nosing at the sweet hay, and stamping in their content. From the shed he

169

then angled up on a new course toward the cabin.

It was an unnecessary precaution, of course, but there was nothing that Richard Kinkaid was fonder of than needless precautions. The public, considering his achievements and regarding his mighty form, were prone to look upon him as a man who advanced headlong upon any difficulty and any danger. But, as a matter of fact, Kinkaid was apt to use the tactics of an Indian. He loved battle, but he saw no purpose in throwing away chances.

From a new line, therefore, he went on toward the house, all because a quail had been disturbed in the hedge behind him and given bobwhite's familiar call. On this new line he went with a redoubled caution, stooping very low, so that no one would be apt to see him from any point of view against the radiance of the lighted window, no matter how dim. Creeping, now, he slipped toward the house, bending so low that he touched the ground before him with the tips of his fingers, and so explored it more accurately than with a light, to make sure that his following footfall would make no noise.

His attention was by no means confined to the house, to which he drew closer and closer, but now and again he paused and scanned everything around him, to either side and to the rear.

When he made these pauses, however, he could hardly have been expected to see the form that slid behind him and also paused, disappearing against the flat blackness of the ground by lying face down.

So the marshal went on until he was in touching distance of the house itself.

All was still inside, except for two sounds, each wonderfully faint, but perceptible by his keen ear. One was the singing of a kettle on the stove, and the other was the occasional soft crackle of paper, as though the pages of a large book were being turned. One of the two occupants was doubtless in bed—hence the lack of conversation. The other sat immersed in his book, allowing something to cook on the late fire.

Kinkaid stood up straight. He was now close against the wall of the house, so that his background would prevent him from being seen at more than a few paces. He stood up, and as he did so, something cold and very hard was laid against the back of his neck.

"Hoist your hands," said the voice of Duval.

The marshal, for a moment, was speechless. He had faced vast dangers in his life, but this was unique in all his tales of war. In that first dreadful flash of apprehension, it seemed to him that he could hear Duval's quietly regretful voice stating how the lurking form had approached his house, how he hailed, challenged, fired . . . And so the end of famous Richard Kinkaid, obscurely shot.

He could not speak; he could only slowly obey the command.

"Wait a minute," said Duval. "I see you're hitched up to a gun. Unbuckle that belt, stranger, and do it slow . . . and don't try to turn, because if you do, you'll turn into a ghost. Salt that idea away, partner!"

"Duval," began Kinkaid, "I'm Richard Kinkaid and . . ."

"And I'm Napoleon," Duval declared pleasantly. "Sure. I understand. Let that belt drop, and the gun with it, or you'll be Kinkaid no more!"

The marshal did not hesitate. The firm, cold pressure against the nape of his neck spoke to him in a more penetrating manner than words could ever do.

He unbuckled his gun belt, and the gun and the cartridges above it dropped with a solid thump to the ground. For the first time in his mature days, the famous marshal was unarmed.

"Now, we'll have those hands up good and high," said Duval. "Think what mamma told you. Stretch yourself and try to pick a star out of the sky, and sashay right around the house, and go in through the front door, big boy. Now, there, walk slow and easy, and don't stumble if you love your life."

Kinkaid neither argued nor protested. He followed these orders exactly as they were given. A man with a sense of humor might even have

172

smiled, but Kinkaid did not smile. He rigidly held his hands above his head and marched slowly, solemnly in advance of his captor. There was only one thing that would have made him fight for his life against even these odds, and that was an audience. But since the soft hand of night had covered the eyes of the world, he was willing to submit. As for the story afterward, who would believe it of the great Dick Kinkaid?

He gained the door, and strode rather awkwardly into the room. Arrived at the exact center of it, he halted. His fingertips were touching the low ceiling, and willingly he would have pulled down that ceiling upon himself and his captor. Yet another thought came into his mind—the consternation of Duval when at last he should know who his prisoner was.

He heard Duval saying: "You can turn around, keeping your hands still resting on the ceiling, partner."

The marshal turned slowly, as he had been ordered, and stood eye to eye with Duval.

The latter stared at him without amazement, with a keen and curious interest.

"Well, Kinkaid," he said, "I can see that folks don't do right by you, calling you a pretty stern and gloomy gent. Here I find you out playing hide-and-seek. Who were you playing with, Kinkaid? You can tell me while you put your hands down."

173

The marshal lowered his hands, but his heart was not lightened. He did not answer, but looked at Duval in a great effort to learn how far the other would carry his point.

"Speaking personal," said Duval, "I always liked to see a gent that would get out and join the kids and be jolly. But I couldn't tell whether you was playing hide-and-seek, or sneaking up to rob a hen roost, or what. Robbing hen roosts was a favorite game of mine when I was a kid. Now, tell me, did you ever do it, Kinkaid?"

"Duval," the marshal said gravely, "you've made a tolerable fool out of me. It's up to me to tell you why I'm here, though, and I'll do it. I'm here because I came for your hired man . . . Henry. Where is he?"

"Henry? You want Henry? Don't tell me, Kinkaid, that you want to play hide-and-seek with Henry, because he never could run fast enough to make you enjoy the game."

"Are you gonna keep this up?" Kinkaid asked sourly. "D'you know who you're talking to?"

"Why, Dick," said Duval, "I guess that I'm pretty nigh the only man in Moose Creek that really knows you, and the playful way you got with you. Other folks wouldn't hardly believe it possible that you've been up here and visited me and played hide-and-seek this way. And with old

174

Henry, too. They'll sure be a pile amused by that. Everybody from Pete the bartender to Marian Lane."

The last name was a thrust at the very vitals of the marshal's pride.

He swallowed hard. "Duval," he said, "I aim to think that you're gonna try to spread the news of this here around?"

"Why," Duval said, "I wouldn't think of talking about the game at all. I wouldn't be dreaming of it. Because most likely all idea of it will drop out of my head. I'll forget it, complete, and I'll ask Henry if he won't forget it, too."

He whistled, imitating beautifully, the call of the quail chick, repeated it, and eventually there was the sound of a footstep outside the house. Henry appeared in the doorway, with an apprehensive look in his face.

"What d'you think, Henry?" said Duval. "The marshal's been up here to play hide-and-seek with you. Like he wanted to tag you, only he got tagged first, and he was wondering if we could forget about it, if the marshal, say, was to forget about your bad finger."

Henry started violently.

"By gravy!" the marshal said through his teeth. "It *was* the old man. What're you trying to do, Duval? Blackmail me to keep me silent? You chump, I'll have you both in jail before the world's a day older."

175

"Jail?" Duval said, flashing a smile at the larger man. "Why, that'd sure wake us up and make us talk, Kinkaid. I figure that everybody would be mighty interested, too, to hear about how Richard Kinkaid, he come slipping along in the dark, like he was after chickens on the roost . . ."

He chuckled, and Henry, suddenly understanding, smiled his crooked smile, his eyes gloating on the marshal.

"I see what you're driving at," Kinkaid said. "You think I'll shut up sooner than have you talk. You jackass, what difference does it make to me what you say? Will people believe you against me?"

Duval took from behind his back the cartridge belt and the gun.

"Maybe they wouldn't believe me," he said, in a soothing voice. "And they'd think that I picked these up on the road, somewhere? Maybe they'd think that. A mighty disbelieving crowd we got around this here town of Moose Creek, old-timer."

At this, as the full point of the remark came home to him, Kinkaid felt his soul shrivel like dead leaves. He was dizzy with rage, and with helplessness.

"I'll tell you, son," said Duval, "the fact is that you and me and Henry are all gonna be friends. I could sort of see it in you when I first clapped eyes on you. The sort of a gent that I'd like to have for a friend. What about you, Henry?"

"I like him right off," Henry said, grinning enormously.

"The mare, too," Duval said, and putting away his gun inside his coat with a swift gesture, he took out a wallet from which he extracted the $1,500 that the marshal had paid him for the horse that same morning. This he extended, with his left hand.

Kinkaid hesitated. It would be a simple thing to throw himself upon Duval—if only he could estimate the speed with which the latter might be able to get his gun out of his coat. Besides, there was old Henry looking grimly on, and the latter decided the marshal on passivity. He took the money that was offered to him.

"What's it for?" he asked. "D'you want the mare back?"

"Wouldn't dream of taking her back," said Duval, "considering the price that you paid for her, but the fact is that you found out during the day that she wouldn't stand up under your weight, and so that was why you come back here to see me. You wanted to know if I'd call the sale off. Wanted to know if I'd give you back the money and take the mare, instead. And Duval, being a kind of poor businessman and a mighty good fellow, he said sure, that he'd take the mare back, and look on today as though it never had happened."

What Kinkaid saw, first of all, was the face of the girl in the store, that morning, as she had looked up to him with astonished excitement—she, his wife to be, helpmate, companion in arms, as it were. When she had seen that the mare belonged to him, it was as though she already saw Duval mastered and his problem and mystery solved.

That satisfaction would have to be surrendered. He saw all the advantages that he already had gained stripped away from him by this polite, cheerful, smiling Duval. And though he strove to struggle against him, he was held by a silken thread.

For he dared not allow Duval to go abroad and show the captured revolver. It was so well known—even the appearance of a new holster in place of the famous old brown and shiny one would cause infinite comment—and the gun itself, wedded to his hand these years, marked with nine small, regular, neat notches. . . .

The marshal burst into a profuse perspiration.

"I know how it is," Duval said sympathetically. "It's a mighty big relief to get rid of a horse that you spent so much money for, after you find out that she really ain't meant for you, as you might say. But you're busy . . . you're mighty busy, Kinkaid. I suppose you'll want to be hurrying away? Can't persuade you to stay here and have a bite of something to eat with us? No?"

Kinkaid gave no answer. Shame, rage, horror overwhelmed him, and he rushed out into the night.

Chapter Twenty-One

When the marshal had fled outdoors with his shame, Duval sat down in his chair, beside which, on the table, lay an open book, the leaves of which, rustled by the wind now and again, had made the comfortably domestic sound that had so lulled the last suspicions of Kinkaid in approaching the place.

"You knew he'd come," Henry said, frowning from his station at the door. "I dunno how you worked that."

"That's simple. He wouldn't have wanted the mare so badly if he hadn't had some way of connecting her with the crime. He came for her. He got her out of me, and I hated parting with her worse than death. I hope she'll be back soon."

"You gave him the money," Henry said, "but you paid him before you got the mare."

"There's no danger," said Duval. "He might slip around with another gun, however, and shoot through the window. . . ."

"Him?" Henry gasped, and jumped.

"No," said Duval. "On second thought, I believe that he won't attempt anything this evening. He'll be contented to return the mare to me and . . ."

"Aye," said Henry. "That's what I thought when he went out. He's finished, and he's flat."

"He is for the time being," said Duval. "He's no more than an Indian without a scalp."

"What does that mean?"

"An Indian without a scalp never can get into the happy hunting grounds. But Kinkaid may come to life later on. He *will* come to life, in fact, and we'll have more trouble with him."

"Then let's get out," Henry said fervently. "If you've won one stake, what's the use of bettin' on every race that's left on the program? Let's go home, sir!"

"What's home, then?"

"Any place on the wing. What's home for the wild geese? Goin' north or goin' south. We better do the same way, eh?"

This suggestion Duval considered quietly for a time, and then he said: "I've had the same idea, Henry, but I don't think that I can go yet. I have unfinished business . . ." He paused, here, and Henry watched him anxiously.

"The marshal knows," Henry said, "and as long as the marshal knows, it won't be long before other folks know, too. It'll be in the air. And then we're both cooked."

Duval shook his head. "Kinkaid can't talk . . . except to us. His mouth is shut." He laughed with a sudden and fierce burst of pleasure. "The giant's down on one knee, and I'm David."

"He's likely to get up and paste you when you're standin' around to crow," Henry suggested sourly. "What should keep you on here, when you came here for safety and quiet, and now you've got neither of 'em?"

"I was getting so tired of safety, Henry, that I hated to open my eyes in the morning and look at the day coming. I was so weary of the good, quiet life, that I was almost delighted to see you come with the mare in one hand and blackmail in the other."

Henry shrugged his lean shoulders as he replied: "I don't know just how you've managed it, but you've kept me away from Kinkaid, and there's no blackmail in my mind now, sir. When a man gets old, he's apt to try bad lines. I'm through with that one."

"Of course you are," said Duval. "Tell me, Henry. Don't you enjoy a time like this, when we can't tell how luck may jump against us the next moment?"

"Ask a new man if he enjoys walkin' a tight wire over Niagara, sir."

"Of course he does, or he wouldn't be there. D'you mean to tell me that you're not an artist in your field?"

"What, sir?"

"D'you mean to tell me that you were talking through your hat when you said that the only thing you wanted was the fun and not the money? No, no. I understand you better than that. Here's a chasm under our feet a thousand feet

182

to the bottom. If we miss a step, we're lost . . . and that's why this is only the beginning of the greatest sport we've ever had."

"I understand what you mean," muttered Henry. "But I've got two hundred thousand up on this race, and I want to win."

"Of course you do."

"Rule that dark horse, that Kinkaid, out of it, and I don't mind."

"You're wrong, Henry," Duval said. "He's not the great danger."

"Not him. Who, then?"

"The pretty girl with the doll's face . . . the beauty of the grocery store . . . she's the tanglefoot that is most apt to catch us." Henry waited for further light, but Duval merely added: "Not with her own hands, but she knows how to use the hands of other people. I would rather have three Kinkaids to deal with than one Marian Lane. How can she be handled? I don't know. That's the problem."

He began to pace the floor. "Here's the marshal," he said, holding up the celebrated Colt with its notches. "I have him in my hand. I suppose he'll say that his gun is in the repairer's hands. But suppose I should put this gun on the bar of Pete's Place . . . why, the reputation of Dick Kinkaid would burn up like a match in no time. And he understands that." He paused before going on more slowly: "The sheriff is a good-natured old fellow. He may have a few doubts about me, but he's willing to put his doubts in his pocket. He doesn't need to be counted in, unless fighting should begin, and then he's as dangerous as the next man. That leaves only the girl with her eternal question . . . who is Duval?" He broke off shortly, saying: "How the deuce is one to handle a woman like that, Henry?"

"Money . . . ," began Henry.

"Don't be a fool!" said the other tersely.

"I dunno," Henry said. "When I was a youngster I never found any way of getting' along with a woman unless she happened to be in love with me. And when she was, then she was a dog-goned nuisance."

Duval stopped in his pacing and raised his pale face in thought. Henry, watching him keenly, began to grin on one side of his mouth, his keen old eyes sharpening to points.

"That dog has found something," Henry murmured aloud. "And pretty soon he's gonna point to the bird."

"Love!" Duval announced. "I hadn't thought about that. Love!" He laughed as he spoke, but he was filled with excitement. "Suppose, Henry, that I can keep the sheriff quiet, the great Kinkaid muzzled, and put the girl in my pocket, so to speak. That would be the hardest thing I ever tried to do. Three balls all in the air at the same time, and never falling. What do you say, Henry?"

"Hello!" exclaimed the other. "You mean to make her think . . ."

"That I can't keep away from her. That she's upset me completely. That I lie awake at night thinking of Marian Lane. That Marian Lane is closer to my heart than my left elbow."

"Well?"

"Why, nothing, except that it may get me what I've wanted to have . . . a quiet summer here."

"All right," said Henry. "You're the boss, but I'd rather try to be quiet with a live coal in my hand than a woman on my mind."

Chapter Twenty-Two

His left hand in his coat pocket and his right hand carrying an envelope, old Henry entered the grocery store in the sleepy quiet of the midafternoon, to find Marian Lane asleep in a chair behind the counter.

She tipped forward to her feet, shook the sleep out of her pretty eyes, and accepted the envelope with a smile.

The letter it contained read:

Dear Miss Lane:

I'd like to talk to you, and the place I'd pick wouldn't have even walls to listen. Will you give me the chance and say where? Henry will bring back your answer.

David Duval

Beneath this, she scribbled instantly:

I'm going for a walk up the creek in about ten minutes, and since it goes past your door, I suppose we could meet on the way.

This she returned to Henry, and watched him out of the store. Then she hurried up the stairs to change.

She never dressed more rapidly, and never with more care. It was to be an outdoors meeting, and, therefore, she put on a short khaki skirt and tan woolen stockings, a white blouse with a broad collar that would be ruffling up against her face in the wind and making her color seem a shade higher than it was. She boxed up her feet in broad-nosed, heavy shoes, because, as all women know, a dainty foot never appears more feminine and small than when it is furnished with masculine boots. She took a hat with a big, flexible brim, which was very useful in keeping her face from the sun and from unnecessary observation. At her throat, she pinned a tuft of blue wildflowers with soft yellow eyes. Lastly, she pulled on gloves of thin yellow chamois and took a heavy walking stick, much scratched and marred by beating about in the brush and being stubbed against rocks, for she was a lover of walking through the hills.

When she was equipped in this manner, she went through a little performance that ten thousand eyes would have been glad to oversee, for she stood before her mirror smiling at her own image, then critically studious, and smiling again. She bowed to herself. She looked up at her own eyes from beneath the bare verge of the hat brim. She turned to view herself, and, without shame, pulled the skirt down a little more snugly about her hips. She stepped back from the mirror and approached it with a light, quick step, and a beaming smile. She repeated the process languidly, with her head drooped a little to one side, picking at the imaginary twigs along the path. Then, close to the mirror, she rolled up her eyes in childish innocence. She gasped with astonishment and clasped her hands together at her breast, and lastly retreated, laughing a little over her shoulder.

When she had ended this little performance, she stood for another moment in profound thought, rubbing her fingers a little deeper into the tight fingers of the gloves. She seemed to be reviewing the weapons with which she was going afield, and finding at last that they were in fair order and of a sufficient number, she passed the tip of a finger across her forehead to make all lines of reflection vanish and went lightly down the stairs and out to the street.

Young Sam Hewitt was across the street from her and gaped at her with such a wide grin of confused joy that he forgot to take his hat from his tousled, sandy head.

Sam was not important, but she felt that she could reasonably count coup one, and she went on more confidently, if that were possible.

Mrs. Clarkson and Mrs. Bill Witter encountered

her at the next corner and paused to talk about the unseasonable heat, "though weather never seems to bother you, darling."

Marian Lane went on, and heard distinctly behind her: "The sweet innocent. Little she knows of the world, heaven help her."

At this the faintest of smiles appeared upon the lips of the girl, and she quietly counted coup two with all the satisfaction of an Indian brave. She began to feel that this was her day, and this confidence added, if possible, to the blue of her eyes, and to the dainty color in her cheeks.

She entered the woodland trail and walked along it none too briskly. By this time, she reasoned that Duval must have been waiting for her fifteen or twenty minutes, so that he must have been brought to a desirable state of mind. A little more waiting, however, would do him no harm, and above all she wished to be composed when she met him, for she felt that a duel was to take place in which she must present her sharpest wits.

She came up the path with many pauses to admire the creaming ripples on the surface of the creek, and the dark swift flow of it over half-visible rocks. Sometimes she stopped an instant to breathe of the pines, and sometimes of the flowers, or to touch the long arm of a vine and set it swinging and trembling, or to listen to the scolding chatter of a squirrel on a branch far above her.

But all the while her mind was flying before her to the encounter that was to come. What was of the utmost importance was that the mare had been returned to Duval by the marshal. He had said that the horse could not stand up under his weight, but she, having seen Cherry flaunt down the street with Kinkaid in the saddle, felt that she knew better. She could not be sure, but something told her that there had been an occurrence between Duval and the marshal in which the former came out the victor. If he could handle Kinkaid, it seemed probable that he could handle any man. As for the women—ah, that was a different matter.

Here the path turned with the bank of the creek, and she saw Duval sitting on a rock, with one knee embraced by his hands, as he stared at the water.

"Hello!" she said.

"Hello!" Duval said, standing up. "I'm delighted that you came."

Her head tilted a little to one side, and she laughed at him. "You've left the cowboy talk behind, I see?"

"I've left Duval over yonder in the cabin," he said. "I'm David . . . Castle."

"It's a nice name," she said.

"I hoped you'd like it better. Shall we walk or sit?"

"I'd rather walk, I think, David . . . Castle."

She made a pause before the last word, smiling a little at him as though she accepted the new name only tentatively.

They went up the path together at a pleasant pace, she apparently only attentive to the trees about them, the bright shrubs, and the lantern rays of sunlight that twinkled on the ground before them or glittered in the upper foliage. In fact, she knew each time he touched her with his eyes, and where the touch had fallen, as distinctly as though his hand had gone out to her dusty shoes, or her swinging stick, or the flowers at her throat, or the red of her lips. So, divinely aware and unaware, she walked on, somehow glorying in her strength.

Duval, in the meantime, was in no haste to begin. But after a time, he said: "How long can you be away?"

"An hour, I suppose. Then I'll have to get back to the store."

At that, he answered: "Then I'll have to start. It will take me the better part of an hour, I should say."

"For what?" she asked.

"Confession," he said.

She stopped short and faced him, with all her airs and mannerisms forgotten. "If you mean that, there's no time limit."

"Good," he said. "I've asked you to come out to hear me surrender."

She did not speak. Her eyes were too busy scanning him, searching, searching.

"The going is too deep for me," he said. "I used to think that I was a horse for all sorts of tracks, but I begin to see that I'm only a fair-weather performer. When the rain comes down, I can't win." He smiled at her. "To begin with," he said, "I'll tell you what I intended to do. I was going to tell you a cock-and-bull yarn about my past, and try to win your sympathy so that you'd send me no more Larry Judes and Dick Kinkaids to look me up. Jude was enough. Kinkaid was a bad one to handle, though."

"Was?" she said.

"For the time being," he said cautiously, "I think that Kinkaid won't trouble me again. I suppose that you've guessed that much?"

She nodded.

"But when I saw you today," he said, "all dressed for the innocent country-girl part, so simple, so excessively sweet, turning up your eyes at me . . . why, then, I lost heart at once. I saw that you're too clever to be fooled, Marian. I have to tell you the whole truth, and trust everything to your mercy."

"You make me out a bad sort of a person," she remarked.

"I make you out a dangerous one to poor fellows like myself who are made of penetrable stuff. I'll even go one step further, Marian, and tell you that I was going to play the fool and the cad wholesale by trying to make love to you." He chuckled. "But, of course, the first glimpse of you put that out of my head. You know entirely too much to be fooled by acting. That's why I'm desperately going to tell you the truth."

"The whole truth?"

"And nothing but the truth."

"Of course, I haven't any real right to hear it."

"You haven't. But you've decided that this fish must be shared and taken out of the water so that you can see its actual colors. Well, the fish has doubled and dodged and safely escaped from two of the fishermen. But the fish is badly frightened. It is afraid that the third fisherman will be entirely too much for it. Therefore, it jumps out of the water of its own accord, Marian. It lies on the bank at your feet and lets you judge for yourself whether you're going to put the gaff into it, or else let the poor thing flop back into the creek."

"You make me feel like an executioner," she said.

"You are," he answered calmly.

"Well," she said, "of course I'm curious. I'd like to hear anything you have to say."

"It will take a lot of time."

"When I'm in the middle of a good story, I can always forget time."

"Mind you, this is no story."

"Nevertheless, I'll guarantee that I'll keep everything I learn a secret."

"No, you'd better not promise that."

"You're right. I can't promise that."

"You're ready?"

"Yes."

"Then prepare yourself. It's police court stuff. I'm going to start at the beginning, as they do in books."

Chapter Twenty-Three

They walked on again, more slowly, Marian sometimes stopping as Duval made a point of interest, he with his hands usually clasped behind his back, while he talked in his soft, quiet voice.

"It was all horses, country life, riding, jumping, hunting for me," he said. "School was a necessary nuisance, that was all. In the summers, my father generally took me West for hunting, and fishing, and bronco riding. 'To rough up my hair,' as he used to say, because a fellow whose stomach had never been tucked up for lack of food will never make a man. He used to start off with me across country with rifle, ammunition, and salt. We killed our food, and if we didn't kill it, we went hungry. We've been so hungry that we had to dig roots and eat them. An Indian had taught him which ones were good . . . but none are very good."

"Your father . . . he must have been a man," she said.

"He was a man," admitted Duval.

"You learned guns that way?"

"What I know about them I learned that way. You have to shoot straight when you feel that your first dinner in three days is inside the barrel of your rifle, you know. Single-shot rifles were what we carried. Father never believed in a second chance."

"I suppose he's right," she said.

"Do you act on the same principle?" asked Duval.

"I?"

"In your hunting, I mean," he clarified.

The gray eyes met the blue, seriously, soberly. Then they both smiled a little, and he went on.

"I was out of college when the break came. Father died. We expected to cut up a fat melon, but instead we found that we had a house, some books, and some horses. That was about all. I'd been the leading spender, and now I had to be the leading provider."

The girl stopped and slashed deftly at some tall weeds, slicing off their pale, flowered heads.

"That's it," Duval observed. "I had to cut off heads to make a living."

"How did you go about it?"

"Father's banking was not a business at all, we discovered. He sat in an office and did what other people told him to do. His real work was riding and hunting anything from a fox to a bear . . . but there's no money in that. And that was all that I was qualified to do. However, he had one other interest . . . a hobby for the evenings."

"What was that?"

"He used to fiddle about as a locksmith."

"Did you learn that trade, too, from him?"

"Inside out. That was why he loved me. He used to say that I could open any door in the world, and, after his death, I remembered that speech of his and decided that I'd turn it into a legacy. Do you follow my drift?"

She whirled the cane and nodded. "I suppose you decided to open doors that had money behind them?"

"That's it. And there's my story, Marian."

"That's only the beginning."

"Do you want me to go on?"

"Of course!"

"Well, perhaps you want to know how I excused myself?"

"Yes. I'd like to know that."

"I was a little younger then. Not quite so able to face the facts. So, I told myself that Robin Hood had done things as bad. He took from the rich and evil. He gave to the poor and good. If I included myself in the latter class, I might be excused for vanity. So, I decided to begin, and I did."

"The first time . . . that must have been rather hard."

"You've picked the one. It was Arthur Burchell that I decided on. He was a member of a mortgage ring . . . the fellows who make a business of throat-cutting, and he'd cut enough throats to fill his pockets with blood money. His third wife was a gold-digger and she was the one creature in the world who knew how to extract coin painlessly from him. Diamonds were her hobby. She used to wear half a million dollars' worth of them, and very little else when she went out in public in the evening. I saw her, decided that this was fair meat, and went to rob the house that same night."

"By yourself?" she asked.

"By myself. I never believed in partners. Do you?"

"I don't see the point of comparison," she said.

"Tools . . . I believed in a few humans as tools and agents, but not as accomplices. Haven't you the same idea?"

"In what way?"

"There was Jude, Kinkaid. They were only errand boys, weren't they?"

She smiled, but did not answer directly. "Do go on," she said.

"It doesn't bore you?"

"I'd like to know how you got at the diamonds that night."

"I didn't. I got to the room where they were kept. It was cold November. There was frost on the roofs. Once I skidded thirty feet into an eaves gutter. The gutter broke the force of my fall, but the fall broke the gutter."

"Did you go clear to the ground, or land in a haystack?"

"The only stacks were chimneys. It was eleven

stories to the ground. No, I didn't fall. I hung on by my hands and swung myself back to an unbroken section of the gutter. Then I climbed up the roof and got in at a skylight. I found my way down through the hotel and got to the door of the Burchells' suite. That was the worst moment . . . I mean, standing there on the plush carpet of the hall breathing the warm air with a taint of perfume in it, as though a woman had just gone by. Every instant I expected a maid or a guest to heave in sight. But no one came. I got the lock open fairly soundlessly, and into the room where the diamonds were in their pet safe."

"Did you carry that away?"

"It weighed about two hundred pounds, I think. No, I didn't carry that, but when I tried the lock, a bell rang, the lights flashed on, and fat Arthur Burchell sat up in bed, gasping with fear. He turned loose at me with an automatic, and I dived through a spray of lead for the door.

"I had sense enough to lock it behind me. The corridor held a maid and porter running toward the sound of the shooting, and I shouted robbers once or twice, and ran as if for help. I needed help, too."

He drew up the sleeve of his left arm and showed her a broad, white dot on the bulge of the muscle of the forearm.

"Burchell had clipped me here, and I was

bleeding pretty badly. But I got away over the roofs, and down to the street."

"That ended the Burchell diamonds, I suppose?"

"No. I got them, all right."

"When?"

"The same night. There's nothing that makes for sound sleep like a foiled attack. I tied up my arm and waited in view of the hotel until the lights in the Burchells' rooms went out at about four in the morning. Then I went back over the roofs in exactly the same way. I got into the room in the same way, too."

"Weren't you frightened to death when you stood at the door?"

"Not the least. This time I was pretty sure of myself. The door opened in an instant . . . I remembered it perfectly from the time before. When I got inside, I squatted down and listened to Burchell's snoring, and hoped it wouldn't waken his wife. I unloosed one ray from the shutter of the dark lantern and pricked the dark here and there with it. Burchell had been having champagne to celebrate his courage and his victory. There was a little table in the middle of the room that looked like a broken iceberg . . . it was so covered with glassware. I let the ray sparkle on it for a minute. Then I found the top of a champagne bottle in the ice bucket, and helped myself. It was pretty flat, but I never liked champagne with too much jump in it. I was very thirsty, you see, from the loss of blood. I hope that doesn't sound like boasting? I mean, the champagne drinking in the middle of the robbery?"

"No, I think you'd do that," she said.

"It was easy to find the electrical connection of the little jewel safe, now that I knew about it. I clipped the wires, and had the safe open in a moment. Just as I raised the lid and had sent a flash of light into the contents, Missus Burchell sat up and gasped. I faded onto the floor. She poked Arthur in the ribs, and when he woke up, she told him that she was sure that there was a man in the room. She'd seen an outline against the stars outside the window."

"That was a ticklish moment," said the girl.

"It was."

"What did you do?"

"Sat still."

"And then?"

"Burchell told his wife that she was nervous and that his sleep was worth more, anyway, than her blankety diamonds. He was snoring in another moment. After a while I went around to her bed to see if she was asleep."

"Br-r-r-r," said Marian Lane. "How did you tell?"

"By listening to her breathing. When I was sure of that, I went back and took the diamonds in their soft little chamois sacks, filled my pockets, and left them to have their sleep."

"Tell me this . . . when you were seen by the maid and the porter in the hall, didn't they see you clearly?"

"Very. The maid described a middle-aged man with a short black mustache for the detectives the next day, and the porter described a burly ruffian who looked like a prize fighter."

"You hadn't hired them?"

"Not with a penny, but in such cases excitement generally corrupts the faithful more thoroughly than a million dollars."

"I suppose it does. So you got off scotfree?"

"Entirely. There was only the cut in my arm. It bothered me for a while, but not as much as the man did who I used as a fence . . . I mean, the fellow who receives stolen goods, do you see?"

"How did he bother you?"

"He paid me a hundred thousand for half a million's worth of diamonds. And, after that, he tried to blackmail me for half of the hundred thousand he had paid me."

"Did he?"

"They have their little ways, the fences."

"What did you do?"

"I killed him," Duval answered. "I was young, new at the business, and thought he meant to do what he threatened . . . about disgracing me, I mean."

"You killed him! You murdered him?" she gasped.

Duval, looking down at her with admiration, said: "When I see you do that, I almost think that you mean what you say."

"What do I mean, then?"

"I'm only a critic, not an interpreter," he said.

Chapter Twenty-Four

It was extremely hard to look at Duval without meeting his eye, for no matter how casual the glance that fell on him, the gray, keen eyes were apt to be turned instantly upon the observer, so that details were wiped out, and there remained only the impression of the pallor of the face and of the gray pupil itself. But Marian, watching him constantly as they walked along side-by-side, was gradually able to build up a more consistent picture of him, point by point. The pallor was the only point of weakness; otherwise, it was the face of an athlete in high condition, lean, with distinct ridges of muscle at the base of the jaw, and all the lines of nose, mouth, and hard chin showing dominance and intellectual sensitiveness together.

She thought of her own soft picture in the glass, and all seemed contrast, and yet there was something in her that flew out to meet his spirit and understood it. He, too, must have had somewhat the same sensation, or he would not have talked in this manner to her—roughly, as though she were a man.

It was a novelty to Marian Lane, and a not altogether unpleasant one.

"You killed the fence," she repeated. "How?"

"In the back room of his place."

"But I mean . . . how?"

"Why, I simply walked in and told him to draw his gun, which he did, and then I shot him through the head. The others made a good deal of noise, but when they saw that he was really dead, they stopped shooting after me and began to loot the place."

"There were others?"

"There were three others, his pet yeggs. However, I had a hundred thousand out of him, and after that I lived very well for a couple of years and kept the old place up, and was complimented on my success in the street." He laughed, without grimness, enjoying the memory, as it seemed.

"Only two years? That's fifty thousand a year."

"I mean that I lived well. Gave to the poor, too, like Robin Hood. Poor relations, I should say, to qualify my praise. But they're the hardest kind to give to. They never know what to expect, except a little more than they get."

"At the end of the two years?"

"Then I saw that I'd have to dig in deeper, and this time I chose the Merrill brooch. You've heard of that, I suppose?"

"No, never."

"Merrill was a real-estate broker. He owned an improvement company, and when he got through improving a town, he had all it was worth for the next fifty years mortgaged to the hilt. Then he moved out and improved somewhere else. Missus Merrill had the brooch. She . . ."

"There was always a woman in it?"

"Even rich men seem to have wives," Duval said. "That's a riddle you may be able to work out for yourself. At any rate, there was the brooch. The Merrills didn't splurge in quantity, but they did in quality. He went to India and came back with five rubies, any one of them worth a fortune. It cost him nearly a million, it was said, and I have reason to know that the estimate wasn't extravagant. The big one was in the middle, and the other four set around it. It was big enough to fill the palm of a man's hand, almost, but the silly woman wore it as a brooch. It shone like a danger signal, and I determined to have it.

"One evening we were sitting at dinner, side-by-side, with a big fireplace just behind us, so I took off the brooch and chucked it back into the ashes. After a while, she missed it. There was a great commotion. Everyone was searched, and all that sort of thing. When the search was ended, and every inch of the room had been combed . . . except the flaming fireplace, of course . . . I raked the thing out with the toe of my shoe while I was kindly building up the fire for the sake of the chilly ladies. And I walked home with that million. Of course, I didn't realize fifty percent, but that was a good deal."

"How long did that last?"

"I increased my scale of living, but still it endured for four years, and would have gone longer if I hadn't had some bad luck with the ponies."

"Four into five hundred is a hundred and twenty-five a year."

"Yes, I had a good time. The poor relations got less poor. But when the four years ended, I saw that I would have to operate again, and this time I decided that I'd take no chances."

"What sort of chances? In stealing?"

"Not that. Unluckily, chances have to be taken in stealing. The business never has been organized past a very amateur standpoint, and, as you can see, I hadn't had enough practical experience to work out a new theory. I mean to say, I decided to make it safe by stealing so much that I could live on the investment and the interest thereof without having to spend my capital."

"How much did you need for that?"

"I wanted to be moderate . . . only to maintain the same scale that I had been living on up to that time. I thought that two million would do handsomely. At six percent, there's a hundred and twenty thousand a year, and I thought that that should do."

"Yes," said the girl, "I should think so."

"But how was I to make that much money in jewels?"

"Why did you have to stick to jewel robberies?"

"The unfortunate limitation of my mind," Duval answered. "Of course, I shouldn't have stayed with that one medium when there are so many others that are easier to negotiate in the open market. Securities that can be turned into cash, for instance. And then there are banks whose lucky vaults are bulging. But, as I said before, I was limited by my experience. Criminals generally are, and I can see how the criminal streak in me controlled me according to the old standards.

"Odd how crimes are repeated in the same way by the same men. There was the good old English wife-killer, who always strangled them in their bath and collected the insurance, I believe. There was I, with the world as open before me as it was before Robin Hood, and yet I had not his delightful variety. Tyros cannot imitate a genius. Robin ranged from highway robberies to the pillaging of castles. Poor David Castle could only do over again what he had already done.

"But he decided that in the first place such a large percentage should not go to the fences. What else to do, then? Why, pearls immediately jumped into my mind. You can take a long string and break it up into units. Not difficult to dispose of them in small quantities anywhere, and at the top market price. So I hunted around for rich pearl collectors, and hit upon Henry Hollinshed at once.

"He'd made his money in opium, poor old Henry. Worked hard, handled it from the growth of the poppy to the distribution of the drug in the States, including the smuggling in. His profits were very handsome. He built a church with part of them, and endowed a school with another part. But he loved pearls. He was a bachelor, was Henry. He collected the great strings and set pieces for the pleasure of seeing them with his own lonely eyes. He used to set them up on velvet like saints on an altar, and worship. Quantities, Hollinshed had, at rock-bottom Oriental prices, and a canny old Arab always collecting.

"I visited Hollinshed, after I'd devoted six months to the serious study of pearls and their values. He kept the pearls in a safe in a corner of his room, a perfectly modern, up-to-date safe, very hard to handle. It was doubly guarded at night, so I went in one noon and blew the door off. It was perfectly simple. I got the collection and disappeared with it through the back-cellar door. Then I went around in front and watched the police arrive, and after them the reporters. I was a plumber, with a plumber's kit . . . full of pearls, now, besides a few tools . . . and a smear of lead on my face that would have disguised me from the eye of the most inquisitive angel. Only my patron demon could have known me.

"Then I went home, and on the way knocked my old grip against a lamppost and spilled out a dozen or more big pearls. Luckily for me they were so big, and I gave five cents apiece for them to some boys who were standing near if they would pick up the marbles for me . . . the ones that had rolled off into corners. I was taking some marbles home to my little boy, you see. I thought I had gathered up all those marbles, but it seems that I really hadn't.

"At any rate, I went on home and examined my catch. I wanted to estimate it, but I didn't need to do that. The evening papers said the gross total was nearly three million, and they were only a few hundreds of thousands out of the way. All was well, but in a few days, I had bad news. One of the boys had liked the look of that lustrous marble better than five cents. He kept it and he even showed it to his mother, and by bad luck she was a court stenographer's wife who had known better days. She recognized it . . . thought it was paste . . . and took it to a jeweler. To a bad one, you'd think . . . to a cheap, around-the-corner chap, you'd say. Not at all. By the further grace of eminent bad luck, she took it to an honest man, who nearly fainted and asked her what she was doing with a twenty-thousand-dollar pearl.

"And immediately there was a hue and cry. The pearl was big enough for Hollinshed to identify it. Important enough for him to dig up the record of its sale, exact description of size, weight, color, et cetera. There was no doubt. It was Hollinshed's pearl. Then who was the greasy, lead-marked young plumber? You see how embarrassing it was for me?"

"Of course I do," said the girl.

"I decided to leave town and disappear entirely. I decided that I'd go where I could rest for a long time, and let the dust settle after this disturbance. For, in spite of what the detective story writers say, the police are as clever as fiends, and I dread them to the core of my soul."

She nodded, her head bent, as it had been for some time.

"And having decided on retirement, what better place than to come West, where I'd spent so many happy summers as a youngster? No sooner said than . . ."

She raised her head, and Duval heard the merriest of laughter peal beneath the gloom of the trees, flooding them with music as bright as the sun.

"Is that funny to you?" he asked. "D'you think I should have picked Paris?"

"It isn't really funny," she said. "It's almost sad that you should have told it to me. But, after all, I'm not really laughing at you. I'm admiring you, David, because you're the most wonderful man I've ever known."

She faced him, both her hands placed on the broad head of the cane, and she needed that support, for she was rocking gently back and forth with her continued laughter.

"As pretty as a bird atilt on a bough," Duval said in appreciation. "But why do you laugh?"

"To think of the waste, David! A mere jewel thief, farmer, and man crusher, when you would have made such a delightful writer of romantic stories."

Chapter Twenty-Five

He watched her mirth, still with unchanged appreciation, still with critical thought. And, eventually, he began to laugh in turn.

When she had ended her laughter and was wiping her eyes, he still was chuckling, but stopped to say: "Did I choose the wrong line, then?"

"It was a beautiful line," said the girl. "I enjoyed every minute of it. Oh, David, how wonderfully you told of that first time . . . and the crystal on the table . . . and the champagne . . . and every little detail, so that it put me into the room. If you write it down, you'll be remembered for it."

And she came closer to him, and gasped her admiration, and clasped her hands together at her breast.

Duval admired her again. "I wish that you'd keep a little farther away, Marian," he told her. "I'm a sedate fellow, a man with a quiet heart, and very much afraid of you. And when you come so close and open your eyes so wide, I grow a little dizzy. You make me feel as though I were standing on a very tall building."

"Do I?" she said.

"You do," said Duval.

She seemed to grow a little puzzled, but at length she snapped her fingers. "I have it!" she exclaimed.

"You have?"

"Yes. You're going to try the other line, now that the first one has failed."

"What other line?"

"You're going to make love to me!"

"Ah," Duval murmured sadly, "you wouldn't believe a word of that either, would you?"

"I did believe part of the first one," she confessed. "And so I might believe part of the second. I'd like to try. Will you begin as we walk on?"

She started slowly up the path, Duval beside her, and, tucking the walking stick under her elbow, she took the arm of Duval for support, her hand resting lightly upon it. She fell in step with him and trudged along at his side.

"Now," she said, "do begin."

"You embarrass me," said Duval. "And you have hold of the arm that I need for gestures. What's lovemaking without gestures?"

"There's something in that," Marian Lane agreed, "but it's the talk that I want to hear. I want to have you unloose your imagination, because I'd bet high on the results. Just for a little jewel robbery, you've had my heels dangling eleven stories above the street, put a bullet through my arm, made me thirsty with loss of blood, and

214

given me champagne . . . that went to my head, too. But for the sake of love . . . how I should like to hear you talk then, David."

"I have quite another way for that," he said.

"Of course you have, and it must be wonderful to hear. What is your other way? I don't presume to guess."

"Oh, very few words. Something manly, direct, and simple . . . the cards all upon the table . . . here I am . . . a poor thing, but your own. You see?"

"H-m-m," she said. "I can see how well that might do, especially with horsey people such as you've known a lot. They're free and easy and love bluntness, and talking to the point."

"They like to be casual," said Duval. "One says to the girl of one's choice . . . 'Mary, why not step off?' 'Where?' says she. 'Give me a cigarette, will you?' 'To a church,' one answers, lighting the cigarette for her. 'How can we find a church?' says she. 'By asking for the minister,' one answers. She yawns, and then wakes up a little. 'Are you proposing, David?' 'Some girls take it that way,' one answers. 'Jolly old David,' says she, 'he *will* make conversation. Let's go out and see the new filly. Jimmy says she's up to my weight.' That's the way proposals go in the hunting crowd."

"But suppose she accepts you?"

"That's just as simple. 'Good idea,' she says. 'Wait till I get my hat.' It's like that."

215

"It wouldn't do out here," Marian advised. "We're romantic. We have long evenings without cards, and that lets us read stories, and that makes us want speeches made. If you'll make speeches for me, David, I don't think I can resist."

"I'd need to work them up a bit."

"You could tell me the themes, though."

"You mean eyes and hair, and lips and throat, and all that sort of thing?"

"Well, for a background that would do."

"But I couldn't shine at that, because you know a lot more about your face than I do. I haven't had time to give it the study that you have."

She gave his arm a slight tug that stopped him.

"I like you better and better, David," she said. "If you leave out the face, what would you find to want about me?"

"The intriguing imp that makes you torment me, Marian."

"We'd better walk on," she said. "You're growing bad-natured. Is there an imp in me?"

They went on together.

"A mysterious imp, Marian. A cruel, wicked, pain-loving, cunning, prying, eavesdropping imp, that has not let poor young Duval alone, who took burning glass and focused it on him, and ever since has kept him writhing and dancing and twisting in the fire until at last he came to you and fell on his knees, as it were, and begged for mercy."

"And heard a long, pretty story," she said.

"If it had been a kind-hearted imp," Duval said, "it would have recognized the worth of labor even in a lie. Such a long lie. Such thousands of words put together, such detail, such embroidery, such passion, such a veritable sun of near truth shining upon it, warming it, making it more like the truth than a mirage on the desert. But this cruel spirit in you, my dear, only skewered me with a sharp accusation and left me in more pain than ever before."

"We'd better turn back," suggested Marian Lane, "because I'm growing uncomfortable."

They swung slowly about and started back. But despite her protest, she still walked with him, arm in arm, swinging along in step in the most companionable fashion.

"Besides," she said, "it really isn't true. I've only shown a perfectly natural, human curiosity."

"Ah, I'm not talking about myself, alone," said Duval. "But there's the rest of the world. All the good fellows about here whose hearts fairly quake when they see Marian Lane, when they speak of Marian Lane, when they so much as think of her gentleness, her industry, her child-like face, her child-like soul. What a wife for any man, and particularly for a cowpuncher, a farmer, a rancher. What a girl to be cherished, to be held in the arms, and her eyes covered from the biting, brutal truths about the world. An Iago would melt in the presence of such a girl."

"But not a Duval," she said.

"Why not? He can see that she has spent her days learning to play this neat rôle, this pretty, guileless part of baby face that looks up to the big strong men, and never changes expression, and never lets her mockery get up as far as her eyes, to say nothing of her tongue."

"But why should I play such a part?" she asked.

"Because if you were yourself, my dear, the acid of your criticism would eat away the sham gold leaf that covers men and let the eye of the world see their true composition of brass and lead. They would hate you for that. Even if you were more beautiful than you are . . . though I shouldn't like to try to improve you . . . men would hate you for knowing the truth about them. For no matter what exquisite care God shows in forming a woman, if He puts a brain in the completed picture, men will not endure it. The first thing and the last that we positively demand of every good woman is that she shall not think."

"But what about the other kind?"

"Well, they're different. And because they're burning themselves up like candles before an altar . . . man being the god in the case, do you see . . . we'll permit them to have brains, poor things, and enjoy reasonable conversation with them. But not from you, good people. No, if your logic goes one scruple deeper than 'because', we're frightened away, and that's why many a lovely girl has mysteriously grown into a charming spinster while her snub-nosed sister marries three times and always picks from a crowd. You knew it, Marian, and you planned your life accordingly. And nothing can save you except one odd chance."

"What's that?"

"Some hundred percent fellow who will sweep you off your feet, make you as dizzy as you've made others, rattle you away to a church, and marry you before your head clears, thereby bringing you in touch with the eternal verity."

"Which is?"

"That we're all such children that none of us need to pretend simplicity."

They went on in silence, after this, until at last she withdrew her hand from his arm.

"Here's the end of our walk," she said. "I see the sun through the trees, and I'd better go out alone onto the road."

"I suppose you had, and this is the one friendly time we'll have together. This is the last time, eh?"

"David, David," she said, "I only wanted . . ."

"Do you have to roll up your eyes like that?" he asked.

"I can't help it," she said. "I've practiced so long that it's deeper than second nature. But I've never wanted to harm you, and I'll never again ask anyone to help me find out who Duval is."

"That's a promise, but I'm afraid you won't keep it."

"So am I," she said.

"Then good bye, Marian. After this, swords out once more . . . but now I'm going to say good bye to everything that's delightful in you." He took her deliberately in his arms. "Do you mind?" he asked.

"Not at all. I'm delighted," she said, and she turned up her face to him, smiling, and with half-closed eyes.

Duval, however, leaped suddenly back from her. A gun flashed in his hand, and then, with a murmur, he made it disappear.

"We've been watched," he told her. "Jude, the sour-faced cur, has trailed us, and I had a glimpse of his eyes as he faded out of sight in the bushes, there!"

"That's not the end of the world," she answered.

"That he's seen you in my arms?" Duval cried, strangely excited. "Don't you see? Kinkaid hates me enough without hearing that. And Charlie Nash, when he learns of it . . . what will Charlie feel about me? Others, too. It'll be spread through the town in no time. I'm the lucky man, and twenty of them will want to murder me for my good fortune. . . ."

He began to laugh heartily but silently. He even

leaned a hand against the trunk of a tree, and the girl, watching him, suddenly yearned to be out of the shadows and in the warm, bright, honest sun. She hesitated, then yielded to a quick panic and fled from the woods out onto the open road.

Chapter Twenty-Six

Into Pete's Place went Larry Jude.

Even his sullen and vicious heart could have made no greater effort than to face the sneers of the men who had seen him, not so long before, thrust ignominiously out of that place. But he came armed with patience and with savagery. That downfall of his spirit that had allowed even a puny bystander to strike him with impunity he now had recovered from to some degree. To face Duval, he dared not at any price, but the very fact that he made the one exception made him despise himself and all other men profoundly.

So he stood in Pete's Place in the late afternoon, when the blacksmith had ended his day of hot labor and stood with elbows on the bar, his red, soot-marked face bowed above a tall glass of beer whose thick and creamy collar he had not yet disturbed. Two cowpunchers had just come in, and Tom Main from his ranch, with a buckboard loaded with broken harness that needed repair—for Tom that morning had tried the unique experiment of hitching twelve mustangs to a gang plow, and when the mêlée ended, the plow was a battered wreck—one mustang had been kicked and trampled to death, and their leather harness was a tangled mass.

When they saw big Larry Jude come in, these men swung half around toward him in dismayed surprise, in disgust, and then, instead of speaking, fell back to their drinks and looked at one another with faint sneers.

Only Pete himself rose to the occasion. For Pete was a gentleman to the core of his heart, and he allowed no malice to overcome him. It made no difference to him that Jude had acted the part of a boor and a brute. The man had had his lesson, and now he was too thirsty to resist the smell of liquor in the air, the feel of soft sawdust underfoot. He asked with a certain amount of solicitude what the big man would have.

"Whiskey!"

It was poured; it disappeared.

"Another!"

It went the way of the first. The third drink stood glimmering on the bar before Larry Jude, a ray of westering sunlight shining in the red heart of the liquor.

Tom Main offered the first general conversation.

"Chimney Creek is in flood," he said. "They tell me that Will Mason's house has got water up to the top of the verandah steps. His chicken coops have gone down the current, and he's lost half a dozen calves. Chimney Creek is a heck of a stream, I always said."

Larry Jude cleared his throat. The others looked

down, bit their lips, and waited for the outcast to speak.

"I was crossin' Chimney Creek one fall," said Larry Jude. "Got in the middle of the dry bed. Warn't more'n a trickle of water that twisted along between the rocks. Give my horse a drink and went on. It was too muddy water for a human. I hear a roar. It's one of them water walls that come crashin' around the curve above me. Five foot of water, leapin' and dancin'. I put the pony to a run. There was a wall of rock each side of the creekbed. I had to sprint him nigh half a mile before we made the bank, and as he climbed up, the crest of the wave hit his hind legs and rolled him and me over and over. But we'd got away. Chimney Creek is a right treacherous bit of water."

This broke the ice, and the others were all willing to chime in with remarks, and similar anecdotes. No matter what they privately thought of Larry Jude, they respected the effort he was making to step back into human society once more. It was not all mere good will, moreover, for they saw in the fixed and glaring eye of Jude, now beginning to relax, that he meant trouble, if trouble were necessary to rehabilitate himself.

"You come from up Montana way, Jude?" asked Pete.

"Naw. But I had a wife up there, once."

"Died?"

"Run away with a half-breed."

He swallowed his third glass of whiskey, but refused a fourth.

"The half-breed died sudden," Jude said. He smiled his crooked, evil smile. "I dunno what come of her."

The others could not help a quiet glance at one another. They could guess what had happened to her.

"Lot of women are that way. You never know what way they'll jump," Pete said, the smoother-over of difficulties. "You see 'em all the time, but you can't tell what they'll do. The younger and the prettier they are, the worse trouble maybe they'll make, the more they'll fool everybody. Ain't I right?"

There seems to be professional agreement among men that the opposite sex is not to be defended. His own wife, his own daughter, may be the exception—but as for all others . . .

So there was a general murmur of assent to Pete's proposition.

"I remember," Tom Main began, "a brown-eyed girl in Tucson, with enough Mexican in her to give her spice. She was one day out with a fellow by name of . . ."

"You don't have to go to Tucson to be fooled," Larry Jude inserted. "What about right here in Moose Creek?"

225

"Aye, wherever there's women, ain't I right?" Pete suggested philosophically.

"You couldn't be no righter," declared Larry Jude, and the evil in him ripened and flowered in his speech. "Take this afternoon . . . I was out walkin' in the woods, and there I seen the blonde kid from across the street . . ." He paused and shook his head with a smile.

An electric shock passed through the bar-room.

"Might you be meanin'," Pete said slowly, picking his words with care and changing color, "might you be meanin' Miss Marian Lane?"

Larry Jude grinned down at his empty glass, turning it methodically between thumb and forefinger. "What else would I mean?" he burst out suddenly. "She's the girl that nobody can touch, nobody can lay a finger on. She ain't got no steadies. Am I wrong?"

"No, you're right," Pete agreed. "There ain't a man that's so much as held her hand, and I'm here to say so. There ain't been a word ag'in' her, and there ain't gonna be."

"Ain't there?" Jude muttered somewhat sourly.

"No, there ain't," Pete insisted, and gripped both his fists as he answered the ominous stare of Jude.

"Lemme tell you what I seen," Jude said slowly. "I was out strollin' through the woods, and there I seen this same Marian Lane that makes the boys so dizzy . . . there I seen her out walkin' with a gent . . ."

Growing hot and white in spots, Pete interrupted, saying: "I seen her start out. I seen her go up the street, and there wasn't no man with her."

"Sure there wasn't," Jude said. "Why should there be? Wouldn't it discourage the rest of the boys a lot if they seen her goin' out with one man, day after day? They'd feel a good deal out of place with her, wouldn't they?"

He paused for an answer, but none came from the troubled company. They looked neither at one another nor at him, but considered in their own minds what protest they should make against this attack on the favorite of Moose Creek.

"Why should she show herself with a man," continued Jude, "when she can walk up through the woods and find a gent waitin' for her?"

Honest Pete gathered his courage and his strength to burst out: "Jude, mind what you're sayin'! You're talkin' about a lady, now, man!"

Larry Jude regarded the bartender with a deadly eye. "Oh, I mind what I'm sayin'," he declared. "I got the facts and the figures, the names and the faces. Would you know what man she'd picked out?"

They did not answer, each feeling that he should speak some disclaimer, and each unable to do so, for the man was fairly trembling now with malice, and with rage.

"What man," went on Jude, "is sort of out-standin' from the rest of the herd, here in Moose Creek? What's the man that's made himself taller than the rest of you? Will you tell me that? You know him well enough. Some of you seen him hypnotize me here in this barroom. You seen him make me take water . . ." Despite his rush of words, he had to stop here and swallow hard. "Because if it wasn't hypnotism, what was it? Who else ever seen Larry Jude take a back step from any man, and who's ever gonna see it happen again, for one Duval, or for twenty of 'em!"

He waited, and, waiting, he struck the bar heavily with his balled fist.

Then Pete spoke again. "I got no better friend in Moose Creek than Duval," he said. "There ain't a girl in the world that we all think more of than Marian Lane."

"Don't I know it?" Jude said fiercely. "Ain't that why I'm here? To tell you what fools you all been about her, and about him. Him that hadn't no time for women, eh? Him that couldn't be bothered with 'em, because he was too busy workin'! Why, Duval, I see him holdin' out his arms to her, and her steppin' into them like a horse trained to step into its collar. Like a fire horse trained to jump into its place!"

He broke off with loud laughter, and, standing back a little from the bar, he glared fiercely around him. Vainly they strove to meet his eye.

"Why don't they come out into the open?" Larry Jude asked. "Why sneak into the woods and make love? What's on her conscience? Because she still wants the whole town to trail around after her, I reckon. What better idea have you got?"

Pete strove to answer, here, but he found the words sticking in his throat.

At this point, old Henry himself walked into the saloon for his afternoon glass of beer. It was his one drink of each day, and now, as he saw Larry Jude, he hesitated for a tenth of a second, mid-step, then went on to his corner place.

Pete, without a word, served him with his foaming glass.

But Jude turned on the old fellow like a snarling dog.

"Tell Henry, too," he said. "He knows enough already, but I reckon that even Henry don't know about the girl and Duval, their spoonin' in the woods together, their sneakin', lyin' way of livin', and turnin' their backs on each other when there's another person in hearin' of 'em! D'you know that, Henry?"

He waited, but Henry, without turning, continued his attention to his beer.

"And tell Duval," went on Jude, "that once he hypnotized me, but, the next time, they ain't gonna be time for him to get in his dirty work. I'm waitin' for him to show his face!"

With that, he left the saloon.

Chapter Twenty-Seven

Having finished his beer, old Henry walked without hurry back up the hill and came to the house of Duval. He found the latter still making the rounds of the narrowing land, with the team at the harrow, and walked down to meet him. He waited until the team had turned the corner and then held up his hand.

"What's wrong, Henry?" asked Duval. "You look pleased, and that's a sure sign that you're full of bad news."

"Is it?" asked Henry.

"It is! A shipwreck makes you feel years younger, and good, honest murder sets you up for a day. What is it, Henry?"

"Why, a lot better than either of those. They say that you're philanderin' with Marian Lane, and her with you. The town won't be talkin' of nothin' else by tomorrow, unless you put on the brakes and keep from rolling downhill."

"Who has told that?" Duval asked, unmoved.

"Why, Larry Jude."

"Jude?"

"Yes."

"Where?"

"In Pete's Place."

"And the boys stood around . . . all those

230

excellent friends of mine, all those old cronies of Marian Lane . . . and listened to that talk?"

"It don't cost a thing to use your ears, sir."

"Pete, too?"

"I think Pete tried to stop him, but couldn't. Jude says that he wants to meet you again, but I think that was just to make the rest of the boys feel good and hopeful. He didn't mean it. His eye wavered when he said it."

"What does it amount to?" asked Duval.

"I stayed and gathered up a few seeds of the story after Jude left the place. Only that Jude had seen her in your arms, sir, out in the woods by the creek."

"Is that all? Is that enough to stand Moose Creek on its head?"

"Her being what she is, you being what you are," said Henry, "it'll make considerable commotion, I should say. Better than a long shot winnin' a stake race. A lot better than that."

"Take the team," said Duval. "I'll be busy for a while. Put up the horse and the mule, and then you'd better wander downtown again and listen to what is being said."

He himself went straight to the corral and saddled the mare.

As he was, with the dust and the grime of the day's work on him, he buckled a gun belt around his hips. swung into the saddle, and cantered Cherry down to the town.

He went to the store, first of all, and as he dismounted, he saw two old women of Moose Creek go by. They turned as though he were a pestilence, and looked bitterly askance at him.

Luckily, in the store itself there were no customers, only Marian Lane at work behind the counter, tidying up her place and refilling the flour bin. She greeted him with the pleasantest and most impersonal of smiles.

"I came down," he said, "to find out how everything goes along with you, Marian."

"Perfectly well," she said.

"Our friend Jude has been at Pete's Place telling his little story, it seems."

"Yes, he has."

"You know about it already?"

"Oh, bad news needs only one jump to go across Moose Creek."

"What's so bad about it, Marian? What sort of a place is this if a girl's painted black because she . . . er . . . ?"

"Kisses a man?"

"Yes. It was hardly that, you know."

"No. We were interrupted. The secrecy . . . the woods . . . and the greatness of Duval, and his contempt for women. All those things helped to make it worth talking about."

"Did they?"

"Naturally. Best of all, it shows that I'm a hypocrite."

"I don't understand that."

"Yes, I think you do. You explained it pretty fully this afternoon, for me."

"I was feeling a bit edgy and said too much."

"You were simply feeling a bit frank, and said what you thought. I don't bear any ill will."

"Will it make any difference to you?"

"To me? Not much."

"But a little?"

"Why, it will cut my business in half, make people talk behind my back, and make the boys sneer in my face. Aside from cheapening me, it doesn't matter a great deal."

He drummed his fingers on the counter. She glanced behind her toward her uncompleted work, as though she were anxious to be back at it, but her smile never varied, nor the soft, wide blue of her eyes.

"Marian, you're really eating your heart out about this."

She looked thoughtfully up at the ceiling, abandoning her smile for the moment.

"No, I don't think I am. At least, I won't for very long. I don't really regret it very much."

"I've come to tell you that I'll do anything you say."

"About what? About Jude and his story?"

"Yes."

"You mean that you'll hunt him down and kill him? Is that why Cherry is standing in the street?"

"Perhaps so."

She shook her head. "Don't be angry, David," she said. "You're keeping perfectly cool and cold. It really would be better if you swore a little to let off steam. As a matter of fact, you're ready to kill now, and that's why I like to watch you so closely. To see that the polite self-control is rubbed so thin, so transparent, that even a child would see enough of David to be frightened to death of him. Don't do anything rash, David. Go over to the saloon and tell them that Jude is a puppy, if you wish. But don't, don't, use a gun to help out your words."

"Will you be serious?"

"I am already."

"If you wish, Marian, we'll announce an engagement. We'll let them know that we're going to be married."

"Married? Oh, then they'd be sure that we really had something important to conceal. Even as it is, I'll have to take a few years to live this down."

"You don't think it's a good solution?"

"Marian Lane, engaged to whom?"

"To me, of course!"

"To David Duval, or to David Castle? Or is it really David Smith, or David Jones?"

"You still stick on that point?"

"I'm afraid I do. I still want to know who is Duval."

He stepped back from the counter.

"Oh, but you've done your duty," said the girl. "You've done it beautifully, and I appreciate that."

He bowed to her, and went slowly out of the store.

The wide street that wound through the village was as quiet as ever, except, just visible around the next curve, a little boy and a small dog playing in the dust, and squealing in voices that were almost identical.

Duval looked up and down the way gloomily. The peace that had been here in Moose Creek like a gold mine for him had not disappeared. But he crossed the street to Pete's Place and went in, to find only Tom Main and Pete himself present.

The saloon was very dim in the dusk of the day, but Pete showed no inclination to light his two big lamps. He was standing there, leaning against the bar opposite Tom Main, and the pair were talking together slowly, softly. By the guilty way they glanced up and then straightened, Duval could guess what had been the subject of their conversation.

He felt also, and instantly, that there was very little use in trying words, so he merely leaned against the bar and took a small whiskey with the two. It was Tom Main who treated.

"Jude has been down here with some ugly talk," said Duval. "Is that correct?"

Pete nodded uneasily.

"I'm not angry, except for Marian Lane," Duval said.

"Sure," Pete said, and bit his lip in anxiety.

It was plain that he wanted to believe whatever Duval would say. It was also plain that he would have a hard time doing so.

"If Jude comes along again," Duval said, "I'd like to see him. My old man used to say there was no way to stop a grass fire except back-firing against it. If he should drop in, and you'd send me word, Pete, I'd take it mighty kindly."

"Why . . . sure," Pete said. "I'd do that, only I reckon that Jude won't be comin' in again. He's done his job."

Both he and Tom Main began to look up anxiously toward the ceiling, as though they hoped to find there some new topic for conversation. But in spite of all the seams and cracks that ran along the ceiling, they could not find words. Silence fell heavily over the old barroom, and finally Duval left.

At the door he paused again, looking back toward the others, and they, anxiously, toward him.

"Look here, boys," he said, "because I was fool enough to try to kiss Marian Lane, and because my friend, Larry Jude, says I did kiss her, is there any reason why he's to be believed above me? If there is, say so!"

They both waved deprecatory hands.

"There ain't any reason in the world, Duval," Main assured him. "Jude's a skunk and he's got it in for you. It's my opinion that nobody'll pay no attention to him."

But the words rang flat as a counterfeit coin, and Duval knew that he had lost this trick in the game as he went out onto the street again.

Ordinarily, it would have been of no importance, for it was only a bit of gossip, and that of the lightest kind. Yet he knew that his position in Moose Creek was imperiled. His strength there had been the friendship of the men of the town and the community around it. That friendship was now endangered, and as he walked back up the hill, Duval made up his mind to leave Moose Creek and start for another region.

Where he would go, he was unsure, and his uncertainty weighed heavily on his mind. Something had been subtracted from the world— some touch of spice and joy was gone from it.

Chapter Twenty-Eight

When Jude left the saloon, he did not tarry. He knew that imminent danger was close at his heels, and, therefore, he went with rapidity straight for the place where he knew he would find Kinkaid. This was back among the hills at a small shanty, long deserted and staggering now to the ground. And he found Kinkaid seated inside on a sagging box, his back against the wall and his arms folded across his chest.

There was no greeting between them. Each was equally distasteful to the other, and through the darkening of the day they looked gloomily at one another.

"Duval is on the skids," Jude began abruptly.

"Duval?" growled the marshal, as though the name were new to him.

"It works out like a card trick," Jude said. He leaned against the side of the door, and as one who has done good work and can afford to relax, he rolled a cigarette, lighted it, inhaled deeply. "It was kind of hard to get at him. He had too many friends. It ain't hard now."

"Go on!" Kinkaid said as gruffly as before.

"They liked Duval. Most of those young gents liked something else a little better."

"What was that?"

"Why, the grocery store girl . . . Marian Lane. She's all they could see at one look."

"Jude," the marshal said, "we're working together on one job . . . Duval. Other folks don't count. We'll leave out the girl, for a beginning, I reckon."

"You can't leave her out, because she's in the town and in the game of Duval."

"She is? Talk straight and talk slow, Jude!"

The latter shrugged his shoulders at the warning in the tone of Kinkaid. "Suppose," went on Jude, "that a gent rolled into Moose Creek and mopped up all the attention of Marian Lane. Would the other young gents have much use for him? Would he be popular, I mean, around the town and along the range?"

Kinkaid leaned forward, then settled back again. "Has Duval done that?" he asked briefly. But there was a change in his voice, and Jude grinned with a sour delight.

"He couldn't get past her baby face. He stopped and looked twice, and the second look was better than the first one."

The marshal said nothing. His silence was a sufficient reproof.

"I trailed him, as I said I would. I watched him all day, and it wasn't no easy job. He was harrowin', but every time there was a stir of the bushes in the wind, he'd whirl around and have a look at it, and his gun is only a hundredth part of a second behind his look, if he means business."

"Go on," the marshal said wearily. "Tell how brave you were, lying on the ground on your stomach and watching Duval. Want me to praise you for that, Jude?"

Jude shrugged. "What you think ain't of no importance to me, but if you ain't watched that cat, you might take a few minutes off someday and have a look at him. He's worthwhile."

"Thanks," said Kinkaid. "I know enough about him."

"Enough to keep clear of him, eh?"

Kinkaid stood up, but then controlled himself and sat down again, as though he realized that it was useless to express his mind to such a man as his present companion.

"Go on, Jude," he ordered calmly.

"Anyway, I trailed him like his shadow, and in the afternoon I seen him meet Marian Lane in the woods."

The marshal briefly exclaimed. "Where?"

"Along the creek. He went over and sat down on a stone. Pretty soon she came along and met him."

"What did they do?"

"Talked . . . and walked along."

"When they met?"

"Nothin' but talk. I was too far away to get hold of that, mostly, and what I did hear was kind of hard to understand. But I found out one thing."

"Go on. You take a year to say nothing."

"You'll think it's something. The lingo that he slings around as if he was fresh off the range ain't his nacheral lingo at all."

"What's the proof of that?"

"He talked like a book to the girl."

"What did he say?"

"I don't remember, except that no schoolteacher could've talked closer to a book."

"Good," said the marshal slowly. "I thought that he . . . but I didn't figure on this . . ."

He controlled himself, but Jude went on: "You thought he was a crook. You hoped that he was a crook. But you didn't guess how big a crook he was. Well, he's that kind. Can use both sides of his tongue as fair as any man in the world. I listened to the talk as much as I could."

"Where did they go?"

"Up the creek a way, and then they turned around and they come back together."

"What's there in that?"

"When they quit each other, they didn't go out onto the road. They said good bye under the trees, where the shadows was thick over 'em."

"Yes?" queried the marshal, with a rising emotion.

"Duval, he steps up and holds out his arms, and she walked right into 'em as if they was home for her. . . ."

The marshal was suddenly erect, and, striding

to Jude, he gripped him by both arms, and forced him back into the open, where, by the last of the daylight, he could dimly read the face of the other.

"Jude, if you're lying to me," he said, "I'll have your hide off you for saddle leather!"

"Leave go your hold of me!" Jude said in angry answer. "I'll not be manhandled by no marshal, even if his name is Kinkaid! Leave go your hands from me, d'you hear?"

The marshal obeyed, because already he was sure of the man's truth in his recital.

"I gotta mind . . . ," began Jude. But he controlled himself, as the marshal had done not long before. "I'm gonna try to keep pullin' in double harness with you," he declared, "but don't you make the job too hard for me."

"I'm listening," the marshal said, and waited again.

"She steps into his arms, and he folds her up in 'em, like a storekeeper wrappin' up a Christmas toy. He folds her up in 'em and leans over, and what does she do?"

"Get done with this, will you?" demanded Kinkaid, his voice harsh with anger.

"Aye, it don't please you none, I can see," said Jude, the expert in pain. "It don't please you none, and it didn't much more please me, neither. But I see when he leaned over her, that she willingly lifted up her face for him to kiss. . . ."

"By gravy!" burst out Kinkaid. "The sneaking, hypocritical, worthless woman!"

Jude broke into a jeering laughter. "That puts the whip on the raw, I reckon," he said. "That'll make you pull a load uphill, eh? Well, I seen what it would do, and when I found out . . ."

"What did you do?"

"Went to Pete's Place, because it was the same as goin' to a newspaper. Went to Pete's Place and I told 'em what I seen."

"You went back to Pete's Place?" Kinkaid drew in his breath through his teeth with an audible whistle.

"I went back there, where he made a cur out of me, where he busted me down almost to cryin' . . . where he kicked me out onto the street! I went back there, and I faced the boys in Pete's. I told 'em what I'd seen." His teeth clicked like a dog's that has snapped up a choice morsel. "They took it hard," Jude continued, "though most of 'em hung onto themselves better than you done. But they was all galled by it a little bit, I can tell you. It hurt. It hurt 'em bad."

"What did they do?"

"Nothin'! What could they do? But now, every man jack of 'em figgers that Duval has got what they all wanted. Henry come in for a part of the yarn. I talked to his face, and I told him that I wanted to meet Duval ag'in."

"You lied."

"Maybe I did," answered the other with a strange frankness. "Maybe once havin' felt his eyes, I wouldn't be no good no more ag'in' him. But I gotta hope, don't I? I gotta hope that someday I can have a chance back at him, and then get him, or else he gets me, and I die like a man, and not like no danged coward."

The solemnity of this speech took the marshal by surprise, but his mind was already too fully occupied with the news he had heard.

"What happened then?"

"As I started out, I went up the road behind the brush, and I seen Duval come slidin' down the hill on the mare, Cherry. He was aimed at makin' trouble. I guess that Henry had gone back and told him."

"Then Henry's alone at the cabin?"

"He is, unless Duval has come straight back from the town."

"He ain't going straight back," declared Kinkaid. "He's gonna wait down there in the town, and try what his talk can do to rub out.what you told 'em."

"He won't have no success at all," said Jude. "You can mistake a lie for the truth, but not after truth has been along and showed its real face at you."

"Wait," muttered the marshal. "Duval gone . . . only Henry in the house . . . what's a better chance than that to get inside the house, I'd like to know."

"You mean to go inside of Duval's house? Why not go and put your foot in a steel bear trap?" Jude asked angrily, and yet touched with admiration. "You'll be tellin' me pretty soon that you got no fear of any man in the world."

"I mean it," answered the marshal firmly. "But now let's go down and get to Duval's place. He may be started back by now."

Chapter Twenty-Nine

It was not pleasant to Jude to return to the house of Duval. Having been there once, he would, as he expressed it well, as soon have put his foot inside a steel bear trap. However, since the marshal would have it so, so it must be.

And they rode down from the hills through the romantic twilight like falling stones aimed at the head of Duval. The pebbles scattered before the flying hoofs of their horses, the dust rose in thick puffs behind them as they plunged down from the last dim rose of the day into the dark of the lower valleys.

As they rushed on, the dry, pure air of the heights, only sharpened by the scent of the pines, departed behind them, and, instead, they entered a moister region, where the earth gave up a sense of coolness, and the air was soft with the breath of growing things. All in the upper region was silence, or sounds so muffled that they were no more than the living pulse of the silence. But in the lowlands, there were the sounds of cattle and dogs, and the very noise of the galloping hoofs flew up more loudly to their ears.

So they came to the verge of Duval's place and dismounted.

"Why are you hanging back?" asked the

marshal roughly as he started into the hedge of shrubs, and then turned back to his companion.

Jude did not answer. He remained in the attitude of one who has taken a step forward and been arrested there by something he has seen or heard. His face was lost in the darkness, and yet there was something that breathed from him of intolerable fear.

The marshal was not peculiarly sensitive to the feelings of others, but this cold of dread he could sense, and he remarked shortly: "Stay here, then. And if there's a sight of Duval coming back up the road, or a sound of his horse . . . you could tell the long beat of her gallop, I reckon . . . you whistle to me, not too loud, and I'll know what to expect."

"Suppose he's there now?"

Kinkaid peered through the hedge. "The house ain't lighted," he argued. "If he was there, they'd be a light . . . maybe . . ."

He left his sentence unfinished, as the possibilities of disaster surged up into his mind. Once before he had gone toward that house expecting to find it tenanted, because the light was shining from it, and that time he had found it empty. Now, again, he was stealing forward confidently because it was dark, and there might be within the thick night of the cabin the pale face and the gray eyes of Duval.

Yet the marshal's spirit, unlike that of Jude, had

not been broken. He hesitated only one moment, and then slid through the shrubbery and walked with long strides straight for the cabin. He did not attempt to stalk the place. He marched straight to the house and beat against that door. He heard the hollow echo of the knock die swiftly inside, so he thrust the door wide and entered.

Within, the hot, close air of the day poured against his face and made him break into a perspiration. But, casting one look behind him at the safe, free outdoors that he was leaving, he unshuttered the dark lantern that he carried and started to work.

He found the trap that led to the cellar, opened it, and descended into the moist coolness of the lower house.

The walls were roughly masoned stone. The floor was merely packed dirt. First, he went around the walls, tapping them cautiously, and listening to find the hollow sound that would mean a cavity within. It was difficult work, but the marshal was an expert.

It was while he proceeded in this fashion that he stepped on what seemed to him a softer portion of the floor, and, turning the full light of the lantern upon it, he was reasonable sure that here the earth was a shade loose, and that it was heaped a trifle above the surrounding level.

Instantly, he was scooping it away. In a moment, he had touched oiled silk. In another instant, there was spread out on the cellar floor a gleaming row of burglar's tools, of the finest steel, of the latest fashion. He regarded them with an appreciative eye, but he did not take them.

Instead, he rolled them up exactly as they had been, and, replacing them in the hole, he cautiously restored the earth, and spent a moment stamping down the soil that he had displaced. Here it occurred to Kinkaid that any warning whistle would hardly reach him as he worked in the cellar. Moreover, had he found enough?

He hastened up the ladder to the house itself and went to the door. But here he paused, uncertain, ill at ease. With all his soul, he yearned to be gone, but an odd thing decided him. Out of the town, he heard the distant barking of a dog, high pitched and sounding uncannily like mocking laughter with caught breath. Laughter at him, for giving up the work when so much remained unlearned, undecided.

He gritted his teeth and turned back to the cellar door. Here, with his hand upon it, the perspiration rolled out on his forehead. Whatever else he did, he could not return to the cellar below, so far from freedom. Telling himself that, after all, that cellar would yield him no more returns, he gave himself to the search of the house itself. He would take the attic later. In the meantime, here were the walls and the floor of the house.

The ray of the lantern began to pass around the

walls, scrutinizing every joint of the logs until it came to the short angling ones that built up one blunt corner, and to tap the logs here, Kinkaid found that it was necessary to reach across the bed.

The very first stroke he made rang hollow on his ear. He had to pause to wipe his face, because the drops were blinding him, but then he started a serious examination of that log. Those above and below it were normal to the ear, but this one was distinctly flawed. At last, gripping it with both hands, he jerked back—and the front face of it came easily away.

Within, he found two things. The first was to him beyond all price, for it was the gun belt that he had lost, the brown-rubbed holster, and within the holster his own revolver with the nine storied niches in its handle. He dragged it out with the joy of an Indian recovering his medicine bag. He trembled with indescribable pleasure, like a child, as he belted the familiar weapon around him, and as the touch of the mother earth trebled the strength of Antæus, so the grip of the belt about him and the sense of the old gun at his hip seemed to double the strength of Dick Kinkaid.

But there remained the second object in this home-made niche. It was a small chamois sack, the mouth of which he pulled wide and poured some of the contents into his hand. He blinked at what he found, jerked the string that closed the sack, and dropped it into his pocket.

He had found all that he wished, a thousand times more. He held Duval in the cup of his hand, as it were, and yet there was nothing to be gained and much to be lost by letting Duval know at once that he was destroyed.

So he picked up the section of log that he had removed, and replaced it. It was while he was pushing it home that Kinkaid heard the whistle and, hearing it, knew that the same sound had been in his ear before.

He had been warned by the whistle of Jude, several times repeated, but unheeded by his conscious mind—except that this might account for the extraordinary tension of his nerves. Otherwise, his absorption in his present work had prevented him from realizing what was happening outside the cabin.

He stood back, therefore, against the wall, as he heard the approaching footfall, and drawing his own revolver, his tried and proved weapon, he gripped it hard, until the notches rubbed into his skin. At that distance, he would not fail.

He raised it, leveled it, and as a footstep approached the cabin from without, he prepared to shoot Duval the instant the silhouette of the man appeared dimly embraced within the rectangle of the door, against the stars of the horizon.

It seemed to the marshal, waiting in a growing self-confidence, that Duval himself must have realized that the end was near, with such a slow and dragging step did he approach the cabin. Then the shadow stepped into the prepared frame, not swiftly, lightly, as Duval usually moved, but with an uncertain waver, like a wounded man, or one whose strength has been strangely sapped.

And a weary voice sounded: "I thought I'd closed this door when I left . . . I'm gettin' old."

The voice of Henry!

In mid-impulse against the trigger, Kinkaid checked his forefinger. And, standing at ease, smiling now, he waited until Henry had lighted a lamp, blown out the match, and was standing back from the growing flame in the chimney.

Then he said: "Henry, don't turn around!"

Henry jerked halfway about despite that command, then controlled the motion.

"Well, well," he said, "if it ain't the marshal come back to pay a sort of a surprise call on us."

"I've come to pay a call," the marshal said grimly. "And I was sorry to find you both out of the place. Where's your boss?"

"Him? Oh, he's gone off on the mare."

"You lie!"

"Look in the corral, then."

"Where did he go?"

"Where you'll never find him, if he don't want to be found!"

Kinkaid could not keep back the curse that leaped to his lips at this unwelcome news. "Gone?"

"I dunno," said old Henry. "I never know what he'll do. But whatever it is, I know that it'll be too deep and hard for you to follow, Kinkaid."

The marshal laughed. "You poor trusting fool," he said. "You jackass! I got Duval in the palm of my hand."

"That's what the feller said that held the prickly pear," remarked Henry, "and then he closed the fingers and wished mighty hard that he hadn't."

"March out the door!" the marshal ordered.

"Me? What's wrong with me?"

"Robbery's what's wrong with you, man."

"Robbery? There's an idea," Henry said.

But, as he spoke, his hand glided beneath his coat. For some reason, the instant that movement began, Kinkaid knew what it meant. He did not fear for himself, but understood Henry's intention was to take his own life. So he leaped wonderfully swiftly for a man of his size, and as the muzzle of the weapon whipped up under Henry's chin, Kinkaid struck the hand away. The next instant, the report of the gun thundered in the room.

Chapter Thirty

The noise of the revolver exploding made Kinkaid hasten his prisoner, unharmed, into the open, merely pausing to kick the door to with a thrust of his heel, and while he did so he heard a guarded whistle from the hedge.

"That's the signal, eh?" Henry said musingly. "That's the warnin' for you, Kinkaid, when you come robbin'?"

The marshal threw a fold of his big bandanna over the mouth of his captive and held it tightly twisted at the nape of his neck. In that manner he effectually silenced Henry, and with his free hand gripping the old man by the elbow, he forced him rapidly forward toward the hedge.

But up from the lower gate came the swinging beat of the hoofs of a horse, and as though sunshine fell upon her, Kinkaid thought he could see the striding of the mare, Cherry. He hurried his prisoner on, therefore, until they came to the hedge. There he paused, fearing to call the attention of Duval by making any sound of rustling in passing through.

Duval, in the meantime, had reached the corral and was inside it, unsaddling the mare.

"Henry!" he called.

There was no answer from the house. It seemed

to the marshal, waiting at the hedge, that Duval might have guessed by the light that streamed through the window of the cabin that Henry was not inside, for to Kinkaid, who knew, it appeared as though the lighted windows were the eyes of an idiot, opening upon the empty soul within.

Yet, to Duval, it probably promised a lighted fire in the stove, a steaming kettle, and the rattling preparation for supper.

"Henry!" he called again.

Then big Kinkaid distinctly heard the other murmur: "The old fellow's losing his ears."

Shortly afterward the whistle of Duval went toward the house, and as the sound grew dim around the corner of the cabin, Kinkaid plunged through the hedge and gained the road beyond.

"One for me," he said briefly to the waiting Jude.

A strangled voice began in Jude's throat and dissolved into the words: "Was that . . . was that a whistle, Kinkaid? I thought that was the gallop of the mare."

"Gimme your horse," said Kinkaid in answer.

And as the other led it up, Kinkaid with his gigantic strength lifted old Henry and literally threw him into the saddle. He mounted his own horse the next instant and rode on at a slow walk, lest the beat of hoofs might convey some message to Duval.

"Walk back behind us," he said to Jude, "and keep your ears open. That cat might see trails in the dark and come after us. Walk far enough back so the scuffing of the hoofs through the dust won't sound in your ears, or the creaking of the saddles."

Jude obeyed. Quakingly he obeyed, and walked with his head perpetually turned over his shoulder, ever and anon seeming to hear the rattle of a gallop on stones far behind, and to see the loom of a horseman after him.

But no horseman appeared, and the imaginary gallop did not actually sound, while they passed slowly down byways to the rear of the town, and so to the back door of Sheriff Nat Adare's sanctum, the Moose Creek jail.

It was opened at the marshal's knock.

"Who's there?" the jailer asked, growling out through a crack of the door.

The heavy hand of the marshal cast the door wide open and nearly felled the jailer. "Kinkaid and a prisoner," he announced. "Show me the cells."

There was no protest against his brutal roughness. The jailer, nursing his head where the door had struck him, mutely showed the way, lantern in hand, until he arrived at the short avenue of cells.

Into the central one of these, Kinkaid had the prisoner locked.

"Got food?" he asked.

"Rice and 'lasses," said the latter. "I'll go get . . ."

"That's good enough for him," declared Kinkaid. "Feed him. Jude, come with me."

He went out to the rear of the jail again, and there talked quietly with Jude in the darkness.

"And . . . him?" Jude asked in a shaken voice, pointing with his thumb over his shoulder. "Duval? Is he gonna go loose?"

"He's got to go loose for a while," said the marshal. "I've got enough to get him . . . but I can't spring it for a while. I've got to get a little extra proof, and then I'll close in on him. But in the meantime, he's gonna find out what I've done. He'll find out before morning where Henry is. He may find out before that what I've taken from the house."

"And run?"

"I dunno," the marshal said thoughtfully, "I guess he won't run, or, leastwise, very far. By the way I write him down, he ain't the kind that'll run out on a partner, and Henry's a friend of his. He'll stand by to try to help Henry. And Henry's the bait that'll be dangled in front of him until I've got the proof that I need and can put the irons on him. If I could've left the stuff there . . . if I could've left the stuff there . . ."

He paused, with a wistful note in his voice, then concluded: "That would've made it easy to get

257

all the proofs I need, I reckon. But I couldn't do that."

He touched the handle of his old gun as he spoke. It was true. He could not let that remain away from him when such a man as Duval was near.

"I dunno what you're talkin' about," said the blunt Jude.

"You'll learn later. What I want you to do is to go back up there and shadow the house."

"Me?"

"Yes, you."

"I can't do it," said the other with calm decision. "I ain't got the nerve to do it . . . yet. Maybe I'll get it later on and try. But just now I'm played out."

The marshal hesitated, breathing hard, he was so angered by this weakness, yet he said not a word of reproof. He himself had been through such a searching fire of suspense that same evening that he could understand the failure in the heart of Jude. He merely laid a comforting hand upon the shoulder of his companion and murmured: "Stay a while and steady up, man. You'll be all right again. Everybody gets the jumps at this game. And Duval ain't a house cat. He's wild. Take your time. If you find that you can get up there later and use your ears and your eyes, I'd take it kind."

He turned away, with this, and went back into

the jail without another word to Jude, leaving the latter standing uncertain in the dark, with fear all around him.

Inside the jail, he went at once to Henry, who was finishing his plate of rice and molasses with proper philosophic unconcern. The marshal remained outside the bars and suddenly thrust through them the chamois bag.

"Ever see this, Henry?"

Henry looked with an impatient frown. "No," he said.

And the marshal believed him, in part, because he wished to believe.

"Henry," he said, "I guess you know how you'll get off with an easy sentence?"

"I dunno nothin'," Henry said pleasantly. He shaded his eyes, the better to see the face of the marshal.

"You know, but I'll tell you, anyway. Tell me where to get the stuff you took from Broom and Carson's safe."

"Broom and Carson's safe? Are you saddlin' that on me?" Henry chuckled a little and wagged his head at Kinkaid.

"You've still got the bandage on your finger, man," said Kinkaid. "It's the pen for you, anyway. The only thing is that if we get the money back, on account of you being old and all, the judge might parole you. Anyway, he wouldn't make it a heavy sentence. I'd answer for that."

"You'd answer, would you?" said the old man calmly. "You double-crossin' sneak!"

Kinkaid started. "You think I wouldn't keep my end of the bargain, Henry?"

"Dang you and all your bloodhound kind," Henry said without special emphasis. "I'll take my chances outside of your promises."

"It's a clear case, Henry," said the marshal with much patience. "The prints of the mare's shoes, and the wound on your hand. How can you dodge that?"

"The law is a good dog, if you know his name," Henry said. "And maybe I can find that out."

The marshal smiled in spite of himself. "If noise keeps your heart up, keep on smiling," he said. "But you know how the facts stand, Henry. D'you count on Duval to get you out of this?"

"Why not?"

Kinkaid knocked against the bars. "Tool-proof steel," he said. "I reckon that's enough of an answer for you, my son."

However, Henry chuckled and shook his head. "You got a wise head on your shoulders," he said. "You know a lot, Kinkaid, but you don't know much about Duval. You've had him with his back to the wall, and he slipped out and was behind you before you could hit him once. And that'll happen again and again. You could have Duval cornered twenty times, Kinkaid, and every time he'd show you how much better he was than you even dreamed that he could be. If you doubt it, you keep on takin' notes on him. Will you? And lemme know the answers, until the answer comes that'll leave you with your tongue still."

"Is he gonna kill me?" asked the marshal, half contemptuous and half curious.

"He's gonna kill you, Kinkaid," Henry said soberly, "as sure as I'm sittin' here in jail. Lay your money on it, and make out your will, and if you got a kind feelin' for anybody in the world, which I sort of doubt, get out a heavy life insurance policy and write in the name of the folks you like. Because they'll collect before long."

"Henry," the marshal said, "I pretty nigh like you, when I hear you talk like this, but lemme tell you that the next time I meet Duval, it'll be face to face, and then heaven help him. He'll go where nine have gone before him. But about you . . . there's one sure way you can get out of jail . . . maybe even without turning in all of the money that you got from Broom and Carson . . . and that's to tell me . . . who is Duval?"

Chapter Thirty-One

Virtue, after all, is a comparative—almost a tentative thing. And the virtue of Henry halted, as it were, in mid-stride, as he heard what the marshal had to say. And the virtue of Richard Kinkaid, which had endured a thousand tests, a thousand offered bribes, now weakened, as he saw before him an opportunity of securing a prisoner who, in his eyes, was worth a thousand Henrys.

He argued, with some reason, that Henry was an old man, near the end of his possibility of doing evil, but if Duval were a criminal, as the marshal had every reason to suspect that he was, then Duval was in the very early prime of his career, with a generation of danger stretching before him. It seemed to Kinkaid only a reasonable thing that he should use one thief to catch another.

He waited a moment for Henry to speak, but the old man was lost in thought.

"Suppose," said the marshal, "everything was returned to Broom and Carson, except fifty thousand dollars . . . that could be put down to commission, say. For the rest of that money, they'd be willing not to press the charges home. You see?"

Henry nodded. Still he was squinting at a most distant thought, and unable to bring it close to his mind. "That would be fifty thousand for me," he said. "Fifty thousand clear, and Duval . . . where?"

"Wherever you could put him. You know where that would be a tolerable lot better than I do. In the pen . . . up Salt Creek. I dunno, but you ought to know."

The eyes of old Henry turned positively green, but in the very crisis of temptation, he suddenly shrugged his shoulders and cast out his hands in a gesture of dismissal.

"You won't do it?" asked the marshal.

"There ain't a thing against Duval," Henry said.

"That's a lie! I saw it in your eyes!"

"I was tryin' to work up a lie," Henry said steadily, "but I seen it was no use tryin'. There ain't a thing ag'in' him."

Kinkaid, having had what he felt would have been a great triumph in the grasp of his hands, now ground his teeth in a fury of disappointment.

"Why, you chump," he said, "you'll get life out of this . . . twenty years, anyway. You'll die in stripes!"

"Stripes ain't on the skin, they're only on the clothes," said Henry. "And they got long sleepin' hours, besides, in a good, up-to-date pen."

"Listen to me," urged Kinkaid. "There's no chance that Duval could harm you. Tell me what

263

I want to know, and I'll have him gathered up in one day and put away in irons."

"Put irons on a ghost," answered Henry. "You talk . . . well, the way I'd expect you to talk." Then he added, while Kinkaid strove to find another argument: "Suppose I had somethin' over his head, what'd he do? Either get me safe out, if he thought I'd play straight, or else slip in and shoot me through the head, if he thought I wouldn't. Don't talk to me, man. I know Duval. You only do a little guessin' about him."

"Then I'll make you this promise," the marshal said fiercely. "If there was a hundred hands on Duval, none of 'em will ever open the door of this cell. If they do, may I die!"

He turned and walked away with great strides, and found the sheriff just entering the jail. Old Nat Adare looked still full of sleep, but he blinked himself nearer awake when he saw the marshal before him.

Kinkaid was too irritated to be diplomatic. He laid his hand on the shoulder of the sheriff and said: "Adare, I've put an old man in that cell, yonder. He ain't gonna do much himself, though he's a lot smarter than you may think. But on the outside, I got an idea the smartest man that ever come over the mountains is gonna try to free him. Can you keep him safe?"

"Extra guards . . ."

"Extra guards can be bought up," said the

marshal. "If you can hire 'em, somebody else can pay a higher price. Ain't that right?"

"I'll be here myself," said Adare. "Who's the outside man?"

"I dunno. I'm trying to find out," the marshal said, and abruptly left.

In spite of his bluffness, he felt a great deal of trust in the honesty and the alertness of the sheriff. He knew the veteran would be on his metal after the challenge that had been delivered, and he felt the odds were nine out of ten in favor of keeping his prisoner securely.

Now he had other preparations to make.

It was almost at this hour that Mr. Broom, of Broom & Carson, stamped away from his dinner table, slammed the door in the face of his anxious wife, and retired to his study, where he paced up and down making many pauses.

Mr. Broom was a man of adroit mind and swift in his thoughts as any ferret. He looked like a ferret, in fact. That is to say, he was a little man with a long neck and a very small head. He looked almost as though he could button his collar and then put it on over his head. His ways were as swift as his thoughts, moreover, and he could rarely stay still for a moment. When he sat down, he was continually twisting from side to side, shifting his feet, jerking his head back and forth, interlacing and then separating his fingers.

In five minutes in his own room, he went through a thousand contortions, and the first problem that he put to himself was—in what manner can I shift the total loss to the shoulders of my partner?

For Carson, bigger and slower than Broom, was infinitely more stupid, just as he was infinitely more honest. Their partnership had been based upon the money of Carson and the brains of Broom. Mr. Carson wanted to be rich, but he wanted to be honest. Mr. Broom wanted to be rich and thought that any means were justified that led to the golden end.

In the beginning, he had been the obsequious servant of his wealthy partner. But now Carson was in a minority. Yet, no matter how he turned the matter back and forth through his mind, Broom was unable to find a way of taking all the loss out of Carson's pocket. His failure to come to this desired end drove him almost mad, and it was while his nerves were jumping at their worst that his wife tapped on his door.

"Well?" screamed Broom, and since one word rarely did for him, he kept on shrieking—"Well? Well?"—several times. It helped him a little to speak in this manner.

"There's a man to see you," his wife said timidly through the door.

He being an incarnate fiend, without kindness, trust, gentleness, or charity, his wife, it followed

266

almost as a matter of course, was sweet-natured, faithful, affectionate, and true. She dreaded her husband almost as much as she loved him.

"Dang the man that wants to see me!" yelled Mr. Broom. "Dang you . . . dang everything! You wanna drive me crazy." He smashed at the door with his fist to emphasize his point.

But he hurt the hand more than the wood, and the pain made him so desperate that he wrenched the door open and leaped out at her with his little ferret eyes one blur of red and his thin lips stretched back from his white teeth.

Mrs. Broom, who seemed to have guessed what would happen in response to her knock and her words, already had shrunk back across the hall, so that Mr. Broom saw, directly in front of him, just inside the front door, the man who had come to see him. He was most rudely dressed in blue jeans that bagged enormously at the knees. He had on no coat, but only a loose blue-flannel shirt, and he carried his slouch hat in his hand.

Mr. Broom, in an ecstasy of rage, began to laugh. He twisted and squirmed in the exquisite height of his fury as he fairly danced toward the stranger.

"You wanna see me! You wanna see me! You wanna job, I guess? You come begging for a job . . . this time of night . . . taking my time. No, I won't take you . . . dang you! Get out! I wouldn't have you . . . not for a gift . . . you danged . . ."

He ceased his speech and his advance at the same moment, not because he had exhausted either his vocabulary or his vindictiveness, but because he was stopped by a short, shrill cry from his wife, who ran suddenly in front of him and caught his arms.

"Archie! Archie! Archie!" she implored. "It's Duval!"

It was the first time in her life that she had taken such a liberty with him, but Mr. Broom did not resent her violence. Instead, he gasped, raised a hand to his face in the manner of one stunned by a blow, and fell back two or three uncertain steps, while he stared at the pale face and the gray, steady eyes of the other.

"Bless me!" said Mr. Archie Broom. "Duval! Duval! Bad light . . . blockheads always coming around for a job . . . day and night . . . no peace . . . no rest . . . always harassed . . . terrible mistake . . . glad to see you, Duval. Terribly glad to see you. Come right in. What can I do for you? What will you have? Heard so much . . . simply delighted . . . this is my wife . . . come this way . . ."

He led Duval into his office, and when the latter was seated, Mr. Broom himself fell into a chair, exhausted for the moment by fear. He recovered almost at once, however, and, sitting up, he consumed every feature of Duval with his rapid eyes, scanning him over and over again for a full ten seconds, while Duval filled the pause by calmly rolling a cigarette. He lighted this and flicked the match out the open window.

"Now, Mister Duval," the lumberman said, "what is there that I can do for you?" He rubbed his hands together. "Honor to have you here, sir. We've heard a lot . . . Moose Creek talks about people, you know. But the man who's with you . . . that Henry . . . that scoundrel! I beg your pardon . . . probably a mistake . . . but said to have been the one who robbed me! Who robbed me . . . almost a quarter of a million! I beg your pardon. No offense to you, Mister Duval. Wouldn't offend you. Let's forget Henry. What can I do for you, sir?"

Duval listened to this rapid, broken outpouring of words without impatience, and then answered: "I don't know of anything that you can do for me. But I dropped in here sort of thinking that I might be able to do something for you, Mister Broom."

The latter tapped himself rapidly upon the breastbone. "You for me? You for me?" he said, delighted and amazed. "What could you do for me then?"

"I don't know if we could make a bargain," Duval said. "But it seems to me a mighty shame that old Henry should be in jail . . . and that you should be out all that money. Don't that sound as though we could meet somehow?"

Chapter Thirty-Two

If by chance the ears of Broom had been so sharpened that they could have heard the music of the spheres, no greater expression of delight could have come into his pink-stained eyes.

He grinned at Duval agape, like a thirst-starved man at a vision of blue, cool water.

"A hundred and eighty thousand dollars! Duval, Duval, you've brought it along with you! Don't say a word. Just bring it in to me. That's all. Not a word. Just bring in the money. I'll dismiss the charges against Henry. I'll . . . have a cigar, Mister Duval. Honor to have you here with me. Delighted . . . no idea how much we've talked . . . everybody talked . . . here's a match . . . don't smoke cigars? But where's the money, Duval? Where's the money?"

He had worked himself forward to the edge of his chair, and though he stopped making vocal sounds, still his lips rapidly and silently framed new words as Duval himself was speaking.

"Well," Duval said, "I reckon the money's safe. My old man used to say that money that was put away wasn't likely to go off and spend itself."

Although Broom wore his collars large, he now freed the one he had on to make his breathing easier. "None of it, Duval?" he said. "None of it spent? None of it split up and gone? Still the whole wad intact?" He joined his hands together. He grew pale, and seemed praying to the saints for a favorable response.

"Not a penny gone," Duval confirmed quietly.

Broom relaxed in the chair, fell back into it, disjoined his hands, which fell loosely into his lap, and exhaled a long breath.

This weakness of joy did not last long. He was presently sitting up again on the edge of the chair, smiling at Duval, and blinking with the greatest rapidity.

"Well, then, let's have it out! Let's have it out! Let's have it out!" he chattered. "I'll be glad to see it all again. Not that I'll forget you, Duval. You'll come in for a commission. Something handsome. That's a mere detail. Settle that later on, eh? But to get the money here . . . probably outside in your saddlebags, Duval?" He gaped with a sort of horrible expectancy.

Duval replied: "You get the money back without a commission subtracted. But what about Henry?"

"I drop all charges . . ."

"Does that mean that Kinkaid will drop all charges as well?"

"Kinkaid? Kinkaid? Why, all the marshal wants to do is to get my money back for me."

"Kinkaid? Money? Is Kinkaid any friend of yours?" asked Duval.

Broom wrung his hands in nervous indecision. "Kinkaid? Friend? Kinkaid is . . . is . . ."

"Aimed tolerable straight at jailing of a crook. He's got the right man, it looks like."

"You admit that Henry did it, of course?"

"Sure, I admit it. The marshal has the proofs, too. Only, Henry really ought to . . ."

"No matter what happens to Henry, you, as an honest man . . . your duty to society . . . your duty to me . . . a fellow man . . . must give up the money, no matter what happens to Henry. You agree to that? Of course, you agree! Can see fine integrity in your face, Duval . . . I . . . I . . ."

"My old man used to say," Duval said, "that there was no use buying a bird that was still on the wing."

He paused, and Broom suddenly winced.

"Ah, you mean the freedom of Henry . . . the getting of an assurance from the marshal, say that the shortest sentence that . . ."

"The marshal never would give away a trick," answered Duval flatly. "He ain't got that reputation. He loves a jailed crook because he's jailed, and that's the only reason. But you don't get a penny until Henry's free, outside of that jail."

"Meaning what? Meaning what?"

"Meaning that no matter what sort of a charge is over his head, if you'll get Henry out of that jail, I'll give you back your money."

"Mister Duval!" gasped Broom. "But suppose after Henry is delivered, something happened . . . something that made you change your mind about paying back . . ."

Duval smiled. "That's a chance you gotta take, Broom. You got my word for it. If you wanna gamble on that, all right. If you don't, I'll step along my way."

Mr. Broom twisted violently two or three times in his chair. "Dear me! Dear me! Dear me!" he repeated rapidly. "I'll have to have a little time. I'll have to think . . . I'll have to see my partner."

"There ain't time for that," replied Duval. "Henry comes out of that jail tonight, or the deal's off."

"What?" screamed Broom. He suddenly leaped from his chair and shouted: "You come here pretending to be an honest man, and you . . . !" He remembered himself, the recovery shocking him back almost prostrate in his chair again. "Duval," he said tremulously, when he had recovered some measure of his self-composure, "I didn't mean that. I'll do what I can . . . but a jail . . . a guarded jail. Kinkaid. Oh, my goodness! My goodness!"

He began to wring his hands. But, even in this dilemma, his keen eyes jerked from side to side as he searched for a new expedient. There was none. Eventually his gaze came blankly to rest upon the composed face of Duval.

"You!" he shouted suddenly. "You would do it, Duval! You could do anything. They all say so. You can get him out!"

"You can't get rain every day," said Duval, "even if there's clouds in the sky, my old man used to say. They ain't nothing they're watching for so close, there around the jail, as Duval. I can't do a thing for Henry. It's up to you, Mister Broom."

Broom, in despair, threw both arms stiffly above his head and kept them there, the hands trembling violently in his excess of emotion.

"What can I do?" he asked.

"You can go to see Henry. They'll let you see him."

"And then what?"

"Suppose I could find a way for you to turn him loose . . . you'd have to show your nerve, Broom. Have you got it on tap tonight?"

Mr. Broom laughed through his teeth. "I've got a hundred and eighty thousand dollars' worth of nerve," he said. "Is that enough? I've got all of that. If there's that much blood in my body, I'll spend it drop by drop. D'you hear me?"

"I hear you," answered Duval, "and it sounds tolerable fine to me. There ought to be just about enough nerve in that to get you through and land Henry out of jail. And then you collect what you've invested, Broom. Is it a go?"

The other stretched out his hand, and Duval, after an instant of hesitation, accepted it.

Chapter Thirty-Three

For not more than a quarter of an hour, Duval was in the house of Broom, talking rapidly, earnestly, with the little man. Then he left, mounted the waiting mare, and galloped rapidly back to his own shack.

He did not approach it with any caution, though he was sure that the little house was being watched by some agent of the marshal, but instead, he galloped through the open gate and straight up to his door.

There he dismounted, and passed inside the cabin, lighted the lamp, and with it examined the room with a sweeping glance. Now he seemed to be considering every possibility of any importance that the place contained, and finally, as though making up his mind that nothing remained of any significance except in one place, he went to his row of books and opened several of them in rapid succession, taking out a few papers that had been lodged among the pages of each.

That done, he went to the corner logs, removed the false half that the marshal had already taken out, and looked with a nod of understanding into the cavity. He replaced the covering wood, and now fastened over his left shoulder a strap that was reënforced by another girded loosely around his breast. Under his armpit, depending from the first strap, he secured a strong clip, and into this he passed the long Colt revolver. Then, picking up a big, loosely fitting coat, he shrugged it over his shoulders.

Wearing it open in front, he walked a few times up and down the room, practicing the draw. To nearly all others the art of the draw was in snatching a revolver from a leather holster on the hip. Their skill was employed in shooting the instant the muzzle was clear of the sheath. An expert would raise the dust, perhaps, with his first shot, but the second one was apt to be in the target. The spring beneath the armpit offered two advantages. In the first place, it was easier to whip the hand to the butt of the weapon; in the second place, as it came out in the grip of the shooter, the gun was more nearly in line with the man's eye, so that from the first bullet he could be firing aimed shots.

Duval, having made sure that his hand was well in practice for this work, next busied himself for a moment in the care of his gun, over which he went patiently, cautiously, as though it were a living thing that required affectionate attention before it could be expected to do its best.

When all was at last in readiness to please him, he extinguished the lamp, and, standing at his door for a moment, he listened, with ear canted down, to every small sound that stirred among the trees, whether of the leaves rustling in the wind, or the boughs softly moaning as they rubbed one another.

He seemed at last content, so went on back to the horse shed, where he saddled that same animal on which he had first ridden into Moose Creek. This horse he led back to the cabin, from which he carried out bacon, coffee, sugar, salt, and flour, some baking powder, and some raisins, and loaded all these provisions into the saddlebags. Behind the saddle, he tied a roll of blankets, wrapped in a big slicker. Into the saddle holster he thrust the long barrel of a Winchester repeating rifle, and over the horn of the saddle he suspended a loaded cartridge belt.

He now appeared content, yet not entirely, until he had stood for a moment in thought. He remembered matches, which were duly added and dropped into his own pocket. A couple of cooking utensils also joined the pack, and at last Duval swung onto the back of the mare, took up the lead rope, and jogged softly down the path to the gate.

This he rode through, turned, and closed behind him.

One might have guessed, from the moment in which he remained at ease, staring back toward the house, that he was prepared to sacrifice it and all that it contained, in his eagerness to leave Moose Creek behind him.

However, he did not turn away from the town but directly toward it, and skirting toward the rear of the village, very much as the marshal had done not so long before him, he came up back of the jail where Henry was a prisoner.

Here he halted, dismounted where the shrubbery stood thick and high as a horse's head, and threw the reins of both animals. Just before him was the office of the jail, and as he stood there a light flickered dimly behind the windows, as though a match were being lighted. Then the illumination waned, steadied, and grew until full lamplight was flooding both the apertures.

Inside, at that moment, the sheriff was saying to Mr. Broom, of Broom & Carson: "You set yourself here and wait a while. I don't like to do it, though, because this here is the marshal's prisoner, and if anything happened to him, I'd never hear the last of it."

"Look here, look here!" snapped Broom. "Am I likely to let the man go free? Answer me that! Am I likely to set him free?"

"It ain't likelihoods," the sheriff said, "that I'm talkin' about. It's the possibilities."

"Is it possible, then?" shouted Broom. "Tell me that, Sheriff Adare! Is it possible? How could I turn him loose?"

"Well, I dunno," Adare answered frankly, "and

if I did, no matter how much I thought of you, Mister Broom, I wouldn't let him come in here and stay alone with you."

"Of course you wouldn't," said Broom. "That's only natural. But as it is . . ."

"I dunno that I can do it, anyway," said the other. "Fact is, Mister Broom, the marshal expects to learn somethin' out of that man, and Henry's promised that if he ain't free before tomorrow noon, he's gonna open up and talk and say some things that the marshal is a pile more interested in than he is in Henry himself and your lost money, too."

"More than a hundred and eighty thousand dollars!" exclaimed the other. "Mind that, Sheriff! Things come to a pretty pass when a federal officer lets a hundred and eighty thousand dollars slide for the sake of what a scoundrel can tell him . . . about what?"

"Aye, Mister Broom, there you are. I ain't one of the deep ones, and I dunno. But Dick Kinkaid, he *is* deep. He's clean over my head, and I dunno what he's drivin' at. But he's mighty smart, and he ain't often wrong in the last count of things. You gotta say that for him, eh?"

"Perhaps, perhaps," said Mr. Broom. "However, let's have your friend Henry in here."

"You think you can do something with him, eh?"

"I think that I can."

"But still . . . it ain't likely that you could persuade him, when Kinkaid himself has such a hard time about it."

Mr. Broom's face twisted in a sudden frenzy of anxiety, and, starting up from his chair, he pointed dramatically out of the nearest window.

"Listen, will you?" Broom said.

"Aye, and what is it?" demanded the sheriff, cocking his ear.

"Rain, rain, rain!" burst out Broom.

Nat Adare, blinking at him, shook his head, unable to make a connection between this violent speech and the preceding conversation.

"Rain, rain!" yelled Broom. "And most likely the money is lying out. A hundred and eighty thousand dollars that's washing and rotting away, because you won't let me have a word with your prisoner. . . ."

"Hold on, hold on," said the good-natured sheriff. "I don't want to do you no wrong, man. Hold on, and I'll come and bring him in here. He'll have to be in irons, though."

"Irons?" Broom said blankly. "Irons? Well, let him be in irons, then, if he has to be, but bring him quickly."

And he turned and looked anxiously toward the windows, past which the rain was seen swiftly coursing down in dim pencil strokes through the lamplight.

The rattle of chains began as the sheriff,

disappearing through the door, took a set off the wall. Then a steel door closed with a jangle, and Mr. Broom, approaching the window still closer, leaned out until he felt the rain soaking through his hair.

He ducked back inside again as the noise of the chains approached the door of the office once more, and in came the sheriff, with Henry herded before him. The wrists of Henry were locked together by handcuffs, and his ankles were imprisoned by other fetters, while he carried in his hands the heavy leaden ball that was his anchor.

At the sight of him, Broom lost all diplomacy and all discretion. He flew at the tall old man and shook his bony little fist under the nose of the captive.

"What did I ever do to you that you should do this to me?" he shouted. "What fiend was inside of you that you should come to me like this, I want to know?"

Henry, blinking at the unaccustomed brightness of the lamp, did not answer, only smiled a little with the patience of one who is nerved to meet even greater misfortunes than he finds.

And Broom, recoiling before that smile, puffing and stammering, stood away, confused, and with lightning still in his vicious face. The sheriff regarded them for a moment with a broad grin.

"I hope you get on together all right," he said.

"I'm gonna leave you alone for a minute. I reckon that was a rap at the front door of the jail."

He withdrew, and as he left, Broom hung suspended for an instant between his desire for immediate action and his fear lest the sheriff should still be within hearing, for the partition was paper thin. However, the withdrawing steps of the official were now audible, and Broom lunged forward at Henry.

"Henry," he gasped, "if you're set free, you'll turn back the money to me? You scoundrel! You thief! You'll turn it back . . . every penny? You'll be an honest man, Henry? Will you give me your promise?"

"Why," Henry drawled slowly, "what the word of a crook and a thief might be worth, I dunno."

"I want your promise. I don't ask anything else. D'you hear me, man?"

"I hear you," said Henry, "though I dunno how you're to get me loose from this unless you've got the keys to the chains."

"You hear me . . . will you promise?"

"Why, then," Henry said, "I might promise. I will promise, if that does you any good."

"You'll swear, man?"

"I'll swear, then, if that makes you rest any easier."

"Then . . . ," began Broom.

But Henry broke in softly: "Here comes your key, eh?"

Through the window swiftly came the head, the shoulders, of Duval. Lightly he swung in and dropped to the floor. He shook himself, and a light spray fell from his wet clothes to the floor.

"You've got your gun, have you?" he said to Broom.

"I've got it."

Broom pulled out a stub-nosed revolver as he spoke. He handled it cautiously, keeping it at arm's length.

"Keep your finger off the trigger," Duval said, dropping to his knees before Henry, and beginning to work deftly on the ankle lock. "Mind when you shoot through the window that you point the muzzle up."

"I'll mind!" said Broom. "Faster, faster, man! My goodness, I think he's coming back now. . . ."

"So," Duval said, and the clips sprang loose from the legs of Henry with a soft click. Then Duval stood up, and transferred his attention to the handcuffs of the prisoner. Scarcely a touch seemed needed, when they sprang open. Duval, locking them shut again, laid them noiselessly on the floor.

"Mind you," he cautioned in a low voice to Broom, "Henry must have slipped the handcuffs, while you were pulling down that first window to shut out the rain. Pull it down now, Henry."

The prisoner obeyed. He had not spoken since Duval entered, but his appearance had changed.

283

There was light in his dead eyes, and color glowed in his cheeks.

Down dragged the window, screeching as it came.

"And getting the handcuffs off, he must have had some watch spring or other to work on the ankle lock. See! There it is on the floor." He threw down a little glittering piece of steel as he spoke. "Now, Henry, out through the window with you."

He set the example as he spoke, slithering through the window and dropping to the ground outside. Henry, more slowly, followed him, and as he hung by his hands, there was a tremendous yell from Broom, who sprang to the window and rapidly fired three shots into the air, screeching: "Help! He's away! Help! He's gone! Sheriff Adare! Marshal Kinkaid . . . !"

The door burst open, and the sheriff ran in, white with fear and excitement. He saw Mr. Broom in a state of frenzy.

"He must have slipped his handcuffs while I was pulling down that danged window against the rain . . . then a watch spring, maybe, for the ankle lock. Good heavens, do something, man! A hundred and eighty thousand dollars gone forever! Do something! Do something! Are you going to stand there and let him go?"

"What in the name of heaven did you do?" gasped the sheriff. "Stood and watched him go?"

"He slugged me from behind," Broom said,

wringing his hands and dropping his revolver. "I rolled over on the floor and shot after him. I think I hit him. I must have hit him. See if there's any blood on the window sill. I'm sure that I put one bullet right into his breast. . . ."

The sheriff leaned out the window for one look into the blinding mist of the rain, then he turned on his heel with a groan and ran back and through the office, tearing down his hat from a peg as he went, and calling loudly over his shoulder: "You've ruined my name for me! I'll never hear the end of this!"

"Your name, your name," Broom said to himself as the sheriff disappeared. "Is it worth a hundred and eighty thousand dollars, more or less honestly made? Is it worth that, you poor sniveling creature?" He laughed, in a fierce ecstasy, then clapped a hand over his mouth and looked around him with haunted eyes, for fear lest someone might have seen him.

After that, Mr. Broom left the jail as rapidly as possible. He went out into the open with no hat upon his head, but a hat was an unnecessary luxury to Broom at that moment, for his heart within him was so strangely warm that he could have laughed in the face of an Antarctic blizzard.

He went with almost a dancing step to where his horse waited for him, and galloped that patient animal into the rain as wildly as any young cowpuncher just in from the range.

Chapter Thirty-Four

Nothing was simpler than the escape of Duval and Henry. They retired to the place where the two good horses were waiting, and Henry, as he swung his leg over the cantle of his saddle, made the cooking utensils clang softly together.

"Hey," he called warily, "does it mean that I'm away?"

"Away . . . yes."

"And you . . . with me?"

"We're heading for the stuff that you buried. What's the right way?"

"It's not fifty yards from the house. Come along! I thought . . . for a while, that you were goin' to be fool enough to turn it back to Broom, if you could."

"Well, could I?" demanded Duval.

"I'd've seen you dead first! A hundred and eighty thousand dollars for that ferret?" Henry chuckled as he spoke, then leaned against the cut of the rain in issuing from the woods.

And there was no more talk as they cantered easily along through the woods and the brush, showers of wet knocking up into their faces as they went on, every time they touched a projecting branch.

So they went up the side of Moose Creek on the now familiar trail, and as they came nearer to the house, Henry stopped his horse and swung down from it. He worked only for a few moments under the bushes, and emerged again, carrying a mud-caked satchel.

"This is the stuff, pal," he said.

"All right," said Duval. "Climb onto your horse. I'll hold it for you." He took the satchel from the hands of the other, and Henry climbed with labor back into his seat.

"Do we stop at the house for anything else?" asked Henry. "Have we got everything with us? Don't look to me as though you're carryin' much of a pack, though."

"Doesn't it?" answered Duval. "As a matter of fact, I'm not leaving, you see."

"You . . . ain't . . . leavin'!" cried Henry.

"I'm not leaving. There's something in Moose Creek worth more to me than your hundred and eighty thousand dollars. However, come along and see that I deliver this satchel where it belongs."

The rain had stopped. There was only the pattering of the water from the wet leaves, sometimes in single drops, sometimes in rattling showers.

"Pal," burst out Henry shakily, "will you tell me the truth? You ain't really meanin' to take it away from me?"

"I'm taking it away from you," Duval stated.

"I didn't think you was that low," said Henry. "I can't believe it still. You're only jokin' with me."

"Follow me, then, and you'll see."

Henry, speechless with miserable astonishment, rode on at the side of Duval, never thinking of resistance to the man with him. Only, as they cut through the woods and came out on the road, he at one point checked in his horse, and cried aloud: "Not back to Broom! Not back to that rat of a man!"

"Hush, Henry," Duval said. "When you call him names like that, you almost tempt me not to live up to my word. I promised him the money back if you went free."

"Promised him!" shouted Henry. "Promised him! Besides, Kinkaid would've let me go for sayin' who Duval is."

His anger, his helplessness, forced the words from him, and Duval replied gently: "D'you think that Kinkaid really would have let you off, Henry? Don't you know that he couldn't? The most he could have done would have been to arrange a light sentence for you. And any sentence for safe-cracking would be long enough to see you die in stripes, old fellow. If Kinkaid lied to you, that's no reason you should lie to yourself."

To this, poor Henry was unable to make any

rejoinder, and he rode on with his head fallen upon his breast.

They kept on up the road for a few miles, then swung aside, and so came down the bypath to the house of Broom.

It was lighted down one side. Voices issued dimly from it, and Duval, the satchel across his saddlebow, and old Henry not far behind him, rode up beside the nearest window.

It was unshuttered, and the blinds were undrawn, so that he could look freely in and there he saw Mr. Carson, his fat, rosy face quite pale and long with dismay, while active Mr. Broom, quick-turning as a rat, pranced up and down the room, talking with both hands and with a barking, squeaking voice.

Apparently he was rehearsing for the benefit of his partner the scene in the sheriff's office, not as it had happened, but as Broom had first narrated it to the sheriff himself.

"I suppose it's gone," Carson said in a voice that Duval, pressing closer, could hear. "You have enough interest in the business to carry you along, but my share of that loss will about squeeze me out."

"Your own fault!" shouted the unspeakable Broom. "Who told you to cut down expenses? Who told you to cut off that list of ailing paupers that call themselves your relatives? I told you. You wouldn't listen. You've been bled white. A fool deserves to stew in his own folly, and you're stewing now. Don't ask me for sympathy. Not a penny's worth of it, for I . . ."

The window here was raised by Duval. As it squeaked up and the moist air of the night blew in, Mr. Broom dropped with a groan of fear behind a chair, but Mr. Carson stood up and turned his face and his breast to the possible danger. One might have said that he was too slow-witted to pay any attention to such danger as was here.

However, it was at his feet that Duval cast the satchel, saying briefly: "Here's the stuff back again. It was only Henry's joke."

Then he was off again into the veil of the night that had covered him even when he was speaking at the lighted window.

Yet he heard, behind him, sharp voices raised in great joy, and he smiled to himself as he went off through the dark.

Henry fell in beside him in an altered mood, and though he did not speak for some time, he eventually said: "Look here . . ."

"Well, Henry?" asked Duval.

"They've got the stuff safe back, then?"

"They have it safely back."

"It was him," Henry said in a puzzled tone. "I generally keep my promises, but to a rat like him . . ."

"Why, I understand perfectly," Duval said.

"Well, now that it's been given back to him, I'm pretty glad of it. It's a sort of a funny weight off my mind."

"Is it?"

"I mean, this way. Every penny that I spent of it, I'd have been sayin' to myself that I was spendin' another man's money."

Duval chuckled. "How much money did you ever spend in your life," he asked, "that was really your own?"

"That ain't what I mean," persisted the thief. "I mean . . . the money that I spent before, it was stole honestly, if you know what I mean, old-timer?"

"Yes, I know what you mean."

"Not promised back, after I had it. Or anything like that."

"Certainly," said Duval. "Not on your conscience, you mean? You forgive me then, Henry?"

"Here's my hand, if you can find it in the dark."

"I never shook hands with more pleasure in my entire life," Duval said cordially. "We'll have no trouble after this, Henry. We understand each other. But now tell me. What are your plans?"

"I dunno. I ain't made any very clear plans, except to skin out from here. I'll go just where you go, I suppose."

"Not that, because I stay here, and this is likely to be a pretty hot corner for you, Henry."

Henry groaned. "I've spoiled your play here. You had everything going smooth, and settled down, and quiet, and happy, and I've broken everything up for you. I've been a curse on you, and that's the fact, sir."

"Tush," said Duval gently. "We won't talk about that. As a matter of fact, I probably couldn't have lasted. It was too happy to last. A man can't live a lie, Henry, even if it's an innocent lie. He has to be himself, and sooner or later I should have been found out. Don't let your part in this trouble you."

"But you . . . you ain't really goin' to stay on here?"

"Yes, I'll stay on here."

"You mean it?"

"Yes, I mean it."

"But now they'll be after you as thick as hornets."

"What have they against me?"

"That you kept a professional thief in your house, and so they'll say that you're a professional thief yourself, the fools."

"Well, perhaps they will. Talking doesn't break the skin, though, as you ought to know."

"I don't like it," muttered Henry, and, swinging his horse closer to the mare, he went on: "You'd better slide out with me. I know how to make tracks from here so's they'll never guess."

"They'll know that I've run, though, and that's the same as a confession of guilt. Isn't it?"

"Dang the guilt! What's the guilt that they could trace back to you?"

"I mean, I'll appear guilty, and beaten, and afraid."

"Mister . . ."

"Not even in the dark, Henry. Not that name even to ourselves."

"All right then. I won't say it. But it looks to me as though you're running a fine chance of bein' tagged by a Forty-Five-caliber slug one of these days. I've had my chance to look around the world and see my share of the hard ones, but I never saw a harder one than Kinkaid. You've beaten him a couple of times at this game, but maybe he'll have his innings before the wind-up. And he'll only need to get you once under his gun. He won't stop to think twice, if he ever gets the upper hand."

"Would he murder me, Henry?"

"Would a cat eat cream?"

"He would, I think," Duval said thoughtfully. "I think he'd kill me out of hand. As a matter of fact, for the first time in my life I'm afraid of a man . . . afraid of the marshal. But still I have to stay, even though I know the danger."

"Will you tell me why you have to stay?"

"I can't tell you. I can't begin to tell you, Henry. You've lived past certain things that still are real to me. Things that are as much a part of me now as my own blood."

Henry was silent for a moment, and then he muttered: "There's such a thing as playin' a game till it ain't a game any longer. It's real. And you're that man, I suppose."

Chapter Thirty-Five

The full noon shone down upon Moose Creek. Even the lizards that lay in the sun on the walls, now slithered away into the shadows as the heat of the day began to take effect, and the pigs could not work deep enough into their wallows. The thirstiest cows would not go out across the flare of the sun-scorched fields to find the water, and the sheep lay passive in the low, stifling shade of the brush. The white dust of the main street of Moose Creek became incandescent, and as Cherry stepped in it, fetlock-deep, she winced from the scalding that her dainty flesh received.

She was stopped in front of Pete's Place, where Duval dismounted. He looked up and down the street, but not a form was stirring. Only, in the distance he heard the mellow clangor of the blacksmith's hammer, sounding musically far away and soothing.

There were two or three other noticeable things, chiefly faint shadows that stirred behind windows, discreetly disappearing; these, he knew, were the heads of the curious who had looked out upon him, but who did not wish to be seen.

It meant much to him, for it told him that he had become one outlawed from the notice of frank, everyday life. He was a banned and forbidden thing and he could guess that it was because of the arrest and then of the flight of Henry. That had damned him, with the whispers concerning beautiful Marian Lane as a background against which the more recent and spectacular action was placed in relief.

Having taken heed of all that was to be seen, Duval turned back into the saloon, and, passing through the door, he saw Charlie Nash, not at the bar, but seated at a small table with his head in his hands.

He started toward Charlie with a smile, but Pete, behind the bar, raised a warning hand and shook his head.

That instant Charlie looked up and, seeing Duval, rose from his chair, shoved his hat back on his head, and came straight up to the older man. Not a word of greeting did he speak, and Duval wondered.

Some of his doubt was removed by the action of Pete who, without waiting longer, hurried down the length of the bar, opened the door that led up to his room, and disappeared. This had happened before Charlie spoke a word. And when he spoke, it was to say in a harsh, husky voice: "Who are you?"

"My name," he said, "is Duval. I am a citizen of the United States. I generally vote the Republican ticket. My height is five feet eleven. My weight is a hundred and sixty-five pounds. My hair is brown, and my eyes are gray. Nose, aquiline. Mouth . . . medium. Chin . . . medium. Characteristic marks, hardly any worth mentioning. Does that answer you, Charlie?"

Charlie Nash groaned. "I might've known that it would be something like that," he said.

But he did not give back. The aggressiveness somehow remained in his attitude.

"What else can I tell you, Charlie?"

"A lot, if you'll talk."

"Oh, I'll talk."

"Then tell me the straight of it . . . heaven knows that I haven't been asking questions about it before . . . but whatcha mean about Marian Lane."

"She'll tell you a lot better than I can, Charlie."

"How can I ask her? You know that. I'm asking you."

"I know you're asking me. What's your right to ask, Charlie?"

"The right of loving her. The right of having stood to be your friend. If those two reasons ain't enough . . . ," he continued, raising his voice.

"Speak soft, Charlie," interrupted the other. "When a gent begins to bellow, it makes his temper climb up the scale. The old man used to say that a loud voice made a hard fist. If you want to know about Marian Lane, will you come over to the store with me? I'm gonna talk to her now."

"Are you trying to make a fool of me?"

"Me? Not a bit. I'm going over there to find out what I can do with her."

"Duval, you ain't stringing her? You mean to marry her?"

"What I mean don't count much with her. It's what she means that seems to be a lot more important."

Charlie laughed sardonically. "As if you couldn't twist her or anybody around your finger. Only . . . what lies in front of you, Duval? What're you gonna offer to her? Is it straight that Henry was a crook? Are you a crook, too? Where'd you get your money? Where'd you come from? What's behind you? Where are you going? Is it a fact that Kinkaid is after you?"

"Why, you want me to talk and talk," Duval said, smiling. "Fact is, everything hangs on what Marian says to me."

Charlie Nash, outraged, furiously gritted his teeth.

"Is it because you care about her, Duval? Ain't it because she's the only one in Moose Creek that's stood out much against you? Ain't it because you wanna show how strong you are with women, the same as you've showed how strong you are with men?"

Duval, flushing a little, stepped back a trifle. "I'm a patient sort of a gent, Charlie," he cautioned.

"But you've reached your limit, about?" Charlie suggested, unafraid.

"About."

"That's to put a chill up my spine, I reckon?"

"Man, I ain't aiming to chill you. Whatcha want, Charlie?"

"Reasonable talk and answers to my talk."

"Or?"

"Or I'll fight."

"I don't wanna fight you, Charlie," Duval said as gently as could be.

"I know you don't," said the boy, a slight tremor shaking his body and his voice. "You'd rather face me down. Maybe that's the way that it would end. But either you come clean to me, or else I'm gonna block your game with Marian. That's the fact."

"As far as running away with her goes," Duval said, "I ain't likely to do that, old son, till tonight. Suppose you come up and have supper with me in my shack. Will you do that?"

"If you'll talk."

"I'll talk, well enough."

"I'll come," said Charlie.

"Then have a drink with me." Duval went behind the bar. "What'll it be, partner? Red-eye or beer? Or red-eye with a beer chaser? What'll you have?"

"I'll eat with you tonight," said Charlie. "I won't drink with you now. I'm sick and sore inside of my heart, Duval. I dunno where I stand. I ain't no use to myself. I ain't no use to the girl I want for a wife. But, by gosh, I'm gonna try to do one thing, even if I die for it."

He turned his back and walked from the saloon, while Duval looked earnestly after him.

Then he poured out hardly more than a tablespoonful of whiskey and stood with the glass raised, facing the new mirror, which had just been installed to take the place of the one that Charlie had smashed during his memorable session in this barroom. The frame was not yet painted, and the newness of it made Duval wonder, for it was a striking proof of the short time he had been in Moose Creek.

In this position, he regarded his own pale face with much serious earnestness, and finally made the little upward gesture of a man offering a toast, then swallowed the liquor. After this he tossed off a small chaser of water and started for the door. A voice called cautiously behind him, as though fearing lest an unexpected ear might overhear it. It was Pete, coming toward him with an extended hand, which Duval freely gripped.

"Duval," Pete said, "I dunno what's gonna come of all of this. Somehow, I work it out that there ain't gonna be a long stay for you with us, after all this trouble. When I first seen you come into this here bar, I aimed to say that you wasn't the kind that waited long around one joint. You

300

looked like them that fly fast and don't nest long. But when you leave us, Duval, whenever that may be, I wanna say that my wishes go along with you. Good luck to you, man, a horse that'll never quit, and a gun that'll never miss!"

With that farewell in his ears, Duval went out into the street, knowing that the second sense of Pete had not been wrong.

The end of his Moose Creek career was before him. Even now he was staying under the shadow of a great danger, and only a perverse stubbornness made him remain.

When he had passed the swinging door, he could not help halting for a moment, with the bitter blast of the sun in his face, and eating through the coat into his shoulders. He looked up and down, as though at any moment he expected a cavalcade to turn one of the corners and come careening down upon him.

But there was no one in sight, no sound. All was still.

He shaded his eyes and, without knowing why, looked up as close as he could toward the sun. High above him he saw small specks against the sky, slowly circling. He knew what they were, and, in spite of his nerves of chilled steel, Duval shivered a little.

Then he crossed the street rapidly, and entered the store of Marian Lane.

Chapter Thirty-Six

It was a rush hour in the Lane store, for there were three or four patrons, including a girl with a braided pigtail, waiting to buy red-striped peppermint candies. The others completed their purchases in haste and left the store at once, with their eyes discreetly lowered to the floor, but the little girl, as she went out with her mouth stuffed with the candies, backed through the door, still gaping openly at the most famous man of Moose Creek.

The door shut with a slam behind her, and Duval could give his attention to Marian Lane.

Her usual manner of baby-faced sweetness she abandoned the instant they were alone, standing back against the wall with her hands folded behind her and looking rather wearily at Duval.

"This," he said, "is the biggest compliment I've ever received."

"Is it, David?" she asked. "What sort of a compliment?"

"You've swept up all your little mannerisms and put them away, and here is the real Marian Lane watching me, a little tired, as I guess by the shadows under her eyes, but finally fairly honest."

"Do you want honesty, David?"

"Of course I do, as long as it's pleasant."

"And suppose it isn't?"

"I don't want to suppose that. Everything leads me to think that you're more amiable today, my dear."

"How do you come to that conclusion, then?"

"Because you're almost beaten. In the game we've been playing."

"I'm not a whit beaten!"

"See now," he said cruelly. "You're trembling a little."

"I haven't slept much, and my nerves are a little upset. That's all."

"But still you're beaten. You haven't done the thing that you wanted to do."

"Will you tell me what that is, then?"

"Of course I shall. You set out to find out all about me. You've managed to drive me out of the town, but you haven't learned."

She started, almost imperceptibly. "Are you going to leave us, David?"

"I am."

"Forever?"

"It matters a little, I see," he remarked without exultation.

"Yes, it matters a good deal. Moose Creek is going to seem pretty cramped and small without you."

"Thank you," said Duval.

"You knocked out the walls and made us live

in a bigger house," she admitted. "But, of course, before the summer's over, it will have burned away everything except a dim memory of you."

"Not dim in you, Marian."

"No?"

"Not a whit dim in you. You'll remember me to your death day."

"That's not like you," said the girl in her cold, judicial manner, which she often showed when she was with Duval. "You don't often betray any vanity."

"It isn't vanity. It's the most profound humility. But I think that it's fair to say that a girl never forgets any man who has thrown himself at her feet."

At this she scanned him a little more closely still, and finally smiled. "Have you thrown yourself at my feet?" she asked.

"Deliberately, devotedly, wildly," Duval said, yawning a little.

"I like to hear you talk like this," Marian said, coming forward to the counter, "because I always wonder how you'll be able to dodge and tack until you've justified what you've said."

"Do you think that I can't?"

"Nothing's impossible for you, of course. Let me hear you."

"The reasoning would go like this. I have never made myself a fool about a woman before . . ."

"Have you made yourself a fool about me?"

"Tell me, Marian. Have I let you scorn me, treat me with contempt, baffle me, hunt me down with your hired men?"

"Hired men?" she echoed. "Hired men?"

"Certainly. Hired by the hope that you would at least smile at them, hired by the trust that you would reward them by taking them in as friends. Am I wrong?"

She did not answer.

"This is my day for frankness," said Duval. "Will you make it your day, also?"

"Well," she said, "I must play with you that far. Yes, they were hired, then, if you wish to put it that way."

"Thank you," said Duval. "We'll get on at this rate. Then you admit that you've pursued me with horses and hounds, as it were, and whips and guns?"

She shrugged her shoulders.

"For no other reason than because I wouldn't tell you who I was?"

"You know that that's only a part of the reason," said the girl.

"Well, perhaps. However, you know that you've had me dodging."

"Yes, A little. But never very far. Never enough to make me think that you were being driven away."

"Driven from my house and my farm that I've invested so much labor in?"

"That's a harsh way to put it. I never intended that, and I haven't done that."

"Haven't you?"

"No."

"If I prove it, will you admit that I'm right?"

"Well, perhaps."

"Look here, Marian. What has driven me away?"

"I suppose you mean on account of Henry's arrest, his escape . . . I wonder how you managed that . . . and because the idiots think that you're what Henry is. But why should untrue things like that drive you away?"

"Because they now think that I'm a thief like Henry. Why should that drive me away?"

"Exactly."

"I'll tell you a few good reasons. One of them is that every man jack in the county who has anything against me, would not hesitate to take a crack at me with my back turned now. I'm under the shadow. I'm no longer wanted. That's the reason. This is dangerous hunting ground if I'm the fox and all the others are hounds."

"You can't blame all that on me."

"Distinctly and definitely I can. Without you, Kinkaid never would have taken up my trail."

"Are you back at that?"

"I am. You expected it, you dreaded it, that's why you pretend that the subject wearies you. Am I right?"

She pursed her lips in contemplation and frowned a little. Then, impatiently, she rubbed the wrinkles out of her forehead and exclaimed: "You'd make an old woman of me in another month, with your talk, David!"

"You haven't answered me."

"I don't intend to answer."

"That's all right. I'll accept every point that's surrendered in this manner. But now to continue with our good logic . . ."

"Which I detest," she said.

"To continue, in spite of all of this hounding that I've heretofore received, here I am throwing myself at your feet, Marian."

"Oh, stuff and nonsense," said the girl.

"Literally at your feet, disregarding the insults and the dangers that you've thrown in my way."

"At my feet," she said. "And there I see you, almost yawning in my face, criticizing me, analyzing me like a chemical compound . . . telling yourself that I'm looking a trifle old today, that I'll wither young . . . that, after all, it's not a very interesting flirtation that you're about to leave behind you, making a last summing up of poor Marian Lane, and her poor little store, in the wretched little town of Moose Creek."

"Wretched, Marian? Wretched?"

"Yes . . . I hate it!"

"Because I'm to go away, and trail along with me a few faint clouds of glory from the romantic outside world. Is that true?"

She struck her hands together, and then she began to laugh. "I would be angry with you and your vanity. Only, it's not vanity. You're simply looking at both sides of everything."

"The fact is," said Duval, "that we're horribly alike in most ways, and that's why we'll miss one another."

"That's not according to the proverb, which says that unlikes attract one another."

"Only in a stupid way, however. Opposites are attracted by the essential mystery. They remain in love, for instance, until they know each other better. But people who are alike have ended the most miserable necessity in life before it becomes a leveled gun at their heads."

"What miserable necessity?"

"That of confession, which overwhelms us, otherwise, from time to time, and makes us talk our hearts out and then feel degraded, but lighter about the conscience."

"You and I, for instance?"

"We know one another . . . the cynicism, the scoffing, the cruelty, the lightness, the bitter selfishness. We understand, we know that we are understood, and, therefore, we are at ease. Pain is removed. Will you grant that?"

She hesitated. Then he insisted: "That's why

it's a restful and a delightful thing to be with one another?"

At this she nodded. "And that's why," she answered, "it's absurd for you to speak of being at my feet."

"Is it? Let me show you."

With that he vaulted over the counter and suddenly dropped to his knees before her. He took her hands as she would have recoiled from him.

"Here you see me, Marian, literally on my knees, my heart bowed down, in the dust of your persecution, your contempt, telling you that I couldn't do without you, that I would miss you more . . ."

"Than coffee in the morning?"

"Are you going to keep on scoffing, and force me to be poetic, eloquent, and pitiful? Or will you leave me a few shreds of self-respect?"

"I'll leave you your self-respect, if you'll go back across the counter."

Instantly he was on the farther side of it, his eyes glittering at her with triumph and excitement. "At least I've made you take me almost seriously," he said.

"Yes, you have . . . almost. What is it that you want to do with me, David?"

"Take you away with me."

"Where?"

"Wherever luck and adventure lead us!"

"Shall I tell you where that would be?"

"Tell me what you guess."

"Your home is back East, perhaps out on Long Island, surrounded with big lawns, gardens, gardeners, stables, grooms. Inside there is a gray-haired lady, your mother, a frosty aunt, with a professional smile, and everything prepared to overwhelm and crush poor Marian Lane."

He drummed his fingers on the counter top. "Suppose that that were not true, Marian?"

"Well?"

"Would you take me seriously? Would you go off with me and give yourself a chance to fall really and truly in love?"

An odd warmth came into her musing eyes, and in her daydream, she looked aside, out the window. That instant her glance changed, and she was shocked back to reality.

"No!" said the girl.

Duval, following the direction of her look, saw through the window the looming bulk of Marshal Dick Kinkaid, who now turned into the store.

"Is it the marshal, then?" Duval said, contempt in his voice. "Does that hard-handed brute of a man mean so much to you?"

"You'd better go," Marian said. "I think that he wants to say something to me."

"On the contrary, I'll stay," said Duval, "because I have something to say to him."

Chapter Thirty-Seven

In the most casual manner, Kinkaid went to the counter, nodded to the girl, overlooked Duval, and asked for bacon and cornmeal, telling her to give him a few pounds of each.

Dust lay thick on his shoulders and in the creases of his trousers. Since rain had fallen the night before, it was plain that he had been riding far away. One had a sense of fatigue about him, too, although there was so much iron in the man that it did not readily strike the eye; it was rather felt than seen.

"Well, Dick," said Duval, "I see that you've forgotten me?"

Kinkaid did not even turn his head. "If you'll wrap that up in some of the oiled paper . . . ," he was saying to Marian. He added: "I remember you, somewhere. I sort of forget your real name, though."

Duval did not watch him, nor he Duval, but both looked at the girl behind the counter as though her eyes were the mirror in which they would be able to see what they wanted to know.

She, eagerly alert, looked from one to the other, fairly on tiptoe with expectancy, her glance fluctuating rapidly.

Then Duval said slowly: "I'm giving a little

supper party at my shack, tonight. Charlie Nash is coming. I hope that you two will both come. D'you accept, Kinkaid?"

The marshal did not answer.

"Marian is going to be there," Duval said smoothly. "And I thought that you might enjoy being present at my last appearance in Moose Creek, Kinkaid?"

Still the marshal did not speak.

"Silence I'll take for polite acceptance. Because, after you've turned the matter over in your agile brain for a time, you'll understand why you must be there, Richard. So good bye until that happy time. By the way, you might ask your chum along, if you care to . . . I mean Larry Jude!"

With that Parthian shot, he retreated from the store, swung onto Cherry, and disappeared at once down the street.

The marshal continued to stare out the window, until the dust that the mare had raised in her gallop blew past or settled down again. Then he turned to Marian Lane. He pointed.

"You're going up the hill, tonight?"

She shrugged her shoulders, studying him.

"You're going up there with him, Marian, to his house?" His voice rose as he spoke, against his will, booming loud and ominous.

And she, watching him with her head canted a little to one side, and an almost meaningless smile on her lips, said: "I hadn't heard his invitation until you came in, Dick."

She paused a little before that familiar nickname, and it came so softly and gently on her lips that Kinkaid thought he never before had heard real music.

"He hadn't asked you, then? You hadn't said you'd go?" the marshal asked eagerly.

She nodded. "But, of course, I'd better go with you, Dick."

The pleasant poison ran warmly through his veins. Still, through a hot haze, he talked sense to her: "Y'understand that it's a challenge that he's sending to me, Marian?"

"I suppose it is, in a way?"

"A sneaking, low challenge, asking you along to see that there's no real trouble started? I never figured it before, but I can see now that he's afraid of me, and, by gravy, he's gonna have reason for his fear."

"Not tonight, Dick."

"Tonight? In front of a woman? No, not tonight. There's plenty of days afterward."

She nodded, still thoughtful, only murmuring: "I wouldn't be sure that he's afraid of anyone . . . hardly even of you, Dick."

But Kinkaid had progressed beyond even the thought of Duval, that somber rival. He said thickly: "I wanna say something to you, Marian, if you'll listen."

She gripped the counter, but she maintained her steady smile at him. "Yes? Of course, I'll listen."

"Marian, there's one grand job on my hands . . . Duval. I gotta finish that job, and when it's done . . . mind you, you steered me onto it . . . I'm gonna have something to say to you that'll mean something. D'you understand?"

She did not answer.

"What I'd like to know now, is there any sort of a hope for me, that you'd take me serious, I mean? I ain't a man that can talk, say pretty things, play the fool around a woman. But you've opened the door and stepped inside of my brain, Marian. You're lodged there, and I could never get you out. D'you believe it?"

She answered suddenly: "I couldn't doubt a thing you say in that way. It's a great thing and a wonderful thing, to have such a man as you are, speaking to me so seriously, Dick. I believe you."

"You couldn't answer me now?" the marshal asked, leaning his elbows on the counter, so that suddenly his bulk was impending over her.

In spite of herself, she glanced up with a frightened widening of her eyes.

Kinkaid was instantly himself again, and standing erect at a little distance.

"I dunno how to talk, I dunno how to do . . . ," he began. "I got no kind of manners, honey, but I could sort of learn. I could sort of study the things that would make you happy, if you'll try to believe that."

"Yes," she said faintly.

"If I look big and rough, and if there's some that call me tolerable mean, maybe they're right. There ain't a thing that's ever stepped inside of my eyesight that's meant much to me. I never was no kid to think much of my pa and ma. My brothers and sisters, they never was anything to me. I never had no friends. I never knew nobody very good. I never wanted to. But you're different. I dunno that I understand you. I don't ask to. What I want is a chance to take care of you, have you, work for you, dress you up pretty slick, set and look at you at the end of the day, find you in the garden when I come home at night. I wanna love you, Marian, though I ain't got the proper kind of words to set off what I'm saying. . . ." He paused, his big, booming voice rolling away like disappearing thunder.

And she, in spite of herself, was only half hearing what he had to say, and marking the manner of his saying. In her mind, as vividly, appeared the picture of Duval on his knees, sneering, laughing, ironically protesting his love.

It was much that such a man as Kinkaid should have confessed as he now confessed, yet in the end such a man as he was doomed. She could have told it in the distance. Any woman could have known that the giant would eventually

315

fall. It only needed a pretty face and a little art to undo him. What, then, did he care for in her? Her grace, her charm of an affected manner, her pretended childishness, and perhaps, also, some touches of shrewdness that he could not have failed to observe in her.

So he loved her. But Duval?

There was a different matter. If he cared at all, it was because he saw her almost more clearly than she saw herself. When she was with him, she felt his sensitive intelligence surround and embrace her mind and her spirit. She was, in a sense, in his hand. And, if she could have felt the same possession of him, would she have hesitated one instant before telling him that she, also, loved him, and far more truly than ever he could care for her. Out of this musing she was drawn by the voice of the marshal.

"I've been blunt . . . too fast . . . too straight to the point . . . and I gotta give you time . . . a kid like you, as though you could make up your mind about a gent like me so quick. I see I'm a fool, but only after I've made myself into one. Marian, you take your time, but in turning me over in your mind, treat me easy, remember that I ain't learned much about the way of putting my best foot forward with the ladies, and remember that here I am talking to you right after that gent Duval has been in here, slick as a kitten, quick and soft as a cat's foot. So, how'll I be bound to appear except mean and rough and ornery?" He retreated a little as he spoke, then came suddenly forward to her. "There's one thing else that I better say to you now."

He took from his coat pocket a chamois bag, drawn tight at the mouth with leather strings.

"We started to know each other because of Duval," said the marshal, "and it's only right that I should tell you now that I figure that I have a lot concerning him here in this. What's more, he knows that I have it, and there ain't gonna be a minute of my life, until he's dead or gone, that'll find me safe and easy so long as he knows that. I still got this. Poison, or bullets, or hired knives, he'd sure try anything to get this here back." He paused, then he went on: "You dunno what's in it. I'd like to have you tell me that you won't look."

She nodded intensely, feverishly curious and excited.

"The reason that I give it to you is just what I say . . . that I dunno whether I'll get to the end of the day, or not. If I don't . . . and if you get the word that I've been snagged somewhere, and killed, nobody knows by whom . . . you'll take this here bag to the sheriff. He's kind of two-thirds a fool, but he's mighty honest, and he's got a good deal of experience. He'll know how to use what's in there, and maybe it'll be from old Nat Adare that you'll hear the truth about this here Duval." He ended uneasily, and mopped his wet

317

face with a colored handkerchief. "I reckon that that's about all, Marian."

"I'll keep it as safe . . . as my eyes," said the girl earnestly.

"Aye. I guess you will. I'd trust you, Marian. Tonight, I'll come for you right after sundown, and we'll go up the hill together, the way that you said."

He was gone, and Marian Lane, the instant he disappeared, turned from the window and snatched up the chamois bag. Despite her promise, her fingers were about to tear open the mouth of the bag, when a shadow, as it seemed to her, moved across the rear window of the store. A shadow like a man's head.

She sank back against the wall, half fainting, for she knew by an extra sense that he who had looked in from the rear window was none other than Duval!

Chapter Thirty-Eight

With a reddened face, Duval was intently at work above his stove. He had on half a dozen little tins in which he was stewing various ingredients to make a sauce. It was delicate work, each of the tins requiring a watchful eye, and he gave to them their due share of attention, only pausing once to add a little wood to the fire.

It was after he had straightened from this occupation that he heard a throat cleared outside his door.

"Hello?" Duval called, without turning.

"You forgot the salad," said the voice of Henry, entering the cabin, his hands filled with greens.

Duval stiffened, but did not look around from his cookery. "Well, Henry," he said, "did the horse break a leg?"

"No, he didn't break a leg. He's a return horse, though."

"How did you find that out?"

"I was driftin' along through the hills," Henry said, "and let the reins hang loose, so's I could think a little better, because I've always noticed that a man can think better when he has both hands free. . . ."

"True," observed Duval.

"And pretty soon I come to out of my thoughts. . . ."

"What were your thoughts, Henry?"

"That I was gettin' old . . . that I was gettin' mighty old."

"Not too old to use a can-opener on old-fashioned safes, Henry."

"But too old to cover my tracks."

"Yes, you made a fairly clumsy job of it."

"Too old to keep out of jail."

"Kinkaid's the sort who might land any fish. Don't be down-hearted about that."

"Too old to hang onto the coin that I steal."

"That's my fault, of course."

"So old," went on Henry, "that I had to take charity money to live on."

"Not charity money, Henry. Friendship money, which I was glad to lend you, or give you, whichever way you'll take it."

"Charity money," Henry insisted, "from the same man that I came out here to blackmail, that took me in, treated me white, and then got me out of jail after I'd spoiled his game and made a fool of myself."

"Well," said Duval, "if you're having an attack of conscience, go ahead and talk, Henry. It does a person a lot of good to talk out things like this."

"So old," Henry continued, "that for the first time in my life, I've learned what it is to be homesick."

"That's a compliment to me, I take it?"

"No. It's only that I'm old, old, old, and ready for a halter and blinders, and a stall in a dark stable . . . jail or not."

Duval whistled. "You have the blues badly. You were saying that you'd waked out of these thoughts of yours . . ."

"And found out that the horse had turned and was wanderin' back in the direction we'd come from, so I simply let him come, and he wound up here."

"Hello! That's interesting."

"Seemed to me that it meant I should stay where I was," said Henry. "That's as much as to say, with you."

"And so here you are?"

"Yes."

"When did you come?"

"A good while before dark."

"Picking salad ever since along the creek?"

"Partly that, and partly watchin' Jude."

"Our good old friend Jude. I'd almost forgotten him."

"If you do, he'll bite you in the heel one of these days."

"I suppose he will, so I'll try to remember. What was he doing?"

"Sneakin' around."

"You followed him?"

"It was a pretty good game," chuckled Henry.

"I followed him around, well enough, and slipped along like a snake, until he began to get nervous, feelin' my eyes. A couple of times, he tried to slip around behind me. But I was too foxy for that. Seemed as though he couldn't be sure that I was there, but just kept on suspectin', and gettin' chills up his spine. It wasn't bad sport, me bein' the nightmare and him doin' the dreamin'.''

"What did he do at last?"

"Got up and run right back at me, blind, cursin' in a mutter, with a gun just glintin' in his hand. He might've run right over me, but he missed me by a foot, and after that, I heard him go rustlin' on through the bushes, and I knew that he'd never stop until he was a long way off from this here cabin. You couldn't hire him to come back into these woods tonight, not with a guard of a hundred men around him, because he knows that the spooks are after him. When you got through with him down there at Pete's Place, you sure left only a shell of him put together, old-timer."

"Some diseases leave a man pretty weak and liable to a new attack," admitted Duval. "Take a hand here and baste the roast, will you?" Then he gathered up the dishes in which he had been cooking the sauce, and put them far back on the stove, where they would only simmer very slowly.

Henry was basting the roast, and singing softly despite the steam that rolled out into his face.

Duval began to prepare the salad, breaking off the tough portions of the greens and shaking the chosen pieces in water to cleanse them thoroughly, then flicking all water from them and waving them through the warm air above the stove to dry.

"There's still Kinkaid," observed Duval.

"Yeah?" the old man drawled as though without any interest in this remark.

"He's quite alive," said Duval, "and he's coming here tonight."

"Be glad to see him again," said Henry. "In a sort of a social way, as you might say."

Duval began to laugh, still working at the salad. "Henry," he said, "whenever I feel myself growing old, you say something that makes me young again. Henry, without you, life would soon become intolerably dull. You're intending to stay here and face the marshal, are you?"

"They've got that law of hospitality out here in the West," remarked Henry, "and I suppose that he wouldn't be breakin' that and gettin' himself a bad name all over the range?"

"Is that what you trust to?"

"There's another law that I trust to," admitted Henry.

"What's that?"

"The law of Duval."

At this, the younger man turned toward him with a broad smile. "You're a diplomat, old fellow," he said. "You can turn me around your finger without the slightest effort. There's no one in the world like you, Henry. Very well. Stay on, then. As a matter of fact, I begin to see that you can be of help to me. There's someone coming up the lane . . . see who it is."

Henry went to the door and instantly said over his shoulder: "Not Kinkaid."

"It's Charlie Nash, then."

"Nash, too?"

"Aye, and Marian Lane."

Henry whistled, then said: "No wonder you want me, then, to keep yourself from being talked down. Nash is walkin' pretty slow. You'd think that he was carryin' a load."

"He is," said Duval. "His brain is loaded so deep that you couldn't see the Plimsoll line. Be kind to Charlie, because he's young, and means better than he can do."

"Aye," Henry said. "He's one of them that nearly win every race but trip on their own heels at the finish. He'd be a champion if he wasn't a dub. Here he is."

An instant later the voice of Charlie Nash sounded at the door.

"Come in!" Henry said. "Come right in and make yourself at home, will you?"

"Sure," Charlie said, a little uncertain. He stepped in through the door and exclaimed: "Henry! You still here?"

"The chief wanted me to help him serve up this dinner," Henry said in careful explanation. "So I stayed a while, not thinkin' that the marshal would miss a meal like this to keep ridin' after me."

Charlie Nash looked around, bewildered. He saw the table laid for four, and his bewilderment increased greatly at the sight of it.

"Duval," he said, "is Kinkaid coming here?"

"We hope he won't be rushed by too much business to let him come," Duval said hopefully.

Nash threw himself into a chair and drew a great breath.

"Tired?" asked Duval.

"No, happy!"

"Glad to hear it."

"I been saying good bye to the world all the way up the hill."

"Good bye?"

"Why, Duval, don't blink at me as if you didn't understand. You know what I came up here for tonight."

"Supper, of course."

"Aye," Charlie growled, "as much supper as the marshal is coming for, but if he's gonna be in the center of the stage, I won't have to be bothered."

"Right," Duval said pleasantly. "You're to be the spectator, this evening, Charlie."

"And the fourth place is for Henry?"

"No, sir," said Henry. "I'm the butler tonight,

because the gents are goin' to eat in style, with a lady."

"Lady?"

"Yes."

"Ah," Nash said with a great gasp. "Duval, don't tell me that I'm right when I say that it's gonna be Marian Lane."

"Yes, she's promised to let Kinkaid bring her up the hill."

"Great guns," breathed Charlie Nash, and sat silently for a moment. "I might have guessed that everything would be over my head," he said at last.

"Not over your head," Duval said reassuringly. "I want you here as a neutral, to look on. Besides, you may reap a fine harvest out of this here."

"Harvest?"

"Why, if the marshal and me kill each other, it leaves you pretty clear in possession of the field, don't it?"

Chapter Thirty-Nine

When Henry had disappeared to fetch a fresh bucket of water, and both Nash and Duval were busy at odd jobs about the cookery, Marian Lane stepped across the threshold of the cabin, with the great shadow of the marshal behind her.

The house was very gay. Some late-blossoming shrubs had been ravished to secure decorations, and the wind that passed through the door stirred the scent of the flowers gently through the room. This mingled with the smell of the cookery, and wild wisps of steam whirled continually upward from the stove and made the beams overhead begin to sweat.

Marian would have begun helping at once, and even the marshal gloomily offered to contribute his assistance, but Duval refused all aid.

"My old man used to say," quoted Duval, "that them that worked on a meal wasn't guests, they was hosts, and I aim to be the host here, tonight. Set down and rest your feet, Marian. You, too, Kinkaid. If you want a bracer to stir up your appetite, here's some honest bourbon that's old enough to be your brother."

The marshal refused the proffered drink with a slight sneer. It seemed too palpable a plant, to him—first to drug his senses with liquor, and then to cause trouble to begin. Yet he observed that Marian Lane seemed a trifle upset by the manner in which he made his refusal, and he qualified it at once.

"I never hardly touch nothing, except after hard riding in winter," Kinkaid said.

"All right," nodded Duval. "You, Marian?"

She shook her head, and so they were ushered to their chairs. She had the one upright chair. The marshal was favored with a stool that had no back, and Duval and Charlie Nash had empty boxes that needed some attention to keep them from slumping to one side or to the other.

Soup began the meal, a soup with a most unctuous flavor, and they fell to it. Their manners were each worth attention, the girl in the first place being all smiles, turning from one to another with the most cheerful remarks. These were answered by Charlie Nash in an embarrassed manner. Charlie was on his dignity, as one unwilling to give away a trick, no matter in what formidable company he found himself, and he was so earnestly devoted to keeping his chin in and his back straight, and his brows slightly bent, that he could hardly speak.

The marshal made little pretense of hearing anything, for he was all eyes. In the first place, before sitting down, he had looked all around him and made sure that the wall was at his back.

Next, he attacked the soup with care, as though he suspected that poison might be in it. And he was continually looking up from it sharply, as though he expected to surprise Duval in the midst of a telltale gesture or glance. At the same time, he was terribly ill at ease, for he felt that he was not appearing to the best advantage in the presence of the girl. Certainly, he was at his worst compared with the smiling ease of Duval, who had a word for everyone, and single-handedly sustained the conversation with Marian.

The soup was ended for the marshal, who now rested his big elbows on the edge of the table and was sullenly on his guard, when the tall, meager form of Henry appeared in the doorway. A totally irresistible instinct at once ruled the marshal. He could not help snapping out his revolver and covering the man he wanted so badly. It was one of the worst blows of his career that Henry had slipped away from him, and although he could blame the loss on the carelessness and gullibility of the sheriff, still that was a cold comfort for him, and his eyes glittered with joy as he drew down on the thief.

"Hello, Marshal Kinkaid," Henry said, smiling broadly. "I'm glad to see you here, sir. Are you seein' a bear behind me?" He glanced over his shoulder, as though he imagined that the other must have taken aim at an enemy behind him.

Charlie Nash had sprung up and almost upset

the table at the first flash of the Colt, but Duval raised a deprecatory hand.

"Kinkaid, Kinkaid," he said reprovingly. "It ain't hardly right, is it, to scare the lady before she's finished her soup?"

The marshal was slowly rising.

"I want him. He belongs to me!" Kinkaid said with much conviction. "I've had him once, and now I'll have him again, and he'll have the stripes on before I ever let him out of my sight again."

"Suppose, Kinkaid," Duval said, "that Henry had wanted to work out his grudge against you. He had a pretty good target through the door, eh?"

The marshal grunted. Then, baffled, his glance wavered as far as the face of the girl.

"This night, Dick," she said persuasively, "there's not to be any trouble, is there? And Henry's such an old, old man?"

"You've brought him here and shoved him under my nose!" Kinkaid said explosively to Duval. "What's the meaning of that, I'd like to know?"

"My old man . . . ," began Duval

"Damn your old man!" said the marshal fiercely. He glared at Duval, but the latter smiled back at him genially.

"My old man," he insisted, "always used to say that a gent that had to wait on himself never had no appetite for what he had before him, and I figured out that Henry would be right useful here to hand the things around. And Henry don't mind."

"Not a bit," Henry said, whose smile would not go off. "Matter of fact, I'd do almost anything to keep the marshal feelin' cheerful."

He was picking up the dishes as he spoke, and the marshal slowly lowered the weapon to its holster. He was infinitely sorry, for two reasons.

The first and least important was that he had exhibited a vicious and unmannerly temper in the presence of Marian, and having begun a job, he had not finished it. The second reason was that he had given to Duval a chance to time with his eye exactly the speed of his draw.

And Duval certainly did not appear dismayed by what he saw. On the contrary, the marshal could have sworn that his sly enemy was secretly smiling in content. He was infuriated, but he knew not what to do or what to say. He had delivered himself, he felt, into the hands of an enemy who was not really of his strength, but who was filled with wiles. He was the lion, and, behold, a fox could annoy him!

However, the end was not yet. He took that comfort to his heart and waited for the current of events to flow on. Somehow, he knew that before this evening had ended there would be a great crisis that would solve the problem with which he was confronted.

Old Henry had cleared away the soup and brought on the next course. But, the marshal hardly knew what was before him. Back in his mind rumbled his oath of office like distant thunder, and his head swam with this impossibility—that this fugitive from justice should be here before him, and yet untouched. And always there persisted the sense that he had been trapped.

There was more clearing of the table, rattling of washed dishes, and then the presentation of a great saddle of venison. The marshal heard Marian Lane exclaiming over it, and he stared at her heavily, for it seemed a miracle that she could abandon herself so heartily to the enjoyment of that dinner without feeling the danger that was in the air.

Yet, when he looked at her with a clearer eye, he saw that she, too, had forced her pleasure. And, in odd moments, her face grew grave and her eye apprehensive.

They came to coffee, at last, and as they reached this, the head of the marshal cleared entirely. He knew what he would do, and drained off the steaming hot contents of the cup at a draft. Then he struck the table with his hand, so that the dishes upon it jumped.

Charlie Nash started violently and uttered a

low cry. Marian merely stiffened in her chair.

"Friends," said the marshal, "it's been a fine party, and I ain't denying that. Never sat down to a better meal, but there's a time come when I gotta go back to my job, and the first sign of it is that I gotta take Henry with me. Henry, put on your hat, because you're coming back to the jail with me. We'll make you right comfortable there."

"Sure," Henry said. "I'll go along, if the boss can spare me from the job, here."

"The boss," the marshal said, looking not at Henry but at Duval, "ain't the man for you to talk to now. It's me that counts here, Henry."

He rejoiced, for he knew that he had brought on the climax that had been impending in the air.

Duval was shaking his head. "I'd like to let you have him, Kinkaid," said Duval, "but if you put yourself in my boots, you'll see how it is . . . I can't turn him over to the jail when there are still . . . so many dirty dishes to be washed, man."

He smiled amiably at Kinkaid, and the latter flushed heavily.

"I dunno what you're driving at, Duval," he said, "if it ain't trouble. And if that's what you want . . ."

"Tut," Duval said. "It ain't trouble that I want, but trouble that I gotta have. My old man used to say that it was better to find trouble before trouble found you, and I reckon that he was right, eh?"

Marian Lane stood up from her chair hastily. "You don't mean that you'll force things, Dick?" she gasped.

"I've been brought here like a fool. I've been set down here with that crook, Henry, under my eye. Something's been planned against me, and I dunno what. But I do know that Henry's going back to the jail with me this night or else he . . ."

"Sit down, Marian," invited Duval. "There ain't gonna be no trouble until you've finished your coffee, and maybe that'll take you another ten minutes. Let's see. It's twelve minutes to eight, now. Say we make it eight, Marshal?"

"Eight for what?" asked big Kinkaid.

"Wind up the clock, will you," Duval said to Henry, "and set the alarm for eight o'clock. That ought to do for a signal, Kinkaid, eh?"

"A signal for what?" asked Charlie Nash.

"For the shooting," Duval answered.

"Is that another of your bluffs and your fakes?" asked the marshal fiercely. "The thing that wore down Larry Jude will never wear me down."

"That's a tolerable ornery and hostile way of putting it," answered Duval. "Why, I ain't upsetting you. All I'm doing is saying that he's gotta give Marian time to finish her coffee."

Charlie Nash broke in: "Marian, I'm going to take you out of this. Duval means what he says."

"No, no . . . ," Marian began.

"She'll stay here," Duval said, drawling the words. "Now that she's started the fun, she'd better stay and see the game finish out."

Chapter Forty

This suggestion struck everyone with amazement. There was a silence, broken only by the creaking of the alarm clock as Henry wound up the spring, and adjusted the hands.

It was he who first spoke. "It'll go off in about ten minutes," Henry said.

"Ten minutes makes a long time, when one wishes to settle up his last affairs," remarked Duval. "You agree to that, Kinkaid?"

"I agree to anything," said the marshal. "Except you're a fool and a brute, if you wanna keep the girl here. This is between you and me. Marian, you go. Nash, take her away!"

"Charlie won't take her away," Duval declared, steadily looking into the white face of the girl. "He'll leave her here where she belongs. I reckon that she even wants to stay. Don't you, Marian?" He smiled at her.

"Do you mean that you're going to stay here in this room and murder one another?" cried the girl. "Charlie . . . Henry . . . !" She paused, realizing that there was no appeal she could make that was strong enough to stop the clash of these impending forces.

"No murder . . . no murder," Duval said. "Because I aim to state the two of us are both first-rate experts. Him that's the fastest is the one that'll win. The first bullet home will be the only bullet shot. It'll be no double murder, I can promise you, Marian. You won't have to sit there and see the room all spattered with red and the furniture shot up, and bullets whizzing around your own head, the way that you think. It'll be neat, quick, and pretty. Only one of us will drop, and that's likely to be me, the marshal being as you might say a professional . . . well, manhunter, you might call him. Bounty-getter. You must've piled up quite a considerable, Dick, taking scalps?"

"I've heard enough of your lingo," said Kinkaid. "Get Marian out of the house. Nash can take her. Then you and me'll finish it out, and the less talking the better."

"Not with Marian gone," Duval said. "You sure want to stay, don't you?"

"Stay? I?" cried the girl. "David . . . Richard . . . !" She ended her appeal before it began. "Oh, Charlie," she said, "is there nothing that can be done?"

"Listen to her," Duval said admiringly. "Now, you'd think, to listen to her, that she hadn't worked all this up in good style. You'd think that it wasn't her that put Dick Kinkaid on my trail. You'd think that it wasn't her that started all this trouble, and now that the showdown is about to come, she blanches a mite, and throws up her hands, and hollers how terrible it is, but down in your heart, Marian, you sure must hanker a lot to see this fight."

"Leave her alone!" thundered the marshal. "You're driving her sick with your fool talk. You . . ."

She had, in fact, slipped limply down into her chair, white and shaking.

"You talk like a grandmother," Duval said to the marshal. "Did she think that I was a soda fountain clerk, or a window-washer? She knew what I could do . . . she had some ideas about me. And she picked you up at the dance, Kinkaid, and pointed you on my trail. To find out who Duval was? Not a bit, partner. She wanted to see could Duval be licked, and now she's gonna find out and watch with her own eyes." He turned to the girl. "Tell us true, Marian. Ain't that the fact?"

"No!" she cried at him. "I only wanted to know . . . but whatever my reason was, I see that it was wrong. It *is* my fault! David, if I go on my knees to you and beg you . . . ?"

"Hush," Duval said. "The old man used to say that after the kid set fire to the barn, he was sure sorry when he seen the flames wagging in the sky. I know you're sorry. But now the game's started, it has gotta finish. And you'll sit there and watch. It'll be something to tell your grandchildren, one of these days, how Kinkaid and Duval fought for you. Kind of primeval-like, and strong and wild, like the cave men that used to go courting, and him that had the longest arm and the knobbiest club, he cracked the skulls of half a dozen other gents, and then he walked off with the prettiest girl in the tribe, mostly taking her along by the hair of the head for a lead rope."

He laughed as he ended and, turning to Henry, asked: "What's the time now, Henry?"

"Six minutes left, sir," said Henry.

"Thank you," Duval said. "Now, Kinkaid, we got six minutes left, and maybe you got some affairs that you'd like to put in order?"

Kinkaid sneered broadly. "I see the game that you're working," he declared. "First, you're gonna have the girl here, and Charlie. And second, you're gonna make a long wait to break my nerve. It'd work with most, but it won't work with me. I see through you, Duval."

"Do you?" Duval asked patiently. "Well, even if I've led you to the water I can't make you drink. But if you got friends, family, relations, you'd better think of 'em now. You could tell Charlie. Charlie would remember. Short messages would be the best, though."

"Fill your hand," answered the marshal. "And we'll finish this off now."

"There's still coffee in her cup," Duval advised him. "Besides, I ain't in any hurry. Charlie, have you got a gun?"

"Yes," Charlie said, barely able to speak.

"Pull the gun and stand over against the wall."

"What for?"

"For seeing that this here fight comes off fair and square. There's a time when that alarm begins that it makes a purring, like a cat lapping milk. Then comes the ring. If one of us was to draw a gun before the ringing begins, shoot him through the head, Charlie. You'll be the judge. You been mighty interested in all of this here game, and now it's your chance to take a part."

Charlie did not hesitate. He walked like an automaton to the side of the room, and drew his long Colt, grimly ready for action.

"What's the time, Henry?" asked Duval.

"Four minutes, sir."

"Four minutes left," Duval said. "You ain't gonna accept my invitation after all, Dick?"

"Your invitation be hanged!"

The marshal sat stiffly in his chair, every muscle rigid, his jaws set, his eyes narrowed to needle points.

"All right," Duval said, "but it looks to me like you're pretty tense, old-timer. The old man used to say that even steel could get tempered too hard, and then you could break it in your hands. I wouldn't like to see you break like that . . . not right here in front of Marian and Charlie. The other time, that was different. There was only me and Henry to watch that."

He smiled genially, and the marshal flared up with hot anger.

"You lie!" he shouted. "There wasn't no other time!"

"Huh?" Duval said. "There's a lady with us, Dick." He turned to the girl. "Now that I am a couple of steps from dying, maybe, I wanna say in front of the world that I loved you, Marian, mighty nigh from the first time that I laid eyes on you. But you threw a scare into me, at first. You knew a pile too much. . . ."

"Leave her be," Kinkaid snapped. "Your time's drawn pretty fine. Leave her be, and if you've got talking to do, talk to me, Duval, you sneak, you thief, you faker!"

"What time is it, Henry?" Duval asked.

"There's about a minute and a half left," Henry announced.

"One moment," Duval said. "I sure don't wanna die like this . . . like a farmer just in from the plow, I mean to say. Gimme your neckerchief, Henry."

He took one from the hand of Henry, whose eyes had grown luminous with fear and doubt, like the eyes of a frightened dog. Duval rapidly donned the neckerchief, and then jerked down and smoothed his coat. He passed his hand over his hair and turned his pale, smiling face to the girl.

"Do I look better now, Marian?"

She could not speak. Frozen with white horror,

she watched him. He saw her swallow and make a mighty effort, but the words would not come.

Charlie Nash, also, was a form of stone against the wall, but with his teeth set and all his mind and body nerved for violent action.

"What time is it, Henry?" came the remorselessly polite voice of Duval.

"One minute, sir!"

"Now, Kinkaid, there's one minute left for any message you might wanna send."

Kinkaid caught his breath audibly. "Charlie!"

"Aye?" said Charlie Nash.

"My uncle, Tom Chalmers in Butte. Send him word that when I died, I said that I never set 'em on the right trail after his boy Les. But if I live, dang him if I'll give him that comfort. He can think what he wants about me and . . ." He clipped off the words sharply, for he knew that the time was coming quickly, and he did not wish to be caught unaware.

"Even Dick Kinkaid had one message to leave behind him," Duval said, and smiled. "What time is it now, Henry!"

"There's less than half a minute," Henry said softly, "and heaven help you, Mister . . ."

Even then the word was not spoken, not that Duval interfered, but because the alarm machinery began to purr softly, with light clicking.

Then Duval heard the girl cry out in a voice

like that of a child, in protest. He himself leaned back a little, and made himself smile straight at the marshal, down whose face he saw the great drops trickling.

"Why blast the house to pieces?" Duval said. "One shot apiece had oughta be enough, Dick. Here's my five." He broke his gun and deliberately rolled five shells out on the table.

"Damn you!" Kinkaid hissed. His fingers fumbled and shook with nasty fear, but he accepted that last challenge, at that last instant, and, breaking his gun, shook out five of the trusty shells. Instantly he thrust the weapon back into its holster, to duly keep the rules of the game, and as he did so, he saw Duval fold his arms.

It was a final, consummate act of bravado on the part of Duval, or was it real contempt for his enemy, and confidence in himself? What the marshal decided was that the man was striving to lure him into a false impression that he would have a shade of extra time because of those idly folded arms. And Kinkaid decided that his draw must be fast as light, if he were to live.

That instant the alarm bell clanged. And with an explosion of convulsive speed, Kinkaid whipped out his revolver and fired, pointblank. Not five feet from the extended muzzle of his gun was the breast of Duval, but still he sat there, unscathed, smiling, his arms still lightly folded across his breast.

Chapter Forty-One

The horror-stricken eyes of the marshal turned down to the five shells that lay upon the table before him, then rose to the pale face of Duval, who was still smiling. Then he saw the hand of the other disappear inside his coat and come forth again, bearing a revolver.

It was instinct that made the marshal half rise, and stand like a crouched bear, ready to rush in. But some deep sense of dignity and of how men should meet their death made him, instead, stand suddenly erect, his hands gripped at his sides, as the revolver swung up and leisurely covered him.

"That's the manhunter, the man-killer, the bounty-getter," said Duval, sneering. "I took your gun from you, once. I could take your life from you now . . . but I'd rather let folks see what you're made of . . . and let you go. Get out!"

Once before, on a night of horror, the marshal had been sent in shame from that cabin. Now he went forth again with his head hanging on his chest. At the door, he gathered himself and, turning, cast a glance like that of a madman on Duval, then went slowly off through the darkness.

Old Henry, Duval himself, and Marian Lane remained with Charlie Nash.

It was Charlie who moved first and, saying

nothing to anyone, poured himself a glass of water. His shaking hand spilled half of it on the floor; the rest he swallowed, and then he blundered out from the cabin and was gone.

"The horses, Henry!" Duval said huskily to Henry.

And Henry slipped away in turn, his eyes like those of men who have seen ghosts walk.

It left Duval and the girl alone, and the instant the others were away, he dropped his face in his hands and gripped the flesh hard with his fingers.

Seconds walked slowly over him, endlessly, as he fought to control himself and keep back the waves of hysteria that were rising.

"Here," said a matter-of-fact voice, "is some hot coffee. You didn't drink your first cup, David."

The fragrance of it and the heat rose to his face. "Very well," he said. "Thank you." He had to make a pause between the words and speak very softly. Otherwise, he could not have been sure of the voice in which he spoke.

When he raised the cup, it chattered foolishly against his teeth. He closed his eyes to shut out the face of Marian, who stood by, watching.

The heat, the stimulus, instantly helped him. But still he dared not stir from his chair, for an odd sense of emptiness occupied his brain, and his body was weak. Weakness, like a sensible thing, ran in his nerves and in his blood.

"Why did you do it?" Marian asked. He shook his head, a convulsive shudder rather than a controlled sign. She came close beside him. "I know," she said. "You wanted to crush me with one last, gigantic act. You wanted to make me see that even the marshal was nothing to you." She touched his hair. "This is where his bullet clipped. Oh, David, David, to risk that for the sake of overwhelming poor Marian Lane, who keeps a country store! That was childish, David."

He found her with his hands, for he dared not open his eyes just now. "Don't talk for a moment," Duval said. "Whatever you say is true. But I'm sick. I want to keep you here this moment. That's all." He had her wrists and drew her hands in against his face. Out of the touch of their softness, calmness poured in upon Duval, out of the perfume, too, with which they were scented, and of which he breathed.

"So," Duval said at last, and stood up before her. He was completely recovered, one would have said, from that instant of utter weakness, though still the girl watched him with a judicial air.

"Childish," he admitted. "That was it . . . plainly childish. But, after all, it worked, you see."

"Not well enough to put you at ease, though," she said. "When I saw you fold your arms, I knew what you'd do, and I wanted to scream a warning, but it was much too late. I . . . there wasn't much left to me by that time." She smiled a wan smile.

"In every way," Duval said, "I was contemptible."

"Hush," said the girl. "You saved a life. Is that contemptible?" Then she added: "As for me, I deserved all the pain that came to me, I suppose." She closed her eyes and shook her head a little to drive the picture of the horror away from her. "But now that it's over, it won't have to be repeated. And you're going away, David?"

"No," he said.

"Is it worth your while?" she asked him, half sadly and half curiously. "Is it worth your while to stay here, when you know that Dick Kinkaid will not stop with this one trial, but will surely come at you again? Is it worthwhile, for the sake of the little game that you're playing in Moose Creek?"

He smiled at her, and, smiling, she felt his eyes travel over her face slowly, like the glance of a painter who will remember what he has seen.

"How little is the game, Marian?" he asked.

"Only you can tell that, of course . . . Mister Smith . . . Jones . . . Brown . . . or Van Astorgrand, or whatever your name is, David."

"But don't you know," Duval said, "that you're carrying with you the proof of who I am?"

"The proof?" she said.

"The very name," he answered. "In the little chamois bag that our friend Kinkaid left with you."

Old Henry, who had just returned, cried in a strange voice: "Are you tellin' her that? Are you tellin' her that?"

"Why, Henry," Duval said, "you heard me say before the world that this is the girl I love. This is she who I intend to marry, if I can. Would you have her marry anything but a true name?"

"Only . . . only . . . ," gasped Henry.

Marian had drawn from the bosom of her dress the small chamois sack, and, holding it for a moment in both hands, she stared at Duval. He nodded at her.

"Kinkaid has no right to ask you to keep that shut, if I ask you to open it."

She, with a little faint cry of excitement, drew open the mouth of the bag and spilled upon the table's face—a creamy flow of big pearls!

She stood frozen with amazement, so that she made no attempt to prevent several of them from rolling from the table top.

Old Henry caught them with lightning hands, whispering to himself so rapidly that it was like a continued hissing sound. Then he replaced them gingerly, with a touch that hated to leave their beauty.

He had ended and stepped back when Duval

said gently: "I think one of them escaped into your vest pocket by accident, Henry."

The old man drew it forth with the same enchanted touch and laid it among the rest, a huge pearl of price.

But Marian Lane had looked up, at last, from the jewels, and stared straight at Duval.

"That wild, wild story you told me . . . ," she said. "That fairy tale . . . that impossible thing . . ."

"It was all true, word for word."

"And you weren't hiding yourself away from me?"

"I was laying the naked truth in your hands to see."

"But you didn't protest."

"Why should I protest? I saw that you wouldn't believe a word that I had to say. I was right, I think."

She raised both hands to her face, and when she slowly lowered them, she was crimson with emotion. "After that," she said, "it seems that everything you said may have had some truth in it. It wasn't quite all a game, then?"

"Do you think that any syllable was a game, Marian?"

"I don't know. I'm dizzy. I'm so dizzy, I can hardly see you at such a great distance."

He came swiftly to her.

"I'm sure you see what it means," he said.

349

"And that instead of being possibly an honorable Mister Smith, or Jones, or Brown, I'm only David Castle, the jewel thief?"

Tears came up in her eyes. "Stuff!" she said. "It means that you are my David. And there's no riddle at all."

"You can bring the horses around, Henry," Duval said. "Then go down to Miss Lane's stable and get her own horse out, and ride it up the northwest trail. We won't be going very fast, and you can overtake us."

"But the store, and everything in it?" she said.

"You can settle that later on."

"And the scandal?"

"We'll put that right at the first minister's house. Because, if I'm to have you with me, do you think that I'll stay here another moment in danger of that juggernaut, Kinkaid? Shall I take one single step that will put me in the danger of the law, Marian? Not from this minute forward."

Henry, tiptoeing, overcome with awe, went through the door, but paused outside long enough to see that which made his old heart young, and sent him off hastily through the dark, chuckling to himself.

"I have to go back for clothes!" protested Marian.

"You can be a boy for a day. I have clothes that will more than fit you."

"But . . ."

"Shall I let you go back to Moose Creek, where they may be waiting and watching for you?" He took her in his arms. "Not a step without me. Not a step!"

"Wait," she said. "I must think . . ."

"Will you tell me that you love me, Marian, and do your thinking a little later on?"

"But there's so much to work out. . . . I'll have to think for two, now."

"Only answer me, first."

She stepped suddenly close to him, and stood on tiptoe to bring her face closer to his.

"As if you didn't know," she said, "from the first moment, that I was only fighting against an overlord."

Chapter Forty-Two

Still, when the morning came, they were toiling upward and northward through the mountains. Their horses were tired. The riders were no less, and Marian Lane swayed a little in the saddle whenever her mount stumbled. She could still smile at Duval when he glanced at her, but it was a faint, twitching smile that strove to be reassuring, and was not.

He called a halt, therefore, in the pink of the dawn, for they had found an ideal spot. The lodgepole pines formed a thin fencing around a shoulder of the mountain where the grass grew well for grazing, and where a small spring welled up into a white sandy basin, then sent a silver trickle winding down the slope. Where the trees would throw their shadow, Duval and Henry made two hasty beds of young boughs, and spread the blankets. One would stand watch while two slept, and Duval took the first turn, while Henry and the girl wrapped themselves in the blankets and were instantly asleep.

The horses lower down on the hill shoulder, but still where the trees protected them from view, were busily, hungrily grazing.

Then Duval began his beat, walking slowly up and down. When he came to one end of his round, he looked back down the winding valley up which they had come to the heights, with its verdure, its soft green haze of meadowlands and the stream in its midst, now shadow covered, now flaring like fire beneath the young sun of the day. At the other end of his pacing, he stood on a cliff from which the eye dropped faster than a rock could fall to a profound ravine below. All was different here. Grass grew only on precarious ledges of crumbling stone. The trees found only a scant footing here and there in crevices where a little soil had been formed by slow-growing lichens that had caught the dust. Everywhere was naked rock. Yet it was not barren.

To the eye of Duval, there was an epic story in the enormous folds of strata, and in the great bald cliffs that had been cleft in the range by the insignificant trickle of water that ran beneath, shaken at the head of the cañon into a thin breath of mist as it fell from a height to the lower valley floor. There were colors, too. Not only those of the dawn as they turned the waterfall to a rainbow, or as they poured rose or gold upon the upper heights of the peaks, but colors in the bare rock itself, yellows and dingy reds, and yonder the strike of a vast porphyry dike, and yet farther beyond this, a pale form distinct in its whiteness, but ghost-like in distance.

Duval, as he watched, threw back his shoulders, half smiling and half fierce, then hastily went back to the place where the girl slept. She was troubled in her sleep. He saw her frown and one hand moved outside the blanket as if in protest.

It troubled him more than he cared to say, and when he saw her lips move, he kneeled to listen, ashamed of such eavesdropping, but humbly and hungrily intent in learning what her sorrow could be. He only heard an indistinct murmur, but still he leaned above her.

She had no need, he thought, to pretend childishness, for she was child enough in fact. It hurt him to the heart to see the slenderness of her hand and the delicacy with which it was fashioned, so that he was on the verge of taking it in his, when she looked straight up at him, wide awake.

"It's your turn to sleep, David," she told him, and tried to sit up.

He held her back. "Hush," he said. "You'll be waking Henry, for he's a light sleeper. You've hardly been here ten minutes asleep."

"An hour and a half. I'm made over by such a sleep."

"Not that long."

"Look at your watch."

He saw that she was right. "I've been coming by and looking at you from time to time," he said. "You've had a troubled sleep, my dear."

"I dreamed," she said, "that I was swimming toward a beach, and you were standing on it, and just as I came to the verge of the sand, just as I could put down a foot and touch it, a strong current took hold of me and drifted me far out to sea." She blinked, and then went on: "You were true to character, even in the dream, David."

"What did I do?"

"Just stood there, and asked me if I were trying to play baby-face again and be rescued from the bold, bad sea."

"May every sea take you no farther away than this," said Duval.

"You look serious," said Marian. "You look actually frightened over my dream."

"Because it gives me gloomy thoughts, my dear. Suppose we love each other to the end, and are married, yet how many hours at the end of the years will we really have been together as we are now, on the mountainside here? For all of these mountains, do you see? And this sunrise, and this wind, and the clouds that are blowing across the sky, and the breath of the pines, and all the picture, Marian, are only a background and setting for you. Do you understand? We'll be like others, and leave happiness and love to cool their heels in a darkened room along with the poets on our shelves, while we give ourselves to the important business of the butcher and baker and the candlestick maker. And yet the mountains and the clouds and the wind and the morning are all full of joy simply because we love one another. And if . . ." He stopped. "I'm becoming romantic," Duval said. "The practical fact is that you must stop my talking by going to sleep again."

"I'm not going to sleep again," she said. "I'm going to lie awake, unless you'll let me get up and mount guard."

"A grand guard you'd be," said Duval.

"Are you going to make the old mistake and think that I have to be tied up in pink ribbon like a stick of candy for a baby? You won't try to make me a picture on the wall, David, will you? Because I'll everlastingly step out of the frame, and rip about, and make trouble, if I can't make good."

"You'll do as you please," said Duval.

"You'll find I can work," Marian said. "Whatever you do, I'll find a way to help you."

"Of course you will," Duval agreed, "but you won't have to work to keep the wolf from the door. The poor old wolf will have to howl in the dim distance. Why, Marian, in that little chamois sack there's enough to banish him forever."

She nodded. "But not for us, I suppose?" she said.

"Not for us?" frowned Duval.

"You see," she explained, sitting up again, "I don't complain of what you did before, as long as we don't live on it now."

"Wipe it all out?" Duval said, his breath

taken. "Millions are what you're talking about. Millions, child!" Then he added, almost roughly: "It's better to let me worry about how the money is made. Now, you go back to sleep."

She did not argue or protest, but lay back again in the bed of boughs with the faintest of frowns, and as she lay, looking up at him and past him, he saw her hand make the same slight motion of protest that he had watched in her sleep.

Duval was instantly on his knees beside her. "You're right," he said. "And I'm an ass. To think that I could keep you with stolen goods. To be fool enough to think that. It goes back to the right owner, and it goes at once. Here, take the stuff. I won't be tempted with the beauties."

She took them. "I wanted to say . . . ," she said, and paused.

"Yes," said Duval.

She took his hand and pressed it. "I wondered how hard it would be, but if this is so easy, I'll never have another thing to ask of you, David. Do you believe that?"

"With all my heart."

"And . . . ," she said.

"Yes?" murmured Duval, after a moment.

But her hand gradually relaxed and fell away from his, and when he looked down at her again, he saw that she was profoundly asleep and smiling in her slumber.

It was much later when she wakened again.

The cracking of a twig underfoot had roused her, and as she sat up, blinking, she saw old Henry standing in the meadow looking anxiously about him on all sides.

When he saw that she was awake, he said eagerly: "Did he tell you where he was going?"

"No," said the girl. "Not a word. Going? David? He's not really gone, Henry!"

The old man pointed. "There's the other two horses. Where's Cherry?"

She was on her feet by this time, all sleep startled from her mind.

And then Henry stretched out his long arm and pointed down the valley.

"Is that David coming back?" he asked.

Chapter Forty-Three

She got her glasses out of her pack. Strong field glasses, they picked up distant objects with wonderful detail. And when she focused them on the far-off rider, it was to exclaim immediately: "A gray horse, that one . . . not Cherry! Looks like a big horse and a big man . . . only I can't be sure."

"A gray horse? Like Kinkaid's?" asked Henry. And then clapped a hand over his mouth as he saw what he had suggested.

She lowered the glasses to give Henry one keen glance. Then she raised them again and spoke with them at her eyes.

"Now that you've given me the idea, it seems to me that you may be right. A big man on a large gray horse . . . riding hard . . . I can see the way he rounds the curves in the trail. Who else would be coming up against the grade so hard and fast? Dick Kinkaid." She lowered the glasses and added: "David has seen him long ago. He's gone down to meet Kinkaid." She passed the glasses to Henry and walked out a distance. "You try to find him, will you?" Then she leaned one hand against a tree trunk and waited, her eyes closed, as the old man searched the upper ravine.

Suddenly he cried out: "I've got him! I see him now!"

"Are you sure?"

"I know Cherry's stride even at this distance! Look, look!"

She ran to him and snatched the glasses away. "Look down into the lower cañon," said Henry, uselessly pointing. "There where the boulder nest begins. You'll see Cherry galloping, and who but him would be ridin' her?"

She found him almost at once. "Get my horse!" she cried to Henry, still with the glasses glued to her eyes.

"It's too late to do any good," Henry said with great decision. "There ain't any use. Because he'll be sure to crash ag'in' Kinkaid in another few seconds . . . now, maybe?"

"He's out from the rocks," said the girl. "They're riding straight at each other. They're meeting near a grove of trees . . . pines, I think . . . they . . ." Her voice choked away, then she began again, chattering the words out rapidly. "I thought he was down, but he'd only slipped down alongside his horse, I suppose . . . that old Indian trick. And now he's up again. I thought I saw the glint of the sun on the guns. I can't be sure . . . they've closed. They're both down. . . . Henry, Henry, they're both down, and Dick Kinkaid has those huge hands on David!"

"Then heaven help Kinkaid's unlucky soul,"

Henry said solemnly. "Because he ain't gonna live to talk about this day. What's happenin' now?"

"They've rolled into the shade of the trees, and I can't see anything. Get my horse . . . my horse! Henry, Henry! Be quick!"

He got the horse swiftly, his own hands shaking with the same nervousness that made the glasses quaver in the hands of the girl.

But at last the saddle and bridle were on. He gave her a leg up, and as she dashed the pony down the hillside, like water leaping with a full head, swerving around big boulders, dodging among the trees. Henry already had picked up the fallen binoculars and, regardless of Marian, was scanning the pine trees eagerly, but nothing could he see.

Never was there madder riding than that which took Marian Lane down to the bottom of the lower ravine. For she told herself that fate would not let her have such happiness as that which had been in touch of her hand. Duval was dead. It must be so, and, therefore, she rode wildly, not caring greatly what came of her in that perilous descent.

She reached the lower and level footing, with the mustang stretched out at full gallop, and came plunging on to the view of the pines under whose shadow she had watched Duval disappear.

Then she saw a man seated on a rock at the edge of the woods, and waving a hat at her.

Duval!

She came closer, and made sure that it was he. But why did he remain there, seated?

On and on rushed the mustang, and now she could tell a vitally good reason, for red ran down one side of Duval's face, and red soaked his torn and ragged shirt, and red streaked his trousers, also.

She was out of the saddle with a leap, like a man, and there was David smiling up at her with perfect peace in his face.

"Davie, Davie, Davie!" sobbed the girl. "He's killed you!"

"He wouldn't say so, if you asked him," Duval said calmly. "He's gone back toward Moose Creek a rather sick fellow, Marian. When Henry comes jogging along, we'll send him after Kinkaid to see that the pieces get home, safely. Dead? I'll live to be a thousand, if I'm never sicker than I am now."

His head drooped back against the tree trunk behind him, however, as he spoke. It was instantly supported in the cup of her arm, and she heard a rapid murmur saying: "I'll live, Marian. No fear of that, my dear, but work fast. The life is soaking out of me. Fast, fast . . ."

And when Henry came, he found Duval with eyes closed, senseless, and the girl working, white-lipped, stern, with determination.

Between them they closed the wounds with bandages. And long after, Duval opened his eyes and gritted his teeth as he felt the binding power that was on his injuries. He mastered himself at once, and was able to smile wanly up at Marian.

"He was down and out, the cur," said Duval. "And he gave in. And after that, he came at me again when my head was turned. He came like a blind beast . . . and I can thank heaven for that blindness, or I wouldn't be living in your hands, my dear. But at last he was done for. He backed away from me, Marian, and ran for his horse . . . and he's ridden out of our lives forever. He'll ride other trails, but never the trail that leads to me again."

This is the history of David Duval as Moose Creek knew it, and, in some respects, a great deal more than all of Moose Creek knew.

As for David and his wife, they never came back to the little town again.

It was said that he was ill for a long time in the mountains, until she and Henry had nursed him back to some shadow of his old strength, and then they resumed their journey north and west to a new land, and to a new life.

To this day, opinions in Moose Creek differ concerning David. Pete the barkeeper is the one who talks the least, knowing as he does the most.

Simon Wilbur is sure that no squanderer will ever come to a good end.

The blacksmith has confidence in the two swift, strong hands of Duval and his good wits to solve all the problems of his life, and Charlie Nash says that the husband of Marian Lane never could fail in the great test.

But all that Pete will say is that David Duval knew a horse when he saw one. Perhaps he knew them too well!

Once a rumor came back to Moose Creek from a wanderer who spoke of a little village in Maryland, a shining sweep of river, wide meadows green as lawns, a spacious grove, a house on a hill, and a happy face at a window that looked strangely like the face of Marian Lane, not a whit older than she had been in the former days.

But there was never any confirmation of this rumor, and now Duval and Marian Lane have both joined the ghostly procession of legendary forms that ride across the imagination of the West.

About the Author

Max Brand is the best-known pen name of Frederick Faust, creator of Dr. Kildare, Destry, and many other fictional characters popular with readers and viewers worldwide. Faust wrote for a variety of audiences in many genres. His enormous output, totaling approximately thirty million words or the equivalent of five hundred thirty ordinary books, covered nearly every field: crime, fantasy, historical romance, espionage, Westerns, science fiction, adventure, animal stories, love, war, and fashionable society, big business and big medicine. Eighty motion pictures have been based on his work along with many radio and television programs. For good measure he also published four volumes of poetry. Perhaps no other author has reached more people in more different ways.

Born in Seattle in 1892, orphaned early, Faust grew up in the rural San Joaquin Valley of California. At Berkeley he became a student rebel and one-man literary movement, contributing prodigiously to all campus publications. Denied a degree because of unconventional conduct, he embarked on a series of adventures culminating in New York City where, after a period of near starvation, he received simultaneous recognition as a serious poet and successful author of fiction. Later, he traveled widely, making his home in New York, then in Florence, and finally in Los Angeles.

Once the United States entered the Second World War, Faust abandoned his lucrative writing career and his work as a screenwriter to serve as a war correspondent with the infantry in Italy, despite his fifty-one years and a bad heart. He was killed during a night attack on a hilltop village held by the German army. New books based on magazine serials or unpublished manuscripts or restored versions continue to appear so that, alive or dead. Beyond this, some work by him is newly reprinted every week of every year in one or another format somewhere in the world. A great deal more about this author and his work can be found in *The Max Brand Companion* (Greenwood Press, 1997) edited by Jon Tuska and Vicki Piekarski. His Website is www.MaxBrandOnline.com.